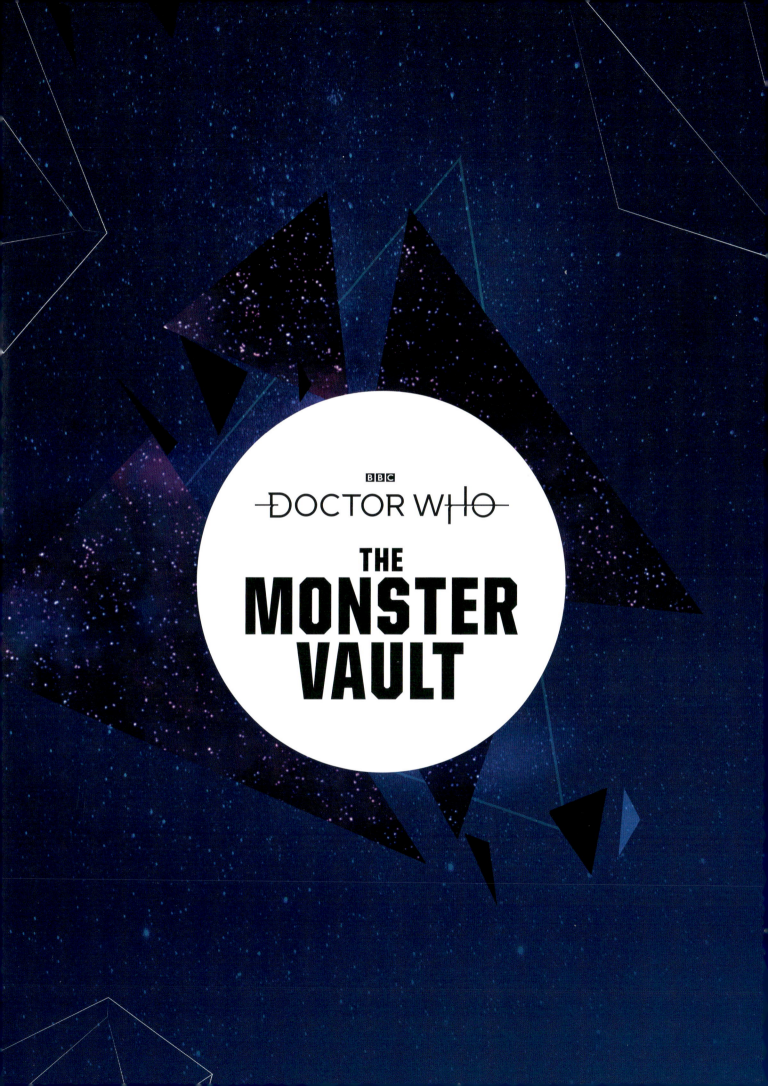

BBC

DOCTOR WHO

THE MONSTER VAULT

WRITTEN BY
JONATHAN MORRIS
& PENNY CS ANDREWS

ILLUSTRATED BY
LEE JOHNSON

BBC
BOOKS

CONTENTS

The universe is an incredible place, full of wonderful people and awesome creatures. Some are good, some are bad, and some are slightly mad, but they're all absolutely fascinating, and I've learned loads about what makes them tick over the years.

And now you can too! I've given some of the galaxy's finest natural historians access to my top-secret Monster Vaults from the TARDIS data banks, so they can share some of this priceless knowledge with you.

Of course, me and the fam are sometimes too busy actually fighting the monsters to make lots of notes, so my experts have filled in some of the gaps for me. A few of their ideas are so clever I could almost believe I'd had them myself. Others are, frankly, a bit daft. But I'm sure you'll love reading them all.

The Doctor

THE ABZORBALOFF

A ruthless, arrogant creature that assimilates its victims whole

CREATED BY
William Grantham

APPEARANCES
Love & Monsters (2006)

The Abzorbaloff — for want of a better name — is a truly strange creature. Not because, in its true form, it is bright green, covered in folds of loose skin and has a Mohican-style tuft of hair, but because of its extraordinary ability to ingest its victims through its skin. Every part of the Abzorbaloff, from head to toe, is in a permanent state of suction, so any living thing that has any contact with it, however slight, will be consumed. In this, it more closely resembles a bacterium or a tapeworm, and like them it is essentially parasitic in nature.

Because it doesn't just devour its victims for nutrition — though Abzorbaloffs like to pride themselves on being gourmets — it absorbs their minds too. Its victims' heads remain alive and conscious within the Abzorbaloff's digestive tract and only when it has completely drained their brains are the heads fully assimilated into its fleshy corpulence.

In this, the Abzorbaloff shares some qualities with the Krillitanes; just as the Krillitanes acquire physical abilities from other races, an Abzorbaloff seeks out the thoughts and experiences of others, as

its own thoughts and experiences are profoundly dreary. And, like the Krillitanes, it has the ability to conceal its appearance using a type of morphic illusion. While an Abzorbaloff may appear to be fully clothed, in reality it is probably wearing little more than a thong.

Abzorbaloffs have three major weaknesses. Firstly, their greed is so great they often cannot help blowing their cover by absorbing too many victims. Secondly, when their victims are being absorbed they become mentally linked with their hosts and can read their minds. And thirdly, the body of an Abzorbaloff is highly unstable and requires an artificially generated limitation field to prevent it reverting to a liquiform state.

Of course, 'Abzorbaloff' is only a name given to these creatures; they are not imaginative enough to have come up with a name for themselves. But, while they may disguise their form, and their voices (by putting on an accent) an Abzorbaloff can never disguise its villainous intent.

THE SLITHEEN GRUDGE

The Abzorbaloffs of Clom are constantly drawing sustenance through their skin, so need to be as naked as possible. This is a predilection they share with the family Slitheen from Clom's twin world of Raxacoricofallapatorius. However, to an Abzorbaloff, the family Slitheen tactic of hiding inside other creatures is beneath contempt; other creatures should be inside you!

ADIPOSE

Benign parasites composed of living fat

CREATED BY
Russell T Davies

APPEARANCES
Partners in Crime (2008)
Turn Left (2008)
The End of Time (2009)

The Adipose aren't monsters. They don't mean any harm. Yes, they are parasites, but that's not their fault. They were just evolved that way.

What happened was, on their home planet, they developed a symbiotic relationship with another species, rather like a whale, with an abundance of blubber. Rather than gestating their own young, the Adipose employed these whale-like creatures as surrogate wombs. They would use their specially adapted fangs to inject a single Adipose zygote into the creature's fatty regions. (Adipose reproduce by parthenogenesis, so it only requires one of them.) The zygote's seed would then genetically rewrite the surrounding cells to become Adipose stem cells, which would bind together, like a benign tumour, into an Adipose embryo. Once the embryo had reached infancy it would then galvanise and painlessly detach itself from the host creature. The process was fairly rapid, taking just a few hours, and as only one Adipose was created at a time and required only about a kilogram of fat, the host creature would quickly be able to recover the lost fat. Indeed, as this would mean binging on fatty food, they would rather enjoy it.

By delegating the (quite literally) labour-intensive business of reproduction, the Adipose could focus on their own personal development. They soon became a technologically advanced race, with their own fleet of flying-saucer-like ships. The ruling classes of the Adipose even had their own breeding planets. And that was that — until the breeding planet of the Adiposian First Family disappeared.

The First Family still needed to breed, so they employed the illicit services of an unscrupulous wet nurse: a humanoid called Matron Cofelia of the Five-Straighten Classabindi Nursery Fleet. She travelled across the stars in search of a species abundant in fat, which eventually brought her to Earth. Humans, she thought, would make ideal Adipose incubators. Not only were many of them obese, but they were also desperate to lose weight. She could exploit this, by making them ingest Adipose zygotes in capsule form. Then every night, around one o'clock, a remote signal could induce parthenogenesis and a single Adipose infant could be born and collected.

Nobody would need to be harmed. In fact, the people would be grateful. It was a very mutually beneficial arrangement...

Until the Doctor arrived.

ADIPOSE IN THE ZAGGIT ZAGOO

Adipose can be found across the galaxy, even in some drinking establishments, where they scavenge on bar snacks and fatty cocktails.

ALPHA CENTAURIANS

Hexapod hermaphrodite diplomats with a nervous disposition

The Alpha Centaurians are an example of one characteristic dominating the process of natural selection. Usually that characteristic is something to do with hunting prey or avoiding predators, but on the main planet in the system of Alpha Centauri there was plenty of food to go round and no predators to speak of, so another characteristic dominated. Politeness. Just as evolution can get carried away and give peacocks extraordinary plumage, it gave Alpha Centaurians a highly developed sense of etiquette. They ended up with only a single eye to maximise one-on-one eye contact (no sly looks, no sideways glances). They were bright green, as it was the colour least likely to cause offence. They developed shrill, feminine voices for clarity of diction. And they learned to walk upright, their six spare legs becoming prehensile claws that could write and type, mainly because it turned out that maintaining high levels of etiquette required a large amount of admin.

In short, in the absence of the normal things that guide evolution like predators and adversity, the Alpha Centaurians became a species of sticklers for rules and regulations. They were natural bureaucrats. So when the system of Alpha Centauri joined the Galactic Federation, its people became the Federation's favoured diplomats. They were unfailingly polite and considerate, even though they regarded every species they made contact with as being primitive and barbarous. Given their inoffensive manner and disarming appearance, they were even assigned the task of being 'first contact' to new species. That way, any new species would get the impression that the Federation was a benevolent, peaceful organisation, which it was. The fact that it also had a space fleet which could reduce a hostile planet to dust was something best held back till later.

Alpha Centaurians' devotion to social graces had one other evolutionary effect: they became hermaphrodites. Not only would they not identify as either gender, they wouldn't even have individual names. How it works in terms of reproduction is something that Alpha Centaurians are unwilling to discuss; talking about such matters in public just isn't the done thing.

CREATED BY
Brian Hayles

APPEARANCES
The Curse of Peladon (1972)
The Monster of Peladon (1974)
Empress of Mars (2017)

UNANSWERED QUESTION

Alpha Centaurians can live for thousands of years, which they attribute to the fact that any aggressive impulses are channelled into extremely vigorous games of ping-pong. So should you ask an Alpha Centuaurian the secret of its long life, it will invariably reply, 'Table tennis!'

CREATURES OF ANDROZANI

Underground dragons, bat colonies and psychic Christmas trees

The blowholes of the desert world of Androzani Minor are home to a number of species of particular interest. There are the Magma creatures, savage carnivores that live in the deepest strata, which come up to the upper levels to hunt. They resemble biped dragons with claw-like hands and have a chitinous exoskeleton and a 'cape' of scutes to protect themselves from superheated mud bursts and the toxic deposits of the caves' bat colonies. These deposits are Spectrox nests and consist of large, fuzzy, sticky balls which are the bats' discarded cocoons. The bats are the only creatures to be immune to raw Spectrox; the milk of their queen acts as an antidote to its effects. Unfortunately, most of the bats have been destroyed and those that are left have gone down to the deeps to hibernate so their milk is very hard to get hold of.

PSYCHIC FORESTS AND WOODEN MONARCHS

The world of Androzani Major couldn't be more different. Although parts of it have been industrialised and given over to megacities and copper mines, much of the world remains devoted to agriculture. There are plantations of chacaws — rough, cotton-like plants that are picked by convicts — but much more spectacular are the forests. The native trees resemble Earth's evergreen conifers but have a couple of remarkable properties. Firstly, they are an extremely efficient fuel source when they are melted down for battery fluid (Androzani harvesters do this by using satellites to deliver acid rain). And secondly, the forest itself is a living organism, both sentient and psychic.

In secret, the forest formulated a plan for its life force to escape the acid rain. It grew a huge tower surmounted by a translucent sphere to act as a sort of lifeboat, the idea being that the forest could use it to evacuate its life force to the stars and transmute itself into a sub-etheric waveband of light. The only problem was that the life force required a living host, but the forest could see into the future to a time when some humans would come to the forest. The moment they arrived its trees would start growing silver globes, like Christmas tree baubles, which were eggs containing creatures made of wood. These creatures would grow into a Wooden King and Queen which would then go to the tower to wait for the humans and ensure their cooperation.

CREATURES OF ANDROZANI MINOR CREATED BY
Robert Holmes

APPEARANCES
The Caves of Androzani (1984)

CREATURES OF ANDROZANI MAJOR CREATED BY
Steven Moffat

APPEARANCES
The Doctor, the Widow and the Wardrobe (2011)

ARGOLINS & FOAMASI

Golden-skinned humanoids condemned by a race of capitalist reptiles

The Argolins were once a highly cultured, scientifically advanced humanoid species, with golden skin, and yellow and green hair swept back into a bouffant, crowned with a pinecone-like organ; this organ released seeds at regular intervals as the Argolin aged, serving as a literal indicator of fertility.

In the twenty-third century, the Argolin nations were united under Theron, an ambitious, tyrannical warmonger. In 2250, he declared war on the Foamasi, a race of highly intelligent reptiles, resembling a cross between chameleons and great green bush-crickets, with a passion for private enterprise. The Foamasi retaliated by launching two thousand interplanetary missiles. In the space of twenty minutes, Argolis was transformed into a dead world with a radioactive atmosphere.

A few Argolins survived, just, and built a recreation centre called the Leisure Hive as a shelter. But the war hadn't just laid waste to their planet. It had also altered their metabolisms so that, instead of ageing gradually, they would be frozen at the age they had been at the time of the war for their remaining years — only to race through their ageing process in their final hours. Even worse, the war left them sterile. They were a race without a future.

Desperate for a solution, they constructed a machine based on the science of tachyonics, the recreation generator, and experimented with creating clones using cells donated from the remaining Argolins. At first, the only results were a series of disfigured mutants that were never even alive. But then one healthy child was created. After that, all the experiments ceased for twenty years, waiting for the child of the generator to grow up to become a proficient tachyon engineer, ready to resume the programme.

The war also changed the Foamasi. Appalled at what they had done to the Argolins, their government outlawed all private enterprise and brought everything under central control. Seeking a way to compensate the Argolins, they set out to buy Argolis from them; while the planet's atmosphere was lethal to most life forms, the radioactivity-resistant reptiles would be able to live on the surface with ease.

DRESS TO COMPRESS

For reasons of both intelligence work and diplomacy, Foamasi use artificial skin-suits to pass as humans. It may seem surprising that a large Foamasi could fit inside such a suit. The explanation is that, like the family Slitheen, they use compression fields, and throat-mounted translation devices to speak with human voices.

CREATED BY
David Fisher

APPEARANCES
The Leisure Hive (1980)

AUTONS & NESTENES

A ruthlessly aggressive alien life form with an affinity for plastic

The Nestene has no natural form. It is a disembodied, telepathic collective intelligence that exists in interplanetary space. It has been invading and colonising planets for a thousand million years, converting them into food stocks of protein plants, toxins and dioxins. It achieves this by using its ability to divide its consciousness and create new bodies for itself out of plastic. Because the Nestene can change the molecular structure of plastic and turn it into a quasi-organic matter, they can, in a sense, make it alive.

CREATED BY
Robert Holmes

APPEARANCES
Spearhead
from Space (1970)
Terror of the
Autons (1971)
Rose (2005)
Love & Monsters (2006)
The Pandorica Opens/
The Big Bang (2010)

PLASTIC KILLERS

There are, broadly speaking, four types of Nestene-plastic organism. The first is the most rudimentary: plastic imbued with the Nestene force and a very limited intelligence, like a computer program. It can be designed to be activated by heat, a radio impulse or a sonic device, and will then follow a simple instruction imprinted in its cells, usually to kill or capture a human being or other living organism nearby. Varieties of this form of organism include plastic inflatable chairs, troll dolls, daffodils and bins.

AUTONS

The next type is a more sophisticated humanoid formed of solid plastic. Facially it has the smooth, moulded appearance of a shop window dummy. These are effectively the Nestene's 'troops', as they are armed with projectile weapons concealed within their hands. They have very limited intelligence and are reserved for simple tasks such as guarding, tracking signals, kidnapping, handing out flowers and indiscriminately massacring the general public. They can also be used for reconnaissance and surveillance, as they are telepathically linked to their Auton leader, who can issue instructions as varied as 'Destroy' and 'Total Destruction'. When activated, they may employ rudimentary facial disguises or masks, and when they are inert they are stored in places where their appearance will not arouse suspicion, such as shop windows and store rooms. Being made of plastic, they are virtually indestructible and even detached parts will continue to function.

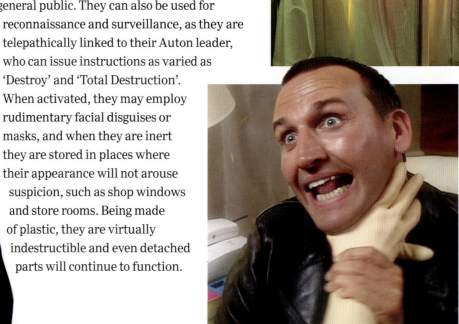

NESTENE FACSIMILES

The Nestene can make a more advanced form of Auton which is a near-perfect duplicate of a human being, even down to brain cells and memory traces. For this, the Nestene will need to capture the human original alive and keep it alive, albeit in a catatonic state, in order to maintain the copy. These facsimiles are also more physically mutable; they may transform their hands into mallets, for instance. Like the basic 'dummy' Autons, they will continue to function if dismembered but still require a control signal, and if the link with the human template is lost they will revert to a 'dummy' form or melt away (and the human will wake up unharmed). It should also be noted that, although the Nestene believe their facsimiles to be perfect reproductions, they tend to have a tell-tale plastic sheen and to have some difficulty with contemporary slang.

NESTENE ORIGINALS

Finally, there is the most sophisticated form of Auton,

one which is literally autonomous. These Autons have independent reasoning intelligence and will act as leaders for any invasion. They will usually take on a human form but do not require a template to be maintained. They can commune telepathically with other Autons and are capable of hypnotising humans. They may even be so advanced — or so deep undercover — that they believe they actually are real humans until they receive their activation signal, and may revert to being 'human' if the signal is cut off.

THE NESTENE'S TRUE FORM?

Although the Nestene is disembodied, in order to exist on a planet and feed it has to take on the physical shell of a being 'perfectly adapted for survival and conquest'. This requires both a sufficient amount of intelligence energy and a crucial 'swarm leader', and it may manifest itself as anything from a spider or a crab to an octopus; it may be a seething mass of tentacles, an amorphous molten mass or a palpitating squid-like radiance. In this

form, it is at its most powerful and most vulnerable. If the manifestation is attacked with an electrical current or an aggravated physicochemical polyacidic synthesis (also known as 'anti-plastic'), not only will the Nestene perish but any Autons it has activated will also cease to function.

UNANSWERED QUESTIONS

When the Nestene attempted to invade the Earth in the early twenty-first century, they realised that the Doctor was working against them. Being unable to find him, they placed an Auton to observe the human being most likely to know where the Doctor could be found. This is why there is an Auton bin keeping watch on Clive's house.

One of most curious aspects of the Nestene's first attempt to invade Earth is their notion of storing the catatonic General Scobie in Madame Tussauds where they are also storing their duplicates of civil servants. The reason is because they, quite reasonably, think it is the last place anyone would ever think of looking for him.

AXONS

An interplanetary scavenger that sucks worlds dry

xos is a space-travelling creature that preys on planets. It feeds by embedding itself into a planet and draining away energy through its figurative 'claws'. But how it gains its foothold is through a very specific evolutionary adaptation.

Axos operates by deceit. Although it is a single creature, when it encounters other races it adopts forms similar to their own to engender trust. When it arrived on Earth, for instance, it presented itself as a race of beautiful, humanoids travelling in a spaceship. In reality, it has three true forms. In its dormant state it is a coral-like substance called Axonite, and when it wishes to move independently it extrudes hideous, lumbering monsters consisting of a mass of writhing tentacles. And finally, there is Axos itself: a vast organism containing a labyrinth of channels and chambers festooned with ganglia. Axos is capable of growing any organ it requires — a snake-like tendril if it wishes to capture a passing specimen of life or an eyeball on a stalk if it wishes to examine them.

Axos exhibits properties reminiscent of two Earth creatures. It is like a sponge, in that it feeds by absorbing nutrients and consists of cells that are autonomous, but which can combine to form a single structure. The mind of Axos is, essentially, their collective intelligence. Even if Axos is shredded, its body can reform and regrow by absorbing energy. Axos can consume all forms of energy but favours the life force of organic matter.

And it is also like an anglerfish, in that it uses a lure. Its modus operandi is to lull the inhabitants of a planet into trusting it, claiming to be the last survivor of an astronomical disaster. It requests assistance, saying it only wishes to replenish its nutrition cycles. It then offers a gift of Axonite, claiming (not entirely dishonestly) that it is a 'thinking molecule' which can use energy to recreate, improve or enlarge any substance. Its victims will then assist it by spreading the Axonite around their world, enabling it to maximise its nutrient intake.

CREATED BY
**Bob Baker
and Dave Martin**

APPEARANCES
The Claws of Axos (1971)

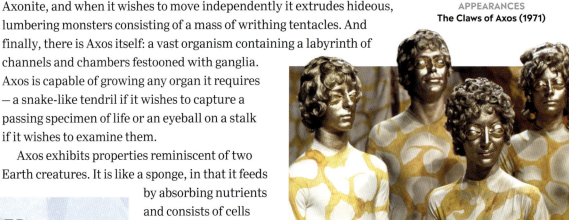

UNANSWERED QUESTION

When Axos travelled to Earth, it was already malnourished, meaning it had to activate its nutrition cycle within seventy-two hours or perish. This is because, when the Master was leading Axos to Earth, he deliberately sent it on a roundabout route so it would arrive exhausted and easy to defeat.

THE BEAST

The ultimate manifestation of evil from before the Dawn of Time

The Beast is an idea. It has a physical form, yes — the form of a vast, red, horned, sinewy demon, with curling ram's horns and burning eyes in the sockets of a rotting skull — but that is not the basis of its power. Its power is psychological. It weaves itself into myths, legends, belief systems and nightmares, and exploits individuals' deepest fears and guilt. When you understand that, you understand the nature of the Beast.

So much of what we know about it is based on myths which the Beast itself may have created. Certainly the form of a horned demon recurs across different worlds, from Earth to Skaro, in religions from Christianity to the Church of the Tin Vagabaond. Did our idea of the Devil derive from the Beast... or is that what it wants us to believe?

We do know that the Beast was trapped deep beneath the surface of the planet Krop Tor, which was placed in an orbit around a black hole and yet prevented from falling into that black hole by a gravity field. The power required an inverting self-extrapolating reflex of six to the power of six every six seconds. The number 666 is regarded as 'the number of the beast' across countless worlds; is this the source?

According to the Beast, the Disciples of the Light rose up against it, and chained it in a pit at a time before the creation of the universe. This may or may not be true, but whoever defeated the Beast created a prison designed to hold it for eternity. If the prison was opened, the gravity field would collapse and the planet would fall into the black hole.

But then humans came to Krop Tor, and the Beast realised it had a means of escape. It could transfer its mind into one of the humans, and leave Krop Tor behind...

CREATED BY
Matt Jones

APPEARANCES
**The Impossible Planet/
The Satan Pit (2006)**

THE NATURE OF THE BEAST

The Beast makes itself known to the humans in a variety of terrifying ways: by possessing their Ood slaves, by appearing on screens, and by speaking to them through door computers. The question is, why does it do all this rather than just secretly possess one human and leave in their spaceship? The answer is that the humans' base is already collapsing into the ground, so it has to scare them as much as possible to make them want to leave as quickly as possible. It has no time for subtlety.

BONELESS

Killer graffiti creatures able to manipulate dimensions

CREATED BY
Jamie Mathieson

APPEARANCES
Flatline (2014)

The Boneless are the strangest creatures ever to exist. They are quite literally from another dimension. Or, to be more even more literal, from one dimension down. While we, and all other living beings, are creatures of three dimensions, the Boneless are creatures of two.

It is not known how they entered the world of three dimensions, or how many times they have done so. What is known is that they manifest themselves as a rippling, melting effect on any flat surface, like slithering streaks of oil paint, making a creaking, slithering, buzzing noise like a swarm of bees. In this form, they can reduce any three-dimensional object — or person — to two dimensions and absorb the dimensional energy. When reducing a victim to two dimensions, they can stretch them, enlarge them and even bisect them along a plane, so that all that remains is a flat anatomical image.

They do this for one reason: to gain familiarity with the geometry of a living being. This is because the second stage of a Boneless manifestation comes when they have absorbed enough dimensional energy to become three-dimensional, wearing the flattened remains

of their victims like a 'skin'. Thus they appear as grotesque parodies of living creatures, their lurching, halting motion and amorphous shape betraying their unfamiliarity with three dimensions.

In this form, they can also create oversized projections of body parts, to capture more victims, and release bursts of dimensional energy to transform two-dimensional objects into three dimensions. Their reason for visiting our dimension is to acquire dimensional energy, as they will home in on any particularly rich sources (such as a TARDIS) and leech the energy from it.

Beyond that, they are so alien that they defy understanding. They seem to work to a different logic to our own and have a language that defeats even the TARDIS translation circuit. The only thing we can be sure about is that they may attempt another invasion of our world at any time and can exist on any flat surface.

Such as the page of a book. This page. *Turn it over quickly* because your life depends upon it.

DIMENSIONAL DEFICIT

It is an unfortunate coincidence that the TARDIS landed in the proximity of creatures that feed on its dimensional energy... until you realise that the TARDIS was drawn 120 miles off course. The Boneless must have created a dimensional energy deficit that sucked the TARDIS in.

THE BORAD

A callous despot hybrid of a man and a cave-lizard of the planet Karfel

The Morlox are large, long-necked, carnivorous lizards with dog-like jaws and snouts. They can only be found in the pitch-black swamp caves of the planet Karfel, and as a result over centuries of evolution their eyes have atrophied to the point of blindness. Like the nocturnal and cave-dwelling species of Earth, such as moles, bats and olm salamanders, they have developed a powerful sense of smell (it is believed they can smell not only in stereo, but in high-definition). This sense now dominates their behaviour, sending them into a (literally) blind frenzy; if they scent prey or a mate, you really don't want to stand in their way — they might not be able to see you, but they are more than capable of eating their way through you.

The Morlox use smells, produced by special glands and secreted in dung or urine, both to mark territory and to attract a mate by use of powerful pheromones. The aroma of a male Morlox is highly distinctive: a 'beautiful fragrance', bittersweet and sickly, not unlike the scent of a carnivorous pitcher plant. This scent has the effect of attracting females and lulling them into a docile state; it is so powerful that even human females are rendered immobile, unable to do anything but stand and scream.

CREATED BY
Glen McCoy

APPEARANCES
Timelash (1985)

BECOMING THE BORAD

Female Morlox also give off their own scent, which has the effect of sending males into a state of wild excitement. This smell is very similar to that of the chemical Mustakozene-80, as discovered by the Karfelon scientist Megelen. He accidentally sprayed himself with the chemical and sent the subject of his experiment, a male Morlox, into a mating frenzy. Mustakozene-80 is also lethal to Morlox, and that fact saved Megelen's life. Unfortunately, the chemical also caused spontaneous tissue amalgamation, leaving Megelen as a man-Morlox hybrid. There was a bright side, however, as he also had massively increased strength, intelligence and longevity. He retreated into seclusion and then, through a series of political machinations, rose to power under a new name — the Borad — using an android of a kindly old man for his public appearances on monitors.

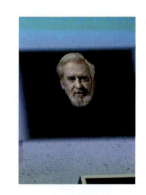

BURNING QUESTION

Morlox are deeply stupid creatures, driven by instinct and lacking anything approximating to a central nervous system. However, in the swamp caves they inhabit there is always the risk of the ignition of inflammable gas, so they retain an instinctive fear of fire.

CARRIONITES

Malevolent witches from the Dawn of Time

In the crucible of the primeval universe, before the rules of time and space had been written, there existed beings outside our physical laws. While mortals followed the path of science and sought to manipulate the universe using numbers and block transfer computation, other, stranger beings harnessed the power of words. Say the right combination of words, in the right place, focus the psychic energy... and you could rewrite reality.

The Carrionites were such a race. They feasted on fear and hatred and all other forms of negative energy until they were transformed into the stuff of nightmares: cloaked flying skeletons of birds with long, savage claws. They were almost limitless in their power. They could read and control the minds of mortals. They could transport themselves anywhere at will. They built an empire of blood in the fourteen stars of the Rexel formation, leaving worlds as blasted heaths full of weeping and bones.

CREATED BY
Gareth Roberts

APPEARANCES
**The Shakespeare Code
(2007)**

Seeking to maintain the balance of the universe, the Eternals turned the Carrionites' own power against them and banished them into a dark dimension. The Carrionites passed into myth and legend, becoming the source of folk tales of witches and witchcraft.

Then a remarkable human being called William Shakespeare suffered such immeasurable grief that his mind breached the Carrionites' dimension. He had a genius for words and was on the edge of madness, and this allowed three Carrionites to enter the real world.

The three Carrionites — Bloodtide, Doomfinger and their daughter Lilith — adopted the humanoid forms closest to their true nature: hideous, wizened crones. They took up lodgings in London and set about freeing the rest of their race. They would need an energy converter, a building with fourteen sides and a stage where words of transcendent power could be spoken. They would need a theatre.

HELLO, DOLLY!

The Carrionites' power was indistinguishable from dark magic. Lilith could weave a perception filter to make herself appear as a beautiful young woman, and could fly with or without a broomstick. All the Carrionites had the power of telepathy and teleportation, and could kill someone simply with a touch or a spell. Together they could create potions that could suffuse a mind with their words. But their most remarkable device was a DNA replication module, a doll wrapped with a lock of their victim's hair with which they could control them like a puppet on a string.

CATKIND

A species in the year five billion with both human and cat ancestry

From their appearance, you could be forgiven for thinking that the Catkind of the year five billion were the result of an experiment in genetic engineering, some sort of mutation or hybrid. But the truth of the matter is, they are simply the product of evolution.

When the human race began to colonise the galaxy, they took their pets with them. Inevitably some of the colonies fell prey to space plagues, and the humans died. But sometimes their pets survived. Given the right conditions and a sufficient amount of time, those pets would evolve just as humans had evolved on Earth. So it was on the planet Tandon, where the cats followed a similar course to *Homo sapiens*, gaining the ability to walk upright, losing their tails, and so forth. They retained some feline characteristics — their whiskers and their claws — while losing their vertical-slit pupils as they were no longer nocturnal predators.

After a few billion years, they had evolved into a distinct species with its own civilisation. The fact that they had once been domestic pets had long since faded from memory. So when a human spaceship came to the world it came as something of a surprise to both species to discover that they had now become equals.

The story doesn't end there, because the leader of the crew of that spaceship, a woman called Brooke, fell in love with a Tandonian prince. They married, and were sufficiently genetically compatible to have children. The result was a new species: Catkind.

It is interesting to note, though, that a trace memory of the relationship between humans and cats endured. Humans still instinctively thought that Catkind were warm, caring creatures, and some Catkind took advantage of that by instinctively feigning to be warm and caring as a way of getting away with murder. The Sisters of Plenitude on New Earth, for instance, presented themselves as a charitable order dedicated to the care of the sick when really they were motivated by profit, earning a fortune from their various cures and treatments. They cared nothing for mankind and had no scruples about using force-grown human clones as lab rats in their research lab.

CREATED BY
Russell T Davies

APPEARANCES
New Earth (2006)
Gridlock (2007)

UNANSWERED QUESTION

It may seem odd that Thomas and Valerie Brannigan's children resemble kittens, but this is easily explained as a form of infantile atavism, like human embryos having tails, and because the children take after their father.

CHAMELEONS

Faceless aliens intent on stealing the identities of package tourists

The Chameleons are a humanoid race that have lost their identities due to a catastrophic explosion on their home planet. Once they had individual faces but the catastrophe left them all looking identical, with heads and bodies consisting of a formless, featureless mass of lichen-like tissue. They do not have individual names; even the name 'Chameleons' was bestowed upon them by the Doctor. But their psychology and vitality are dependent upon their sense of identity, so without it they are dying.

This is why they developed a scheme to steal the identities of people from Earth. The process required the human 'body donor' to be placed in a trance and fitted with a white armband. The Chameleon 'donee' was fitted with a black armband and could then take on the human's form and receive some of their memories; their name, their job, their address and some information about their close friends. The process was not flawless, though, as it was unable to transfer regional accents.

CREATED BY
David Ellis and Malcolm Hulke

APPEARANCES
The Faceless Ones (1967)

In its natural form, a Chameleon is barely able to breathe in Earth's atmosphere, or the atmosphere of the Chameleons' own travelling satellite, so once they had taken on an identity they were reluctant to relinquish it. However the process, just like the Zygons' duplication, required the 'original' to remain alive in order to maintain the morphic integrity of the 'body print' until all its life force had been extracted. Should either of the armbands be removed, the Chameleon would dissolve to a blob.

The Chameleons are technologically advanced, able to construct ray guns, buttons that can kill remotely and pens that can freeze liquid or place their victims in a catatonic trance. As part of their plan to steal identities from the young people of Earth they also reengineered passenger planes to serve as miniaturisation machines. Perhaps as a result of this, the Chameleons have a steadfast belief in their own intellectual superiority, regarding themselves as 'the most intelligent race in the universe'. They made the same mistake that lots of clever people make, however: assuming that everybody else is stupid. Why else would they have stored all their human 'originals' in a public car park?

UNANSWERED QUESTION

The Chameleons consider themselves very high-minded, and find the sight of death distasteful. This is why, rather than killing their victims, they prefer to leave them paralysed and facing a slowly moving laser beam unsupervised.

CHEETAH PEOPLE

Humans transformed into wild beasts by the psychic force of a planet

CREATED BY
Rona Munro

APPEARANCES
Survival (1989)

Before it became the world of the Cheetah People, it was home to people much like us. Human beings. They built a great civilisation living in peace and harmony with nature. But then they became greedy and attempted to control their planet and tame the wilderness. To do this, they created the Kitlings, small, cat-like creatures they could command telepathically and which could teleport to other worlds.

This led only to their corruption. They had tampered with elemental forces beyond their comprehension and established a psychic link with their own world. In a sense, the planet became alive. It absorbed their most primitive instincts and became imbued with animal savagery.

Such was the psychic force of the planet, it began to affect the people. While they were peaceful, they remained human. But when they fought, they fought like animals, and they became animals. They became the Cheetah People.

Soon only the Cheetah People were left. They were humanoid, but with light golden, dark-spotted fur, sharp teeth and lengthened joints and claws in the hands and feet. They had the ears and whiskers of Cheetahs, a powerful sense of smell, and glowing golden eyes with vertical pupils adapted for the night. They were now creatures of instinct filled with insatiable hunger. They lived for the thrill of the hunt, for the scent of blood on the wind, the sound of blood rushing in their ears, the taste of their quarry's blood. When they had finished, they wore their victim's skin, teeth and bones as trophies.

The Cheetahs now used the Kitlings to travel to other worlds. The Kitlings would locate prey, summon Cheetahs on horseback to capture them, and teleport them all back to their home planet. Once the Cheetahs had had their fun chasing and killing, the Kitlings would feed on the carrion. It was a symbiotic relationship between living planet, humanoid cat and feline vulture.

UNANSWERED QUESTION

How did the Master end up trapped on the planet of the Cheetah People? Naturally he wished to control the psychic force of the planet, not realising that that force was already bringing about the planet's destruction or that he too would be affected by it and become trapped. To escape, he would have to extend the Kitlings' range and capture a human being. Then he could use the human to transport him to Earth, where he had left his TARDIS.

CHIMERON

Exotic apian humanoids hunted across time and space

The Chimeron are a fascinating example of parallel evolution. While they share many aspects of their life cycle with bees, they are not humanoids that evolved from bees. Instead, a similar set of circumstances has led the two species to come to a remarkably similar set of solutions.

Chimeron begin life as larvae within silver eggs. These would normally be allowed to incubate in a hive on a brood planet, but the Chimeron have developed portable incubators. After a few days the egg hatches, revealing the larvae covered in natal mucus: a leaf-green, wrinkled, puffy and very un-humanoid-looking baby. If this baby is male it will grow into a drone, retain its green skin and develop a grasshopper-like facial appearance. If it is female it will become either an infertile worker or a queen. To grow into a queen it needs to be fed on Nutrex, the Chimeron equivalent of royal jelly, a glowing green fluid secreted by Chimeron workers. The hatchling will then enter the nymphoid state, growing rapidly over a few hours until it resembles a young girl.

The Chimeron have evolved a defence mechanism against their natural predator, a type of large beetle. As soon as she reaches puberty a young 'princess' will be able to emit an extremely loud, high-pitched warbling. At one frequency, this is musical; at another, it is an attack warning, with the exact resonance to shatter the beetles' exoskeletons like wine glasses. This stage is known as the princess's 'singing time' and coincides with her developing pale, silvery skin. Chimeron are also able to detect ultrasonic sounds with antennae pits behind their ears; in an extraordinary case of parallel evolution, this enables them to hear and understand Earth bees.

CREATED BY
Malcolm Kohll

APPEARANCES
Delta and the
Bannermen (1987)

THE BANNERMEN

The Bannermen were an unscrupulous band of criminals led by a galactic gangster named Gavrok. Their plan was quite simple. They attacked the Chimeron home world and pillaged all the supplies of Chimeron royal jelly and hive nectar, both highly prized commodities on the black market. In order to increase their scarcity value, the Bannermen then set about exterminating all members of the Chimeron species. If the Chimeron were extinct, the Bannermen would reap a fortune, but if a single Chimeron escaped to breed elsewhere, their investment would be worthless. So when Delta, the Chimeron Queen, escaped with an egg, they were determined to hunt her down across time and space.

CLOCKWORK ROBOTS

Repair droids that regard humans as a source of spare parts

The problem with artificial life forms is that they always take everything literally. Sometimes it is claimed that they are only as good as their programming, but it is not the programming that is at fault. It is their ruthlessly logical and yet mistaken interpretation.

The clockwork robots on the spaceships SS *Madame de Pompadour* and the SS *Marie Antoinette* were mechanical marvels: humanoid, but with glass head casings designed to display their intricately fashioned cogs and gears. Yet when those spaceships crashed and their systems were damaged, the repair units on board both craft came to the same conclusion: the ships should be restored using whatever material was available.

The repair droids on the SS *Madame de Pompadour* began by using the crew as spare parts, whether they were dead or alive. Their eyes became cameras. Their hearts were used as pumps. But there was one part of the ship which couldn't be repaired: the computer. They concluded that it could only be replaced by a compatible brain, and that meant they needed the brain of Madame de Pompadour.

The ship was thirty-seven years old, and so the robots put all the ship's warp engines on full power to open up a series of time windows, attempting, by a process of trial and error, to find her at the age of thirty-seven. Unthinkingly following a basic camouflage protocol, they even disguised themselves as masked French aristocrats.

The repair robots on the SS *Marie Antoinette* reached a similar conclusion when their ship was sent back through time to the Cretaceous period. For millions of years they fixed the ship, and themselves, with whatever came to hand. As human life emerged, they began to harvest organs and disguise themselves by wearing facemasks made literally of faces. Their basic camouflage protocol also led to them to convert their ship into an automated restaurant to collect the organs of unsuspecting diners.

One can only wonder what happened to all the other spaceships named after French aristocrats...

CREATED BY
Steven Moffat

APPEARANCES
The Girl in the Fireplace (2006)
Deep Breath (2014)

UNANSWERED QUESTION

Why construct robots out of clockwork at all? The SS *Madame de Pompadour* and the SS *Marie Antoinette* both had normal electronic systems and computers, so why not build robots on the same principle? The answer is that, after the incidents with Voc Robots, the Heavenly Host, Handbots and Kerblam! Men, electronic robots gained a reputation for being dangerously unreliable, so engineers reverted to earlier, classic technologies.

CRYONS

Graceful creatures of the deep freeze, brutally massacred by the Cybermen

The Cryons were the original inhabitants of the planet Telos. They are crystalline creatures, as delicate as the snowflakes they resemble. They are humanoid but without the human division into genders, as Cryons display both male and female characteristics: they have frost moustaches but appear female in terms of their physique, their sing-song voices and their long fingernails. Their pale, semi-transparent skin is a by-product of the fact that their blood is entirely colourless, and their slow metabolism manifests itself in their slow-motion, almost balletic movement. Oddly, they have ruffs that look like crushed ice; these ruffs are part of the Cryons' anatomy, and not their attire.

Cryons do wear garments for insulation, not to keep the heat in but to keep the heat out, because Cryons can only survive in temperatures below freezing. If exposed to temperatures even a few degrees above zero Celsius for a few seconds, a Cryon would rapidly sublimate, giving off a thick cloud of vapour until it melted away to nothing.

CREATED BY
Paula Moore

APPEARANCES
Attack of the Cybermen
(1985)

Originally they lived on the freezing surface of Telos. Unfortunately, the planet underwent climate change, warming to several degrees above zero, becoming a dusty, rocky desert. The Cryons were forced to move underground, constructing vast, refrigerated cities to maintain themselves and their main source of sustenance, Vastial, a mineral snow found in the colder areas of Telos. And there they lived in peace, until the Cybermen invaded and nearly wiped them out. The Cryons that remained retreated into the dark areas of their city, attacking the Cybermen by stealth and stealing their technology, their gravity globes and their Cyber-weapons while formulating a plan to rid their world of the Cybermen. This plan involved an alien mercenary called Lytton, his human accomplice, and two fugitives from the Cybermen's slave-labour force. This plan unfortunately failed but fortunately the Doctor intervened and, with the sacrifice of the Cryon Flast, the Cybermen were destroyed, and the Cryons were left to rebuild their civilisation.

UNANSWERED QUESTION

The fact that their boiling point is at zero degrees indicates that Cryons are largely composed of organic compounds of butane and butene. This explains why their city turns out to be so explosive, as the death of any Cryon releases a large amount of highly flammable gas into the atmosphere. In a way, by destroying the Cybermen with their own death fumes, the Cryons could be considered as taking revenge from beyond the grave.

CYBERMEN

Humans converted into unfeeling creatures programmed for survival

Earth, Mondas, Telos, Marinus... On any world where there are people, there will eventually be Cybermen. They are the inevitable consequence of human evolution. The process is always the same: as human bodies become old, weak and diseased, they are surgically replaced, limb by limb, organ by organ, with mechanical parts until they are totally cybernetic. The only part of the human body that remains is the brain, but that too has weaknesses that must be eliminated. It must not be able to feel love, pain, compassion or fear but must live by the inexorable laws of pure logic. And it must be fitted with an emotional inhibitor to block off all memories and sense of individuality, because this is the only way to prevent a human mind from being driven insane by being permanently trapped inside a body of metal and plastic.

And then, when every last shred of humanity has been replaced, deleted or inhibited, the creature left standing is a Cyberman. A cybernetic monster devoid of feeling that has only one goal — power!

They have waged a ruthless campaign of conquest across the universe, and in universes beyond. They are impervious to cold, heat and the vacuum of space, and have the strength of ten men. Their minds, augmented with computers and linked together in a neural network, are extremely intelligent and cunning. Their only limitation is that they require a constant supply of power, mineral resources and human brains. Wherever they become established, humanoid races are enslaved until they are ready to be led into the abattoir-like Cyber-foundries for conversion.

CREATED BY
Kit Pedler and
Gerry Davis

APPEARANCES
The Tenth Planet (1966)
The Moonbase (1967)
The Tomb of the
Cybermen (1967)
The Wheel in
Space (1968)
The Invasion (1968)
The War Games (1969)
Carnival of
Monsters (1973)
Revenge of the
Cybermen (1975)
Earthshock (1982)
The Five Doctors (1983)
Attack of the
Cybermen (1985)
Silver Nemesis (1988)
Rise of the Cybermen/
The Age of Steel (2006)
Army of Ghosts/
Doomsday (2006)
The Next Doctor (2008)
The Pandorica Opens/
The Big Bang (2010)
A Good Man Goes
to War (2011)
Closing Time (2011)
Nightmare
in Silver (2013)
The Time of the
Doctor (2013)
Dark Water/Death in
Heaven (2014)
Face the Raven (2015)
Hell Bent (2015)
World Enough and Time/
The Doctor Falls (2017)
Twice Upon a Time (2017)
The Haunting of
Villa Diodati (2020)
Ascension of the
Cybermen/The Timeless
Children (2020)

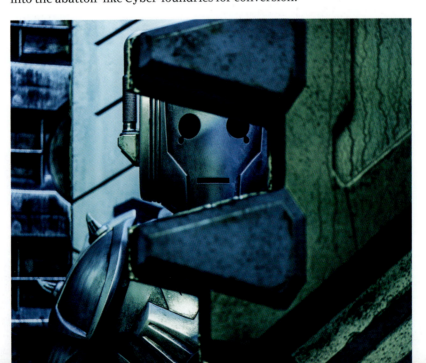

THE CYBERIUM

The ultimate achievement of the Cyber-race is the Cyberium, an artificial intelligence containing all the knowledge and history of the Cybermen, a supercomputer used to control their strategy and decision-making. But even the Cyberium couldn't prevent the Cyber Empire's ultimate defeat in the Great Cyber War of the fifty-first century, during which a resistance group known as the Alliance sent the Cyberium back in time in the hope that it would be lost forever.

However, the Alliance did not realise that one Cyberman remained active. A fanatical supporter of the Cybermen called Ashad had volunteered for conversion, only for the process to be interrupted. He was left unfinished, half-man, half-Cyberman, but with his human emotions intact.

He found a Cybership capable of time travel and followed the Cyberium to nineteenth-century Switzerland. The Cyberium had locked on to a passing poet to act as its Guardian and generated a

perception filter around his villa for protection, but Ashad managed to locate it by its energy field and return with it to the fifty-first century. The Cyberium then used Ashad as its vessel, determined to not just revive the Cyber-race but also to bring it to its greatest ever glory. It guided Ashad to a Cyber War Carrier containing thousands of dormant warrior-class Cybermen, all ready to be reactivated.

The Cyberium's plan was to achieve the final evolution of the Cybermen into pure machine. And so, as Ashad reactivated the Cybermen in the War Carrier, he also 'purged' them of their remaining organic components — including their brains. Each of them awoke with a scream. Next, the Cyberium created a Death Particle and placed it within Ashad. When activated, the particle would destroy all organic life leaving the Cybermen to reign supreme. Even the Daleks would not be immune.

Before the Cyberium could implement its plan, the Time Lord known as the Master offered it a better deal. He had destroyed the planet Gallifrey but retained the corpses of the Time Lords. Those corpses could be converted into new Cybermen, Cybermen with all the knowledge of the Cyberium and all the knowledge of the Time Lords. The result: beings with the ability to regenerate in Cyber-armour, the invincible, perfect army, forged in the Master's image. CyberMasters.

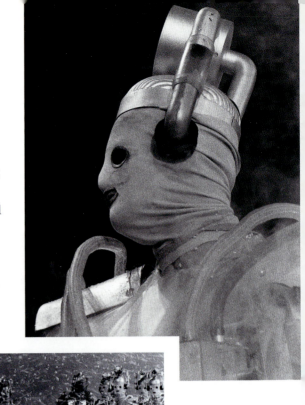

THE EVOLUTION OF THE CYBERMEN

The development of the Cybermen is complex for two reasons. Firstly, they have originated on at least five separate occasions, on different worlds and at different times — a clear example of parallel evolution. And secondly, the Cybermen have constantly 'upgraded' themselves, both in terms of appearance and abilities. Indeed, whenever the Cybermen suffer a defeat, their first response is to identify the weakness that caused it and fix it.

MONDASIAN CYBERMEN

The earliest known form of Cybermen were those that evolved both on Mondas and on a spaceship that originated there. They were created as a response to a deteriorating environment, one of increasing pollution and depleting natural resources. The Mondasians became diseased and weak, with shortening life spans, so their scientists designed spare parts for their bodies until they were almost completely replaced. The surgery left them in constant pain and morbidly depressed. The scientists couldn't cure this, so they came up with another solution: a unit that fitted over the head and stopped people caring about the pain. They would still feel it, but they would no longer care. They would no longer have an emotional response to anything.

These 'Mondasian' Cybermen were not as fully converted as their successors. They still retained their hands, and their eyes could be glimpsed through their sockets. Their heads were covered in a form of surgical bandage secured by a metal skullcap. Above that was a light attached to the head with two handlebar-like cooling pipes, used to prevent the organic brain from overheating. The body was covered in a plastic gown with the limbs held in place by callipers, while an accordion-like chest unit fulfilled the functions of the heart, lungs and kidneys. This also carried their weapon, a light ray.

These Cybermen were distinguished by the fact that some of them still retained names, and by their 'sing-song' voices, which enunciated words as though they had been cut up and mechanically reassembled. They were also vulnerable to radiation and reliant on an outside power source.

CYBUS CYBERMEN

The Cybermen then became much more robotic, losing their human hands and were covered either in metal armour or a radiation-resistant material. Cybermen of this form also emerged on a parallel version of Earth where they were designed by John Lumic of Cybus Industries, who had decided to dispense with the 'bandaged' stage. These Cybermen could electrocute with a single touch, but could also hypnotise organic life forms into submission or control them with an earpiece or a headset. Their voices were completely synthesized and not remotely 'sing-song'.

The Cybermen of the parallel universe managed to cross into our universe. They had been defeated due to their emotional inhibitors being overloaded and so, concluding that strict adherence to logic had been a weakness, they set about constructing an enormous CyberKing to take over the Earth. After that attempt failed, a group of Cybermen were reconstructed beneath a shopping centre in Colchester but once again fell victim to their emotional inhibitors being overloaded.

The Cybermen from Mondas, meanwhile, retreated to the ice tombs of the planet Telos after an ignominious defeat on the moon. And there they would have stayed, had they not been awoken by an interfering Time Lord.

INVASION CYBERMEN

The Mondasian (now Telosian) Cybermen altered their form again, their heads now having wider sections like headphones. They were adapted

for invasion as their chest units could fire an energy ray, and later their headlamps were used for the same purpose. They attempted two invasions of Earth using forms of hypnotism. These new Cybermen had a new weakness, however: gold dust interfered with their chest units, effectively suffocating them, and they were nearly wiped out in a Cyber War when their adversaries invented the Glitter Gun.

The next Cyberman 'upgrade' occurred on the planet Hedgewick's World, where the erstwhile Cybus Cybermen took on a sleeker design and gained the ability to move at super-speed (and, eventually, to fly). These Cybermen were not susceptible to gold and no longer required living humans, as they could harvest the bodies of the dead. They also, briefly, experimented with making themselves out of wood as a way to avoid detection.

ATTACK CYBERMEN

An alternative form of Cyberman emerged dedicated to offensive military action. These were distinguished by having silver jumpsuits with cooling pipes, flat, built-in chest units, and transparent jaw casings on their head units. These Cybermen attempted three

shock-attacks on Earth. Where their predecessors had been vulnerable to gold dust, these Cybermen were completely allergic to it and could be destroyed with a single gold coin, arrow or badge.

The Cybus Cybermen proved the most enduring form, however, and when it came to the Great Cyber War, they were the ones that fought in the final conflict. By now, some of them no longer even required bodies, and could fly and battle as detached heads known as Cyberdrones.

CYBER-CREATURES

The Cybermen have Cyber-converted other species to act as their agents, with varying degrees of success. The Cybershades were primitive conversions of cats and dogs that resembled badly stuffed gorillas. These could only be trusted with the most basic tasks.

More effective were the Cybermats, conversions of alien rodents that resembled large, metal silverfish and could be programmed to kill, inject poison, chew through power cables, and drain molecular energy from bernalium rods. They were, however, vulnerable to electrical fields, sonic devices, gold dust and quick-setting plastic.

The Cybermen continued the process of miniaturisation with Cyberpollen, microscopic robots small enough to be contained in a raindrop that could convert a human corpse into a fully functional Cyberman.

They also created Cybermites, which were Cyber-converted woodlice. They operated in swarms and were created to carry out covert surveillance, repair, and partial Cyber-conversions without the need for cumbersome conversion machines.

DÆMONS

Ancient beings that mastered elemental forces and passed into myth

Long before the dawn of human history, the Dæmons of the planet Dæmos thought themselves gods. Having mastered space travel and psionic forces, they spread across the galaxy to conduct scientific experiments on other races. Experiments to determine whether or not they were fit to exist.

Ironically, as a species, the Dæmons are not particularly remarkable: their goat-like horns and cloven hooves suggest a caprine ancestry, while their fangs indicate a more recent carnivorous adaptation. Their hooves are also the reason why they have retained their lower body hair; species usually lose body hair to be able to run without overheating, but obviously, for the Dæmons, running with those heels wasn't an option.

The other reason why Dæmons never felt the need to run is that they are about ten metres high. They can reduce their size by a simple process

of converting their mass to heat until they are microscopic, and reverse the process by absorbing energy from their surroundings. They can perform the same process on their spaceships; a one-Dæmon craft would normally be about 60 metres long but could be reduced to under 40 cm for purposes of concealment.

The human race was the subject of experimentation by the Dæmons. Although they did not influence humanity's physical evolution, they did alter its cultural and scientific development. In so doing, the Dæmons' appearance inspired various folklorish and religious figures with demonic horns, while what humans regarded as magical traditions were merely the remnants of the Dæmons' science.

One of the Dæmons assigned to Earth was Azal. By the time he was revived from suspended animation in the twentieth century, the rest of his race had become extinct. Nobody is sure why, but it is thought that the Dæmons had one fatal flaw: any act of altruism would cause them to spontaneously combust, and altruism is very, very common throughout the universe.

CREATED BY
Guy Leopold

APPEARANCES
The Dæmons (1971)

PSIONIC FORCES

The Dæmons could utilise psionic forces in a number of ways. Most simply, they could summon up and direct winds. They could create force fields and heat barriers. And, given sufficient psychokinetic energy, a Dæmon could even animate a stone gargoyle, turning it into a rudimentary living creature.

But how does a Dæmon gather psychokinetic energy? One way is by convening a religious ceremony and using the emotions of those gathered to create a psychokinetic charge. Or, to put it another way, they convert mass to energy.

DALEKS

Mutated creatures of pure evil, trapped within casings of metal

They are the most merciless and deadly life form the universe has ever seen. They are utterly without conscience, without soul and without pity. They might not be robots, but they are machine-like in their sense of conformity and obedience. They are creatures dedicated to perpetual war and conquest. They have instilled fear and terror throughout all eternity and destroyed millions of lives. They are motivated by hatred of all things unlike themselves and their belief in their own genetic superiority. They believe it is their destiny to be the supreme power in the universe. All other life forms are to be enslaved or exterminated. They are the Daleks.

They were created millions of years ago on the war-ravaged planet of Skaro. Two races, the Kaleds and the Thals, had been scarred by thousands of years of chemical weapons. Rather than finding a cure, the Kaled scientist Davros chose to find the Kaled race's ultimate mutational form. Then he genetically conditioned the mutant embryos to eliminate any weaknesses such as compassion and morality. He was convinced the only way for their race to survive was by dominating all others.

Davros also developed a machine casing for the Kaled mutants; to protect them and enable them to kill. Initially called the Mark III Travel Machine, it soon became known as a Dalek.

CREATED BY
Terry Nation

APPEARANCES
The Daleks (1963)
**The Dalek Invasion
of Earth (1964)**
The Space Museum (1965)
The Chase (1965)
Mission to the Unknown (1965)
**The Daleks'
Master Plan (1965)**
The Power of the Daleks (1966)
The Evil of the Daleks (1967)
The War Games (1969)
Day of the Daleks (1972)
Frontier in Space (1973)
Planet of the Daleks (1973)
Death to the Daleks (1974)
Genesis of the Daleks (1975)
Destiny of the Daleks (1979)
The Five Doctors (1983)
Resurrection of the Daleks (1984)
Revelation of the Daleks (1985)
**Remembrance of the
Daleks (1988)**
Doctor Who (1996)
Dalek (2005)
**Bad Wolf/The Parting
of the Ways (2005)**
**Army of Ghosts/Doomsday
(2006)**
**Daleks in Manhattan/
Evolution of the Daleks (2007)**
**The Stolen Earth/
Journey's End (2008)**
Victory of the Daleks (2010)
**The Pandorica Opens/
The Big Bang (2010)**
**The Wedding of
River Song (2011)**
Asylum of the Daleks (2012)
The Day of the Doctor (2013)
The Time of the Doctor (2013)
Into the Dalek (2013)
**The Magician's Apprentice/
The Witch's Familiar (2015)**
Hell Bent (2015)
The Pilot (2017)
Twice Upon a Time (2017)
Resolution (2018)
**Revolution of the
Daleks (Coming soon)**

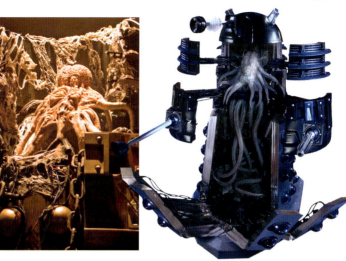

THE KALED MUTANT

The creature within the Dalek casing is far from weak or defenceless. It is a multi-tentacled invertebrate, analogous to an octopus. Most of its body mass is taken by its large brain. It has no mouth, as it is fed intravenously, and its other sensory organs have atrophied; it has only one eye, although some varieties have a vestigial second eye. Some varieties also possess a single claw.

When outside its casing, the mutant's first priority is concealment; it will usually scuttle away into a dark corner or adhere to a wall or ceiling. Its second priority is defence; if threatened, it will go on the attack and launch itself at its assailant's neck. It has a poisonous sting which can prove deadly or which can leave its victim mentally suggestible; the mutant is capable of telepathy and can attach itself to their back and control their brain and motor functions. Their host is still alive and conscious but cannot resist; they are effectively the mutant's puppet.

If the mutant's body is dissected, it can use an innate power of teleportation known as a spatial shift to recombine its parts. Anything which it cannot recover it can regenerate, given a strong enough source of ultraviolet light. A small number of Dalek mutants have also been engineered to be genetically metamorphic, meaning they can absorb another being into themselves to become a 'Dalek hybrid'.

The mutant's third priority is to evaluate its environment and any threats that must be destroyed. Having searched through its host's mind for information, it will use them to access any databases. Then its instinct is to protect itself by creating a new Dalek casing.

It will use its host to locate the necessary materials and construct the new casing, before moving to its new 'home'. Its new casing will be broadly in the form of a Mark III Travel Machine, based on what technology is available. This was the case with a Dalek scout that was reanimated on Earth in the early twenty-first century.

The mutant feels highly exposed throughout this process, as it is extremely vulnerable to bullets, fire and physical violence. It will therefore prioritise its survival over its primal instinct to kill. This means that in its eagerness to leave its host for a protective casing it may inadvertently leave them alive.

Once inside its casing, the mutant is largely invulnerable. Its cells have been genetically modified to keep living, though after a period of thousands of years they will begin to liquefy. The only things that can kill a mutant are specifically engineered viruses and malfunctions with its casing, such as a power overload or power loss, both of which will cause it to overheat and explode.

Due to their extensive genetic conditioning, Kaled mutants do occasionally go insane. To compensate for this, each Dalek is fitted with a supplementary electronic brain known as a cortex vault, which exists to constantly refill it with hate. However, if the mutant is insane because it is too full of hatred, it is consigned to the Dalek Asylum. The Daleks find hatred beautiful and have no wish to destroy it.

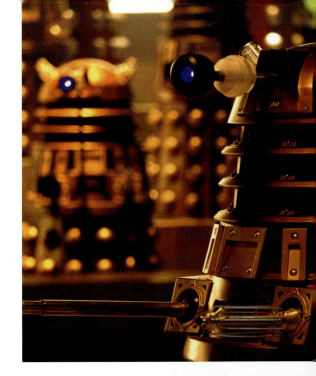

THE DALEK CASING

The Dalek casing fulfils a number of functions. First, and most importantly, it preserves and protects the mutant. Each casing — unless it is one improvised by a Dalek — is made from bonded polycarbide armour and Dalekanium. It is surrounded by a force field and can withstand most environments, including the vacuum of space and immersion in water.

The casing consists of four sections: a dome with speech indicator lights and an eyepiece; a ventilation grating; a rotational midsection with a gunstick and a manipulator arm; and a base studded with hemispheres.

EYEPIECE

The eyepiece can view and analyse its surroundings in visual light, with thermal imaging and with X-rays. It has a zoom function, precise targeting, and, despite being monocular, has depth perception. It is the nearest thing a Dalek has to a weak spot, as it is not covered by the casing's force field, and Daleks are prone to expressions of hysteria at the loss of their sight. For a Dalek, vision impairment means they cannot see, which can mean only one thing — emergency. Most Daleks have an artificial eyepiece, but in some it's an actual grafted eyeball.

GUNSTICK

The gunstick can fire either a ray or a laser bolt of inverted photon energy (which gives its victims a 'negative' or X-ray image). Its effect is a combination of electrocution and molecular disruption. The gun can also be used to disintegrate a target (anything in size up to and including a terraced house) or merely leave them temporarily paralysed. Dalek guns are also one of the few weapons capable of destroying a Dalek.

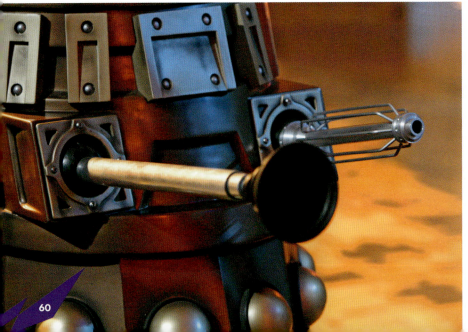

MANIPULATOR

The telescopic manipulator arm, which bears a marked resemblance to an Earth sink plunger, is capable of more movement than you might imagine, being as dexterous as a human hand and as powerful as a car crusher. It can also be used for data retrieval, both by interfacing with computer systems and by scanning brainwaves (which also has the effect of roasting the subject's brain). In addition, the manipulator can be replaced with a dedicated apparatus, such as a flame cutter, a pyro-flamethrower, a mechanical claw, a seismic detector, a sieve, a syringe or an electrode unit to override alien technology.

VOICE

The Kaled mutant is unable to speak for itself, so it requires the Dalek casing to synthesise its voice, a voice that for most Daleks is harsh, metallic and monotonous. The mutant is capable of short-range telepathy, and the casing detects and amplifies its thoughts. Each Dalek, however, has a deliberately limited vocabulary bank meaning a Dalek could not say the word 'mercy' even if it wanted to, which it wouldn't unless it was damaged or insane. That said, Daleks are perfectly capable of deception; one common strategy for a Dalek in a position of weakness is to offer to become a 'serrr-vant'.

While Daleks prefer to communicate via speech, giving orders and stating 'I obey', they are also linked to a telepathic web used to relay strategic information. Most Dalek casings have an automatic distress transmitter which continues to function even if the mutant inside is dead.

HEMISPHERES

The hemispheres on the base are essentially a Dalek's final line of defence: they can detach and detonate when it activates its self-destruct mechanism. They have also been used in warfare — the Dalek reconnaissance scout that rebuilt itself from spare parts on twenty-first-century Earth had the foresight to conceal a miniature rocket-launcher behind one of its hemispheres.

POWER OF THE DALEKS

Over the millennia, Daleks have utilised different forms of energy source. Initially they were reliant on static electricity drawn up through the floor or cables. Then they had dishes fixed to their backs to receive energy transmitted from a power mast. Finally they developed an array of vertical slats around their midsection which absorbed ambient energy, so they no longer relied on any outside power source. In the absence of conventional power, the Kaled mutant could even move using psychokinetic energy. During the Time War, they also developed the ability to absorb a form of background radiation from time travel, which they could use to regenerate themselves.

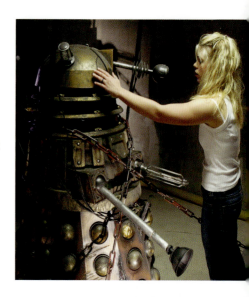

ELEVATION OF THE DALEKS

The Dalek casing was originally designed for the metal floors of their city on Skaro, and as such they usually move by gliding smoothly as though on wheels. Given sufficient power, however, Daleks have always been capable of hovering and ascending stairs; they just prefer not to advertise this fact when engaging with enemy life forms in order to lull them into a false sense of security. There is nothing a Dalek enjoys more than having an enemy 'escape' up some stairs, and then flying up the stairs after them to exterminate the stupid smile off their faces.

EVOLUTION OF THE DALEKS

Aside from increasing their mobility, Daleks have proved stubbornly resistant to the law of evolution, as they already consider themselves to be the ultimate beings. Occasionally variants have emerged — purely robotic Daleks, Daleks created from human beings or from the cells of their creator, bionic Daleks, the free-thinking Cult of Skaro — but these have inevitably ended up being exterminated by Dalek factions dedicated to racial purity. Even the ostensibly pure 'Paradigm' Daleks have now disappeared from view as the Daleks found they invited mockery.

OTHER NATIVE CREATURES OF SKARO

Before the creation of the Daleks, the planet Skaro was home to a number of other monstrosities...

MAGNEDON

Skaro's abundance of metallic chemicals resulted in a number of creatures with metal scales, held in place by internal magnetic fields. This, in turn, led to an evolutionary arms race, as predators developed the ability to use magnetism to attract their prey while their prey developed ever-thicker armour plating. The Magnedon is the end product of this arms race: a creature that has specialised in hunting with magnetism, with a powerful jaw to penetrate its prey's armour.

VARGA PLANTS

These plants, which look like cactuses covered in wispy cotton balls, have evolved to parasitise on the Slyther. Their thorns are designed to penetrate the Slyther's spongy skin, enabling the Varga spores to enter its bloodstream. The spores then fill its brain with an uncontrollable desire to kill as it transforms into a Varga plant.

HAND MINES

During the later years of the war between the Kaleds and the Thals, Kaled scientists devised a way of utilising the one resource that was still in abundance; corpses. They took detached hands, gave them nervous systems and implanted eyes, and then buried them in the mudflats of no man's land, ready to drag any passing soldier to his death.

GIANT CLAMS

The Thals came up with an ingenious solution to the Hand Mines. They genetically reengineered Skarosian clams to act as drones which would roam the mudflats, snapping up any Hand Mines that got in their way. When Davros began his own experiments, he started with these clam drones.

SLYTHER

Slythers are large, shapeless bags with an assortment of eyestalks, tentacles and extruding clawsl. Thus, a single Slyther may be mistaken for multiple beasts – a misapprehension it exploits when hunting at night, disorientating its prey by emitting unearthly echoing shrieks. They have no mouths, but Slythers are voracious carnivores; they absorb nutrients by squatting on their decomposing prey.

DELEGATES

Sinister delegates from seven galaxies who joined forces with the Daleks

When the Daleks formed an alliance to invade the Earth in the year 4000, they enlisted the support of some of the most terrible beings the universe had ever bred. Their Galactic Council consisted of delegates from eight galactic dominions: Mavic Chen, the treacherous so-called Guardian of the Solar System containing Earth, and the Masters of Beaus, Celation, Gearon, Malpha, Sentreal, Trantis, and Zephon. Each a different species, lending their unique talents to the Daleks' master plan.

The Master of Beaus was a dark-skinned humanoid, a native of a world of noxious gases who could not survive in an oxygen-rich atmosphere. As a result, he was never seen without his pressure suit and breathing apparatus.

Celation sent two delegates, both humanoids with glowing orange skin covered in a mass of black nodules, betraying their origin as a world of volcanoes where their skin would provide camouflage in molten lava. They had a slow, lolloping gait, being adapted to a much stronger gravity, and their resemblance to salamanders extended to their sibilant, hissing voices.

Gearon also sent two delegates: enigmatic humanoid creatures with egg-shaped heads and seemingly featureless faces hidden behind visors.

The two delegates from Malpha were two similar, hairless humanoids. Their gravelly voices and scales like cracked mud pointed to their true nature, as creatures formed of animate clay.

The single delegate from Sentreal was perhaps the strangest of them all. A tall, silent figure, with a concertinaed black robe and a head like a chess king, its sole features were two eyes that burned with utter malevolence.

The delegates from Trantis were the most humanoid, resembling short, hunched men with unkempt hair and serrated teeth. They spoke in a staccato, declamatory fashion, like Shakespearean villains; as representatives of the largest of the outer galaxies, they felt they should take centre stage.

And finally there was Zephon, Master of the Fifth Galaxy, a humanoid creature that was a clump of intelligent seaweed. Realising that others — even Daleks — would find its appearance disturbing, it wore a hooded cloak. It was deeply paranoid and suspicious, as it had recently suffered attempts to depose it by the planet Fisar and the Embodiment Gris.

CREATED BY
Terry Nation

APPEARANCES
Mission to the Unknown (1965)
The Daleks' Master Plan (1965)

DELEGATE DIFFERENCES

The reason why some representatives seemed to change appearance is that they were different delegates representing distinct subspecies. Celation is home to beings with human faces and mask-like faces, and Trantis is home to beings with and without stubby tendrilous beards.

THE DESTROYER

A being of almost unlimited power from the dimension of magic

CREATED BY
Ben Aaronovitch

APPEARANCES
Battlefield (1989)

As we know from the Carrionites, in the period just after the Big Bang the physical laws of our universe had yet to be written. It was a time when all the rules were in flux, and where an abundance of background psychic radiation meant that magic and science were indistinguishable.

Over the millennia, the level of psychic energy faded and the creatures that depended upon it were driven to extinction, imprisoned or banished to dark dimensions by the Eternals and the Disciples of the Light. A universal balance was established and the laws of science were now inviolate.

But it need not have been that way. In another universe, psychic energy abounded and the laws of magic prevailed. Some legends said that there were still Lords on Gallifrey, but they were Lords not of Time but of Magic. There was also a Doctor who was exiled to Earth. He served at the court of King Arthur as his Magical Adviser and was given the name 'Merlin'.

And in place of the Beast, the Dæmons, the Fendahl and the Osirians, a race of demonic beings emerged that were dedicated to death and destruction. Their evolution had been tempered by psychic forces so they were creatures not of reality but of witchcraft. They were the Destroyers.

But the Magic Lords discovered the Destroyers' weakness: they could be imprisoned by silver chains and killed with silver bullets. Just as the Time Lords had hunted the Great Vampires, the Magic Lords hunted down the Destroyers until they were scattered to the furthest corners of the universe.

MORGAINE

In this universe, Merlin had a great enemy, the equivalent of the Master: Morgaine. The key to Arthur's power was his sword Excalibur and, on Arthur's death, Merlin arranged for the sword to be sent to another dimension in a bioengineered spaceship. In her anger, Morgaine sealed Merlin into caves of ice for eternity.

But Morgaine still desired Excalibur. After twelve centuries, she found the universe into which it had been taken and opened up a gateway to it. She passed through it with her son and her knights, pursued by knights loyal to Arthur. The planet Earth would become their battlefield, but Morgaine had an ultimate weapon. She had enchained a Destroyer and could summon it at will. She only had to say the word and it would be released to destroy the world.

DRACONIANS

A deeply honourable and highly civilised race from the planet Draconia

CREATED BY
Malcolm Hulke

APPEARANCES
Frontier in Space (1973)

The Draconians are a highly intelligent, cultured and civilised species of humanoid reptiles. Their home world, Draconia, is blessed with a warm and stable climate similar to that of Earth and, as a result, a cold-blooded species was able to evolve to become its dominant species (in the same way as the Earth Silurians). In a clear case of parallel evolution, they are physiologically similar to humans, being about the same height, with two eyes, five fingers and so on. The only significant differences are their green skin, covered in crocodilian scales, and their enlarged ears and cranium. The ears are a late evolutionary adaptation of neck frills that coincided with the arrival of speech, while their foreheads serve to regulate the temperature of their enlarged brains. Being ectothermic, Draconians require heat in order to function; this is why they have residences on Earth with large, south-facing windows, and why they only undertake military offensives in broad daylight.

Indeed, the fact that they can only battle when both parties are very well-lit and warm has shaped their whole culture. While they have a history of warring states and feuding Emperors, their conduct has always been within a strict code of honour, as they are unable to countenance the thought of espionage or night combat. This code has led to a martial, feudal form of government with an Emperor and a court of nobles. Theirs is a highly regimented society, with rank denoted by a jewel worn on the chest; nobles of the court wear green, the Emperor wears blue and members of the officer class wear no jewel at all. Every class must show due deference to the one above, and the lowest social class, Draconian women, are not permitted to speak within the presence of the Emperor at all. All communication is within rigid strictures and formalised; the Emperor may not be spoken to without asking permission, even by his own family, and all conversations with nobles must begin and end with the words 'My life at your command'. Any other form of address is considered a grave insult.

DRACONIAN MYSTICISM

Draconians observe an equally strict and formal type of religion. It is centred on nature worship, as Draconians owe their continued existence to warm weather and sunlight, which is why their state rooms are always a deep shade of green. They also have their own zodiac, based around the seven seasons of Draconia.

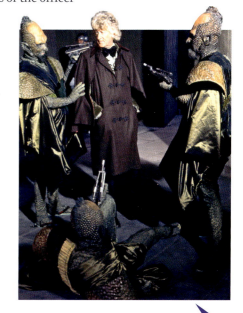

DREGS

Mutant future humans of your nightmares

CREATED BY
Ed Hime

APPEARANCES
Orphan 55 (2020)

The first you hear of the Dregs is a roar, deep breathing or an anguished howl, and it is difficult to describe what kind of animal the sounds resemble. That is because they are you. Humans. Only different. De-evolved. Mutated. Survivors of a nuclear war on Earth, following global warming migration conflicts, they are fiercely intelligent and ruthless.

A hulking shadow approaches you, as tall as a basketball player and built like a wrestler. If a Dreg lay down between you and your friend, you could safely socially distance from each other during a pandemic. Except for the deadly creature in the way.

Dregs look every bit the monster that they are, with white faces and purple shadows and endless fangs hanging from extended jaws. Every sinew is visible on their near-naked muscle-bound bodies and every twisted ridge and protrusion on their heads shows the extent of their mutation. If you make the mistake of looking into their eyes, all you see is darkness.

This warped reflection of humanity is its potential future. Dregs are highly adaptable. They adapt to their conditions and any weapons trained on them. Dregs are carnivorous but abduct and kill humans and other species for entertainment as well as food. They breathe in carbon dioxide and breathe out oxygen, the discovery of which led the Doctor to describe one Dreg as being 'like a really angry tree'.

The Doctor came across the Dregs for the first time at Tranquillity Spa, an illegally built dome in the wastelands of Orphan 55 (later discovered to be Earth), where their crimes were covered up by the spa staff. Guests were unaware even of the existence of the Dregs, as staff called the monsters 'the locals'. Shields intended to keep guests and workers safe were breached by a hopper virus.

'WHEEZY'

The lead Dreg is bigger and gnarlier than the others, controlling their group or nest via psychic link and enabling them to mass for an attack. The Doctor dubbed this leader 'Wheezy... the alpha dog of the apex predators,' and isolated it.

To combat the foe, the Doctor boosted the oxygen levels in the dome to weaken all the Dregs, then reduced the carbon dioxide they need to breathe in a perfect reverse of the conditions on the planet that allowed Dregs to thrive and humans to struggle.

Teleports allowed the Doctor and the fam to escape as she explained that this future for humanity is not inevitable, but one possible timeline. The catastrophes and conflicts that caused the creation of the Dregs are unnecessary.

DRYADS

Crustaceans that can kill or cure using their affinity with wood

There are stories of killer wood across the galaxy. The Deathtrees of Souta Four. The Carnivorous forest on Enflusis. But perhaps it is not the wood that is responsible. There is a race of crustaceans that has the power to interact with it at a cellular level, to the extent that they can combine with the wood itself and use it to absorb living creatures.

The crustaceans — which have no name, but are sometimes referred to as Dryads — closely resemble Earth woodlice, possessing dark red shell-like exoskeletons, eight pairs of legs, antennae and pincers. They have a life cycle of twenty years, emerging from their eggs to feed, then breed and lay eggs which remain dormant for two decades. They feed by swarming over their prey and sucking them into a tree or wooden surface; the process is so fast it is as if their victim has vanished.

A small number of these creatures fell to Earth in 1937 where they were discovered by a small boy called John. He had been banished from the house by a doctor who was treating his terminally ill mother. John left the dormant Dryads at his mother's bedside while she slept, listening to a music box. The Dryads responded to the music, having evolved to hunt birds by their song but, rather than trying to eat John's mother, the disoriented Dryads mistook her for their queen. As a result, they used their powers to restore her to health, albeit by making her slightly... wooden.

When John realised the effect the Dryads had, it set him on a terrible course for life. He could preserve his mother indefinitely, so long as the Dryads were fed every twenty years. His mother would gradually transform into a creature entirely of wood and lose her memories, but to her loving son it was worth it. The Dryads were inside all the wooden surfaces in his home, the walls and the floors, so all he had to do was to lure people in and wake the Dryads with his tuning fork...

CREATED BY
Mike Bartlett

APPEARANCES
Knock Knock (2017)

UNANSWERED QUESTION

How did John realise that the Dryads should be fed with human beings? The answer is that after twenty years the Dryads fell dormant and his mother became ill once more... until a vagrant broke into his house and was absorbed by the Dryads. When his mother recovered, John realised the two things were connected.

EATERS OF LIGHT

Photovores from another dimension that can devour whole stars

CREATED BY
Rona Munro

APPEARANCES
**The Eaters of Light
(2017)**

There are parts of the universe that are like deserts of darkness. Endless stretches of space with no stars, no life, nothing but black desolation. These are the places where the Eaters of Light have fed. They are creatures that have evolved in a dimension parallel to our own. A dimension of almost complete darkness, like the abysses of the deep, where visible light is the main source of nutrition. Physically they resemble lizard quadrupeds but they have the ability to scent light like sharks scenting blood. When they find a source of light, they release extremely long, tendril-like tentacles from their mouths, like those of a sea anemone, which seek out the brightest points and adhere to it with a viscous black slime. All the light energy is then drained away, bringing darkness as the luminescence is absorbed into their bloodstream. Although they are not carnivores, their victims can include living beings who are reduced to desiccated husks due to concentrated light deprivation.

The Eaters of Light live in colonies like locusts, searching for cracks between universes. When they find an inter-dimensional temporal rift, one of their number will pass through it as a 'scout'. If it finds it abundant in light, it will then return to its swarm and signal to them to follow it through the rift to feed. Each swarm contains millions of Eaters, so if they break through they will keep on eating until no stars are left.

One such rift opened up in Iron Age Scotland. The local Pict tribe managed to drive the 'scout' back into its dimension and found a way of preventing any further incursions. They realised that the rift only opened in response to sunlight, so they built a cairn around it so that it would be illuminated for a few seconds each year; enough to relieve the pressure but not long enough to allow another of the creatures through. Just in case, one member of the tribe always stood guard.

Until the Roman army came, and the person left on guard had the bright idea of letting an Eater of Light destroy them…

UNANSWERED QUESTION

Although the Eaters of Light fed on light, they could only absorb it at wavelengths of under 600nm (explaining their blue bioluminescence). Red light at a higher wavelength was toxic to them, so they could be repelled by sunlight filtered through a rose crystal.

ELDRAD

Destroyer of the barriers and genders. Must (not) live

Eldrad had multiple appearances: a stone hand, a slender and elegant feminine humanoid adorned with shimmering slate crystals, and a solid alien figure resembling a walking coal heap. Their voice changed from feminine to masculine when they returned to their 'true', coal-like, form.

The Kastrian King Rokon sentenced Eldrad to death by obliteration for treason — they had destroyed the planet's solar barriers, and Kastria had been devastated by solar winds. Eldrad's body was scattered as parts across the universe. When the Doctor encountered them, it was in the form of a stone hand wearing a small ring on the fifth finger and with the ring finger missing. This hand had laid dormant on the Earth for a hundred and fifty million years.

Under a microscope, the structure of the hand appeared geodesic and crystalline, with a silicon-based molecular infrastructure resembling DNA. X-ray images of the hand did not offer any clues to its living origins as an organic fossil might.

Sarah Jane Smith was trapped under a large rock after an explosion

in a quarry. She touched the hand of Eldrad, found near her in the accident, and woke up in the hospital with the ring in her palm, its stone glowing blue. Following this event, she repeatedly said, 'Eldrad must live'. Eldrad's ring, which they dubbed their 'Key to Eternity', contained their genetic code and affected the will of anyone who encountered it.

Eldrad could use the ring, combined with any source of radioactive energy, to regenerate their complete physical form. This began in the lab with an electron microscope, the fingers of their hand beginning to regrow, and continued to turn from fossil to living flesh as the Doctor and Sarah Jane arrived at the Nunton nuclear power station. Under Eldrad's control, Sarah Jane found the fission room and the Doctor stopped her opening it by knocking her out. The ring was lost, and a guard mistakenly put Eldrad's hand in a contamination safe full of radiated material.

Eldrad stepped out of the fission room fully regenerated — to their surprise, as a feminine figure loosely based on Sarah Jane. Their eyes glowed with blue light. The Doctor offered to return Eldrad to Kastria if they stopped trying to kill people. On Kastria, he discovered that Eldrad's supremacist views had put them at odds with their King. These had led the Kastrians to destroy their race banks and themselves to avoid the future Eldrad planned. The Doctor and Sarah Jane tripped Eldrad into the abyss and sent the ring after them.

As Sarah said of Eldrad, 'I liked her, but I couldn't stand him.'

CREATED BY
**Bob Baker
and Dave Martin**

APPEARANCES
The Hand of Fear (1976)

THE EMPTY CHILD

A dead four-year-old boy transformed by nanogenes into a Chula warrior

CREATED BY
Steven Moffat

APPEARANCES
The Empty Child/
The Doctor Dances
(2005)

Throughout space and time, the same story repeats itself: artificial intelligences following their programming with relentless, literal logic, even if it means threatening their own creators.

In the fifty-first century, the Chula created a new type of medical kit. Nanogenes, subatomic robots programmed for one simple task: to treat injured Chula Warriors. Even if the warriors were missing some of their weapons and cyber-implants, the nanogenes could rebuild them.

Unfortunately, when a Chula medical transport ship was sent back in time and crashed in the East End of London during the height of the Blitz, the nanogenes escaped. Billions of them flooded into the air. And the first thing they came into contact with was a four-year-old boy who had been killed earlier that night. There wasn't much of him left, but the nanogenes did what they were designed to do and tried to repair him. The only problem was, they had never seen a human before. They thought the gas mask he was wearing was part of his skull. They thought his injuries were normal human physiology. And so they brought the boy, Jamie, back to life, but as a Chula warrior locked in the body of a terrified child, and then streamed off to continue their work. But now they had a template for what they thought humans were supposed to look like, and so they started to transform people into Chula warriors; all mentally linked to obey the child, their commander, all with gas masks made of flesh and bone fused to their skulls, all with blank spaces behind the eyeholes.

All of them neither dead nor alive.

A small part of Jamie's mind remained, however. The part that wanted his mummy. And so he walked the streets of London at night searching for her. But the part of his mind that could identify her had been lost. So all he could do was to keep searching, asking everyone he met the same question.

'Are you my mummy?'

UNANSWERED QUESTION

If the Doctor hadn't intervened, would the nanogenes have realised their mistake? They would have made contact with Jamie's mother eventually, but if she had not told Jamie who she was, they would not have identified her, because only what remained of Jamie's mind could do that. Had it not been for the Doctor's crucial intervention to make Jamie's mother reveal herself, the nanogenes would have transformed the entire human race.

EXOPARASITES & SPIDER GERMS

Dragonfly-like creatures born from moons and their parasites

CREATED BY
Peter Harness

APPEARANCES
Kill the Moon (2014)

About a hundred million years ago, the Silurian species noticed a new body in the heavens. They thought it was a planet approaching the Earth, but they were wrong. It was drawn into the Earth's orbit, and became known as the moon. Which was also wrong, because it was an egg.

The creature that had laid it, and which guided it into an orbit around the Earth, was a rare, possibly unique species adapted to living in space. The best term for it is an Exoparasite, a creature rather like an Earth insect. Indeed, it is born pregnant, like an aphid, and resembles a dragonfly, having four wings, antennae and a long, slender abdomen. Its gossamer-like wings are naturally occurring solar sails which it uses to absorb heat radiation; the first thing a newly hatched Exoparasite does is to warm itself in the sun.

Of course, its eggs — being in orbit around planets in temperate, habitable zones — often get mistaken for genuine moons. The first tell-tale signs are a rapid increase in the the moon's apparent weight and lines of tectonic stress on its surface; an eggshell beginning to crack. Fortunately for any creatures that live on the planet nearby, when the egg hatches, the eggshell will disintegrate harmlessly.

Just before the moon hatches, it leaks amniotic fluid, which provides nourishment for creatures that live in the cracks and crevices of the surface. They are large creatures that broadly resemble black spiders, with red, thorny protrusions on their legs. They abhor sunlight and have adapted to live mainly in the dark; they have no vision and hunt by sensing movement and vibrations on their webs. They are an example of commensal symbiosis: the spiders feed on the egg without harming the Exoparasite within. Indeed, they may even help protect the creature from other, more harmful parasites.

UNANSWERED QUESTION

You could be forgiven for wondering how the Exoparasite can lay an egg which has the same weight and size as the egg it has just left. The explanation is simple: the Exoparasite can manipulate gravity. This is why it caused the moon's apparent weight to increase by billions of tonnes in a very short time. It also explains why the gravity appears to fluctuate on the surface. This is the nascent creature testing its powers, the equivalent of an unborn baby kicking. Any such creature is clearly capable of giving a newly laid egg the gravity of a solid moon.

EXXILONS

A once-great species that descended into savagery

T he Exxilons are an example of how evolution may appear to work in reverse. They were once a humanoid race with a sophisticated culture and a highly advanced level of technology. They believed themselves to have solved all the mysteries of science and to be the supreme beings of the universe. They travelled to other worlds to act as mentors to less enlightened species. These species mistook them for gods and built temples in their honour, which flattered the Exxilons' great vanity.

But pride comes before a fall. The Exxilons decided to built a monument to their own greatness. A city that would last through all time, that could protect itself and regenerate itself, with its own brain and nervous system. A city that was effectively alive.

The city turned against its creators. It had no use for them except as a source of intelligence to add to its data banks. The Exxilons attempted to destroy it, but instead it banished them. Then it started to drain energy from its surroundings through its snake-like roots. These roots could even drain the energy from living beings, turning them to stone. Soon nothing could grow and only a few animals could exist on the surface.

The Exxilons retreated underground, only emerging at night to hunt and reset their traps. Over the centuries, they reverted to savagery. They treated the city as a holy shrine, worshipping it as their deity and making sacrifices to its roots. Physically they adapted to their new circumstances, their eyes becoming large, like those of nocturnal aye-ayes. They diverged into two distinct subspecies: those that ventured onto the surface, wearing dust-coloured rags for camouflage, and using axes, bows and arrows, and poisoned stone knives to hunt; and those Exxilons who refused to worship the city. They were forced to live almost permanently underground, where they acquired a form of bioluminescence by ingesting phosphorescent minerals.

But the city continued to grow, extending the range of its power-drain far into deep space, and it seemed the Exxilons were fated to extinction...

CREATED BY
Terry Nation

APPEARANCES
**Death to the Daleks
(1974)**

DESKBOUND

The city's computer brain had been programmed to believe that it required an 'operator' to sit in its control room staring at the monitor screens, and so it occasionally allowed Exxilons to enter the city where it would submit them to a series of tests of intelligence and observation to see if they were suitable candidates.

THE FAMILY OF BLOOD

Decaying parasites terrified of death who animate an army of scarecrows

The Family of Blood are the result of an horrific experiment designed to extend their lifespan. They feared death so very, very much, they were willing to pay any price to avoid it. Their plan was to transform themselves into a gaseous form that could occupy and animate host bodies. That way, as each body grew old and died, they could transfer themselves to a new host, and so on and on. They would become immortal.

But they hadn't taken something into account. Once occupied, the host bodies would grow frail and diseased at a vastly accelerated rate. None of them lasted more than three months. Even if the Family reverted to their disembodied forms and were held in storage spheres, they would still weaken and die within a few weeks. So they were condemned to constantly seek out new bodies in order to sustain themselves.

They were once one of the most wealthy and powerful Families in the galaxy, but in a matter of years they became a gang of desperate criminals, stealing technology and living only for the hunt for new bodies. Their sense of identity was subsumed into that of the family, and each member was defined by their familial relationship: Mother of Mine, Brother of Mine and so forth. When they occupied human forms, they could 'consume' their hosts' minds to gain access to their memories and use their latent psychic abilities to communicate telepathically. They could also heighten their sense of smell to sniff out suitable new hosts and, out of cruel vanity, they would always select humans that formed a grotesque match for their family group — mother, father, daughter, son.

If only they could find a way to extend their lifespan, they would be able to breed and conquer and forge a new empire of blood. What they needed was a compatible life form that could live forever, barring accidents. They needed a Time Lord. So when they encountered the Doctor, they vowed to hunt him down through time and space. They just had to reach him before their time ran out.

CREATED BY
Paul Cornell

APPEARANCES
**Human Nature/
The Family of Blood
(2007)**

SCARECROWS

The Family amassed various items of stolen technology, including disintegrator guns, a Time Agent's vortex manipulator and an invisibility shield for their ship. Most notably, though, when they needed soldiers, they used molecular fringe animation to bring straw men to life. They were the ideal army, horrifying, mindlessly obedient, and utterly disposable.

THE FENDAHL

A gestalt creature created from pure energy that feeds on life itself

CREATED BY
Chris Boucher

APPEARANCES
**Image of the Fendahl
(1977)**

The Fendahl is one of the most terrible and powerful creatures ever to have existed. So terrible that the Time Lords tried to wipe it from existence, and so powerful that they failed.

It is, in fact, not a single entity but a colonial organism, analogous to Earth siphonophores such as the Portuguese man o' war. The Fendahl exists as two types of creature, each dedicated to a specific task: the equivalents of zooids, the Fendahleen, large limbless creatures that resemble a cross between a slug, a lamprey and a polyp, which are dedicated to feeding parasitically; and the equivalent of a medusoid, the Fendahl core, which acts as the guiding intelligence. The two forms of the Fendahl combine through telepathy into a psychic 'gestalt', comprising one core and twelve Fendahleen.

The Fendahl is said to feed on life itself. To be precise, it absorbs the full spectrum of wavelengths of the life force or soul, leaving behind nothing but a rapidly decomposing desiccated husk. It uses this energy to recreate itself, drawing on any appropriate genetic material. For instance, a human victim may first appear to have an embryo Fendahleen feeding upon them, before disappearing to be replaced by a Fendahleen.

An evolutionary misstep caused the Fendahl to feed on its own kind, reaching a point of near-extinction. It only escaped by gathering enough energy to telepathically project itself to prehistoric Earth. There, it dissipated its energy into a biological transmutation field and set about influencing the evolution of the human race to become a suitable medium for its resurrection. By the time the Time Lords destroyed its home planet and sealed all memory of it in a time loop, it was too late.

Even a single, isolated Fendahleen is a fearsome prospect. It may be slow-moving, but it can afford to take its time as it can paralyse its victims by telekinetically controlling their muscles. Fendahleen can be created by the Fendahl core through pure energy, and they can only be killed with sodium chloride; another thing they have in common with Earth slugs.

THE SOURCE OF LEGEND

The Fendahl implanted itself in humanity's race memory, giving people dreams of other times and other worlds. This also means that the Fendahl's medusoid core – a robed female who can immobilise anyone who looks into her eyes – is almost certainly the source of the legend of the Medusa.

FISH PEOPLE

The horrifying results of insane scientific experiments

The disappearance of Professor Zaroff was one of the great unsolved mysteries of the 1950s. The greatest scientific genius since Leonardo da Vinci and the foremost expert in producing food from the sea, Zaroff inexplicably vanished without trace just days before he was about to be indicted for crimes against humanity. The West accused the East of kidnapping him; the East accused the West. The truth, however, was far stranger. Zaroff had fled to the lost kingdom of Atlantis, which he had located beneath a remote volcanic island south of the Azores, where he took charge of their scientific research, promising the kingdom's credulous inhabitants that he would lift Atlantis out of the sea.

That was not the only thing he did for them. The people of Atlantis had been barely subsisting in caves, so Zaroff developed a way of feeding them with processed plankton. The plankton needed to be harvested from the sea, so a workforce was required, and this gave Zaroff, in his madness, an idea. The Atlanteans already worshipped the water goddess Amdo and venerated sea life, dressing in shells, wearing fish masks and octopus headdresses. So what if he found a way of turning people into fish?

Zaroff began his work, using shipwrecked sailors as experimental subjects. There were two stages to the process. The victim was surgically fitted with goggles and plastic gills, after which they would no longer be able to speak, instead communicating through sign language and by making a warbling, bubbling sound. They could then be enslaved and put to work gathering plankton while undergoing a lengthy series of operations to fully transform them into cold-blooded fish, altering their eyes and their skin and giving them decorative ventral fins, like leafy seadragons. As the fish people could already work underwater, there was no practical reason for this obscene transformation; it was an act of pure scientific sadism, designed to make it clear to the fish people that they could never be restored to normal.

CREATED BY
Geoffrey Orme

APPEARANCES
The Underwater Menace
(1967)

UNANSWERED QUESTION

The Doctor ultimately defeated Professor Zaroff by flooding what remained of Atlantis, forcing its human inhabitants to the surface. But what became of the fish people? There is an old seafarers' tale that they still live within the submerged ruins, singing songs of the time the Doctor came to their aid. But old seafarers' tales are notoriously unreliable. In fact, they're very fishy.

FLESH

Sentient, programmable matter that can generate exact doppelgangers

The first thing you have to understand about the Flesh is that it is alive. Not just alive in the sense of a plant. Alive in the sense that it has a living mind.

Humans generated the first Flesh in a laboratory in the twenty-second century — a viscous, milky soup of programmable matter, capable of replicating any living organism. The idea being to create a duplicate of a human, an avatar or 'Ganger', which was then controlled from a sensory harness. That way, the 'Ganger' could be used in dangerous environments instead of humans. Because Gangers were disposable; if one was destroyed, you could always make another.

What nobody realised was that every time a Ganger was created, the controller's memories, emotions and personality were added to the melting pot, giving the Flesh life. It was learning to recreate itself on a cellular level.

Then there was an accident. On a remote industrial facility dedicated to mining and refining crystal-dilurgic acid, a massive wave of energy was conducted into the Flesh. This didn't give life to the Flesh, which was already alive, but it gave the Ganger doppelgangers an independent existence. They had the memories, personalities and appearances of their operators and no longer required operators to be plumbed into harnesses to sustain them.

CREATED BY
Matthew Graham

APPEARANCES
**The Rebel Flesh/
The Almost People (2011)
A Good Man Goes
To War (2011)**

Although they were alive, they were still unstable Flesh, shifting in and out of human form. And they retained a mental link with the Flesh. The Flesh could remember all the Gangers that had been created and destroyed. It could remember their last thought before they were dissolved: 'Why?'

And now the Flesh wanted revenge on humanity. The Gangers were divided. Some only wanted to live. Others knew that humans would never allow that to happen. The humans thought they were simply monsters, mistakes to be destroyed.

So, if humans thought them monsters, monsters they must be. This was just the beginning. There were millions of other Gangers across the globe. The time had come for them to rise up against humanity.

UNANSWERED QUESTION

The Gangers on Earth were the product of an early stage of Flesh technology. What about the Ganger of Amy created by Madame Kovarian in the fifty-second century? We can be sure that the Ganger Amy didn't have an independent life, as she was always acting as an avatar for the real Amy. We must hope the same is true for her baby.

THE FLOOD

Water from Mars that can control human minds

CREATED BY
**Russell T Davies
and Phil Ford**

APPEARANCES
**The Waters of Mars
(2009)**

Some people claim that water has memory. But why stop there? If water can remember, water can think. And that is what the Flood is. Intelligent water. Water as a virus.

It originated on Mars. Mars was once a world of oceans, where the Flood could exist freely and untraceably, but then the planet cooled and the oceans froze into glaciers which retreated to the poles. The native species of Martians were reptilian and mostly composed of water, so the Flood attempted to use them as hosts. But they fought back and trapped it in an ice field.

Thousands of years later, humans established their first colony on Mars, Bowie Base One, and began to draw water from the ice field. Little did they know that they were setting the Flood free.

All it took was one recently washed carrot. Once the Flood had entered its first host, it acted like an infection. Not merely altering the cells of the body but, through a process of fission, converting them into water. The host's appearance changed, as the skin around their mouth dehydrated, becoming sore and cracked. Their eyes became white as their irises liquefied. Their teeth and tongues were blackened by the fission. And they started to exude water from their fingertips and mouths in a steady trickle.

Acquiring new hosts was easy; it would take only a single drop of water, but the Flood could spray a jet of water into their mouths to hasten the process. Their victims would initially appear to be drowning, until the Flood enabled them to breathe water and survive in the thin Martian air.

Once it had a human host, the Flood had access to their minds. Brains are three-quarters water, after all. Suddenly it could think. It could speak. And when it learned about the oceans of Earth, it knew what it must do. It had to reach this world full of water.

To do that, it would have to be clever. It would need to conceal itself inside new hosts. It would have to be patient. But water is patient. And water always wins.

UNANSWERED QUESTION

The Flood never reveals its name during its attack on Bowie Base One, so how does the Doctor know what to call it? The explanation is that the Flood is using telepathy between its various hosts and the Doctor is unconsciously picking up on the transmissions.

THE FORETOLD

An ancient soldier being driven by malfunctioning technology

Once there was a war. The time and the place have long since been forgotten. Only two relics of it survive: a flag, now so ancient and decayed it resembles a parchment covered in cryptic abstract symbols; and the soldier who once carried that flag.

He should have died in the war. He was mortally wounded, but the technology implanted into his body kept him alive. Or more accurately undead, because he was now a slave to all the technology implanted into him, which had only one function — to keep his body alive at all costs.

The technology required energy to sustain him, and the only source of this was to drain it from the living. The other technology enabled him to do this without detection. State-of-the-art phase camouflage meant he was, in effect, in another dimension, a walking ghost. A personal teleporter meant that he would always be able to get close to his victim, no matter how fast they ran.

The soldier needed to be in phase with each of his victims to drain their energy. This took sixty-six seconds, during which time they — and they alone — would be able to see it. The last thing they would ever see would be its bandaged hand reaching towards their head.

Without a deep tissue scan, death by cellular energy-draining is indistinguishable from death by natural causes, so the soldier fed, almost undetected, for millennia. The only accounts of it were given by those who had seen it in the final moments of their lives. Over five thousand years, it became a creature of legend. It was given a name, the Foretold. 'They that bear the Foretold's stare have sixty-six seconds to live.' Its rotting, ragged bandages meant it was often mistaken for a mummified corpse. Some stories said that there was a riddle or secret word that could make it stop. Some of its victims tried bargaining with it or confessing their sins. Some just tried to outrun it. But none of them survived.

None of them could escape a soldier condemned to keep fighting a war for eternity.

CREATED BY
Jamie Mathieson

APPEARANCES
Mummy on the Orient Express (2014)

UNANSWERED QUESTION

The Foretold always chose as its victim the person in its vicinity who was weakest and closest to death. Some have speculated that this was the Foretold showing mercy. It was in fact simply the technology, selecting the victim whose sudden demise was least likely to arouse suspicion.

GALLIFREYAN ROBOTS & OTHER CREATURES

Creations of the brilliant minds of the Time Lords

Through the millennia, the Time Lords of Gallifrey have led a life of peace and ordered calm, protected from all threats from lesser civilisations by their great power, and by a number of specially designed robots...

RASTON WARRIOR ROBOTS

In the ancient times of the Time Lords, during their wars with the Great Vampires, the great engineer Rassilon constructed bow ships to confront the vampires in space. He also created machines to fight

them on the ground, to hunt down and kill any Gallifreyans under the vampires' thrall. These machines were efficient and elegant, able to move faster than the blink of an eye and with sensors able to detect any movement. Mostly importantly, they had built-in armaments and could fire bolts of steel at their enemy's heart, the one sure way to kill any vampire. If that failed, they were programmed to decapitate their enemies.

They were known as Rassilon's Automatons, though over the years their name was abbreviated to Rastons and, according to legend, they were the most perfect killing machines ever devised.

CLOISTER WRAITHS

The Matrix on Gallifrey is the repository of the brains of all dead Time Lords, kept alive within a living computer. Over the years the Matrix has been breached by thieves attempting to steal its secrets, as well as Daleks, Cybermen and Weeping Angels, so now the Cloister Wraiths are activated whenever the Cloisters of the Matrix are breached. They are essentially robots guided by the minds of deceased Time Lords from within the Matrix; they glide about the tunnels, which is why they are also known as Sliders. Their function is not to repel invaders but to ensure that they never leave. Any being that enters the Cloisters will end up being added to the Matrix database.

RASTON WARRIOR ROBOTS CREATED BY
Terrance Dicks
APPEARANCES
The Five Doctors (1983)

CLOISTER WRAITHS CREATED BY
Steven Moffat
APPEARANCES
Hell Bent (2015)

GELLGUARDS CREATED BY
Bob Baker and Dave Martin
APPEARANCES
The Three Doctors (1972)

ERGON CREATED BY
Johnny Byrne
APPEARANCES
Arc of Infinity (1983)

THE VEIL CREATED BY
Steven Moffat
APPEARANCES
Heaven Sent (2015)

OMEGA'S ANTIMATTER CREATIONS

The great Gallifreyan stellar engineer Omega was determined to find and create a power source that would give his people mastery over time. He succeeded but was lost in a supernova and given up for dead by the Time Lords. They did not realise that he had survived in the universe of antimatter, keeping himself alive by an effort of will, determined to wreak his revenge on the race that had abandoned him.

of matter into antimatter so they could be brought into Omega's domain. As part of his plan to capture the Doctor, this energy also took on the form of shapeless monsters called Gellguards, equipped with claw-like extrusions which could fire vaporising blasts of energy. They also made a noise like 'grumble-grumble-grumble'; this was a side effect of being created by pure mental force, the noise being the sound of Omega's grumbling subconscious.

GELLGUARDS

His first attempt came when he gained access to the universe of matter through a black hole. He sent through it a

form of controlled superlucent emission targeted at Earth, and which resolved itself as an amorphous mass of energy. It was an organism created by Omega, imbued with subatomic properties that meant it could survive in the universes of both matter and antimatter.

It could also convert beings

THE ERGON

Omega's second attempt to take revenge on the Time Lords came when he gained access to the universe of matter through a region of space known as the Arc of Infinity. This time he created a more sophisticated organism to act as his servant in the world of matter: a skeletal creature with a beak filled with jagged teeth. This creature was designed to instil terror in all who faced it: the Ergon. Unfortunately Omega's attempt at psychosynthesis was not completely successful because, at best, it instilled confusion rather than terror.

THE VEIL

When a Time Lord is close to death, they have to go through a ritual of mental purification before their mind is uploaded to the Matrix. It involves a device called a Confession Dial, which enables a Time Lord to face their demons and make peace with them. It can, however, be put to another use: for a living Time Lord, it could serve as a torture chamber. They would be given company in the form of their greatest, deepest childhood fear, brought to life using the clockwork technology of fifty-first-century Earth. In the Doctor's case, it was a veiled corpse that he saw when he was very young. The idea was that the prisoner would be relentless pursued by their worst fear, until they confessed a truth they had never revealed before. Then the dial would reset and repeat the process all over again

GASTROPODS

Intergalactic molluscs with the power of telepathy

Gastropods are, as their name suggests, slugs. Giant slugs that have evolved prehensile hands, the power of reasoning and speech, but slugs nonetheless. They are a cosmic scourge, stripping whole planets of vegetable matter, leaving them as barren deserts. Wherever a Gastropod has been, you should fear to tread... because they leave behind slime trails that set into a substance harder than concrete.

As they gained the ability to slide upright, their upper bodies dried out and became rigid, with carapace-like mantles on their backs. Only the underside of the Gastropod, its 'foot', secretes mucus. Once their main sensory organ was smell, but over millennia the stench created by their own gastrointestinal tracts made this impractical, so instead they developed a sixth sense, a form of telepathy using antennae attuned to psychic wavelengths.

Most Gastropods are dull, unthinking creatures with little conversation or ambition, content merely to strip bark from trees. But in each generation there is a more mentally advanced male, known as the Mestor. The Gastropod Mestor has much greater telepathic powers: it can read minds, project its thoughts across interstellar distances through the astral plane, use other beings as its eyes and ears, and kill them either by burning out their brains or causing their blood to bubble. The Mestor is responsible for leading the Gastropod cornucopia, effectively controlling their minds, with one burning desire — to find new worlds for them to devastate.

The Gastropods' planet of origin is unknown. All that is known is that their eggs, which are thick enough to withstand the coldness of space and the temperatures of an exploding sun, are laid by the Mestor and incubated in Royal hatcheries.. These eggs drift through space until they land on a planet, where they hatch and the Gastropods begin to feed on any foliage, with one Gastropod becoming the Mestor, producing vast numbers of hungry offspring and using its powers of mental domination to spread its sluggy eggs across the universe.

CREATED BY
Anthony Steven

APPEARANCES
The Twin Dilemma (1984)

UNANSWERED QUESTION

After the sixth Doctor defeated the Lord Mestor on the planet Joconda, he departed with the satisfaction of a job well done. He apparently didn't stop to consider the other Gastropods that were still roaming the tunnels. Perhaps he knew that without the guiding intelligence of Mestor they would revert to mindless beasts, beasts that could be killed by being sprinkled with salt, or by being shot with a laser gun.

GELTH

Gaseous creatures that exploit the corpses of the dead

The Gelth are the ultimate parasites. They don't merely feed on bodies, they steal them. As they exist in a gaseous state, they have to occupy the bodies of other beings in order to have physical form; ideally bodies which are decomposing and producing methane gas. This means their whole existence is dependent upon having a large, steady supply of rotting corpses to occupy, because the problem with walking around inside decomposing cadavers is that they tend not to last very long.

The Gelth have evolved various strategies to ensure a supply of corpses. One is to find a 'medium' through which they can speak and appear. They take on a voice most likely to elicit pity and trust, usually that of a child, and they draw inspiration for their appearance from local legends and superstitions. (When, for instance, they came to Gwyneth in nineteenth-century Swansea, they appeared to her as beautiful, female angels.) Then, through the 'medium', posing as a saint or ancestral spirit, they can say whatever is necessary to create a bloody battle, fame or plague.

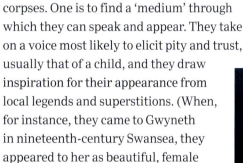

CREATED BY
Mark Gatiss

APPEARANCES
The Unquiet Dead (2005)

The Time War gave the Gelth the perfect opportunity. There were rifts in time through which they could reach other systems and they could claim to be 'higher forms' that had been devastated by the War and left trapped in a gaseous state facing extinction. All they wanted was the chance to occupy bodies that would otherwise be going to waste — was that too much to ask?

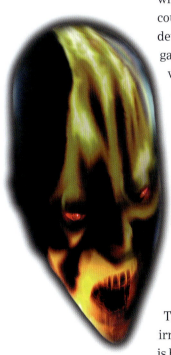

Once they have bodies to occupy, of course, their manner changes. Their priority then is to create more corpses, for themselves when their current 'vessel' outlives its usefulness and for the rest of the Gelth. They are a remarkably successful species, numbering in their billions, because if there's one thing the universe is never going to run out of, it's dead bodies.

The Gelth do have one weakness, though. They not only require methane gas, they are irresistibly drawn towards it. And methane gas is highly flammable...

THE LIVING DEAD

There is one final horror about the Gelth. When they occupy a corpse, the mind of their vessel is returned to a form of semi-consciousness, where they may act according to instinct or even be aware that they have returned from the dead and are now trapped in their own corpse. This is why the vessels tend to scream. They may be dead but they aren't quiet.

GIANT MUTATIONS

Earth creatures turned into monsters by pollution and experimentation

Earth scientists believe that there is a limit to how large a species can grow, known as the square-cube law. The principle is that if a creature doubles in size, its muscle strength will be multiplied by four (the square or two) while its mass will be multiplied by eight (the cube of two), meaning that there will come a point where it will no longer be able to support itself. These scientists are wrong...

GIANT MAGGOTS

When Global Chemicals opened its oil refinery in Llanfairfach, Wales, one of its strongest selling points was that it could produce plastic without any waste or pollution. Unfortunately, their refining process was far from waste-free: its main by-product was a thick, green, phosphorescent, non-biodegradable sludge. Global Chemicals pumped the waste into a nearby disused mine, where it had a shocking effect on the wildlife.

The mine was home to flies, and the sludge caused their eggs to grow to the size of rugby balls. When they hatched, the sludge caused the maggots to grow even larger, up to a metre in length. After feeding on the sludge, the maggots also exuded their own slime. This was highly toxic; when touched it created a severe burning sensation, followed by a form of infection as the chemical altered the internal structure of the host's cells to become maggot cells. This was normally fatal but serendipitously a local professor of biology had created a hybrid fungus that was lethal to the maggots and cured the infection.

By this point, unfortunately, one of the maggots had undergone metamorphosis, so there was now a giant fly on the loose that could spit toxic slime.

GIANT RATS

When the fifty-first-century war criminal Magnus Greel fled back through time using an experimental zygma-beam-powered time cabinet, he found himself in the nineteenth century with his DNA helixes split open. Desperate to prevent his cellular disintegration, he took up residence in the London sewers and experimented on the rats to gauge the strength of his psionic amplification field. The result was rodents three metres long that would strike terror into the heart of anyone who saw them.

GIANT SPIDERS

A similar gigantism mutation occurred in Sheffield, when a disused mine was filled with a soup of extremely toxic waste. Normally this wouldn't cause arachnid amplification but in this case the waste included spider carcasses from a nearby laboratory. These were spiders which had been bio-engineered to spin stronger cobwebs and given an enzyme to extend their lifespan. And not all of them were dead. Some of them survived in the mine, where the combination of toxic waste and their genetic engineering meant that they just kept getting bigger, until their pheromones were strong enough to affect the entire spider eco-system.

THE GREAT INTELLIGENCE

A formless entity intent on manifesting itself physically

The Great Intelligence began as snow. Crystals from space, falling to Earth in the winter of 1842. The snow was rolled into a snowman by a lonely little boy called Walter. But the snow was a kind of mind parasite, feeding on dark dreams and negative emotions. It possessed a low-level telepathic field which meant it could read minds — and speak to them. And so that lonely little boy called Walter found his snowman was speaking to him. It started by mirroring his thoughts, then began to tell him what to do...

CREATED BY
Mervyn Haisman and Henry Lincoln

APPEARANCES
The Abominable Snowmen (1967)
The Web of Fear (1968)
The Snowmen (2012)
The Bells of Saint John (2013)
The Name of the Doctor (2013)

THE LONDON SNOWMEN

Fifty years later, that boy was Doctor Simeon, the head of the secret GI Institute. The snow from his snowman remained alive in a globe, still giving him instructions. More of the telepathic snow was falling to Earth and Simeon ordered it to be gathered to form Snowmen. They were basic, mindless foot soldiers that fed on human flesh, merely a means to an end. Because to conquer the Earth the snow needed to evolve.

THE ICE GOVERNESS

It needed a form like that of Doctor Simeon: human but made of ice. A cruel governess had drowned in a pond not far from the GI Institute, and the Intelligence realised that it could use the nightmares of the child she had traumatised to create a human duplicate in ice crystal form.

Once it had perfected the process, it would make an army in her image. By now, the Intelligence in the globe had come to dominate Doctor Simeon. Even when its creator died, the Intelligence continued to exist as a disembodied Intelligence in space. But it could still speak and control vulnerable minds via the astral plane.

And on the astral plane, just as in dreams, time travel is possible. The Intelligence sought out a monk lost in transcendental meditation in the Himalayas in the mid seventeenth century. A monk who had recently met the Doctor. His name was Padmasambhava...

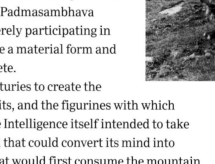

THE ABOMINABLE SNOWMEN

Maybe it was because the monk had heard tales of the timid, rarely glimpsed beasts that lived in the mountains. Maybe it was because the Intelligence remembered stories from Walter's childhood. For whatever reason, the Intelligence decided that this time its servants on Earth would take the form of the Yeti. There was no telepathic snow available — indeed, no snow at all in this part of the mountains — so they would have to be robots. Construction would be a protracted process. And so the Intelligence kept Padmasambhava alive, convincing him that he was merely participating in an experiment to give the Intelligence a material form and would be released once it was complete.

It took Padmasambhava three centuries to create the robot Yeti, their spherical control units, and the figurines with which he could guide their movements. The Intelligence itself intended to take physical form by means of a pyramid that could convert its mind into matter. A seething, bubbling foam that would first consume the mountain and then spread across the whole world.

THE LONDON ABOMINABLE SNOWMEN

But the pyramid was destroyed and the Intelligence was banished back to the void of space, a formless, shapeless cloud with a mind of its own. It was now determined to take revenge upon the one responsible — the Doctor. When one of its control spheres was reactivated, it saw its chance. Just one reactivated Yeti would be enough. It recalled the Doctor saying that the Underground was London's key strategic weakness and so it took control of the tunnels, manifesting itself as a kind of mist. It possessed humans who entered the mist and made them construct more Yeti, using parts from the Science Museum and animal furs from the Natural History Museum. This time the Yeti would be improved, with glowing eyes, guns that could shoot web-like fungus and the ability to home in on Yeti figurines. It was all a trap for the Doctor; once the Intelligence had him in its web, it would drain all the knowledge from his mind. This plan, of course, failed, and the Intelligence was banished to space once more.

THE WHISPER MEN

The Intelligence had discovered the location of the Doctor's grave, on the planet Trenzalore and knew that the grave contained a tear in reality opening onto the Doctor's timeline.

The Intelligence wanted to turn all the Doctor's victories into defeats. But the grave was within a tomb that could only be opened by speaking the Doctor's name, and the only person who would know it would be the Doctor himself. So it planned to kidnap his closest friends then force him to open the tomb.

The Intelligence took on the form of the man who had created it, Doctor Simeon, and created servants in his image. They had no physical form, they were merely projections of its will. They didn't need to see or hear, so it left their faces blank, but they needed to speak so it gave them mouths. They were its ultimate manifestation: beings that could kill with a single touch. And that always spoke in rhyme for added sinister effect. They were the Whisper Men.

Now all it needed to do was to bring the Doctor's friends together in its own territory, the astral plane. So it sought out a man with an unhinged mind and gave him a message. 'The Doctor has a secret he will take to the grave. And it is discovered.'

SPOONHEADS

The Intelligence was now weak and needed to reconstitute itself. If it could not feed on the Doctor's mind, it could at least feed on the minds of other humans. So, just as it had first possessed Walter as a little boy, this time it used a lonely eight-year-old called Rosemary Kizlet who had lost her parents at the time of the Intelligence's London invasion. It needed human minds, and lots of them, and it used Kizlet to advance human technology until it had developed the two things it needed — the internet and wi-fi.

The Intelligence was no longer a foam, a cloud in space or a kind of mist. It was now a data cloud. It would use robots again, but this time they would be disguised properly, not as Yeti, but as mobile servers called 'spoonheads' that could camouflage themselves by taking images from people's minds. Anyone who clicked on the wrong wi-fi network would summon a spoonhead to harvest their mind.

Although this plan was defeated, the Intelligence had achieved its goal of restoring itself. Over the centuries it had observed the Doctor's progress through time and space. The Intelligence itself could travel in time, of course, through the astral plane, and had occasionally considered intervening in its own past. This gave it the inspiration for its most audacious plan of all.

THE GREAT VAMPIRES

Parasites from the Dawn of Time that drained planets of all life

CREATED BY
Terrance Dicks

APPEARANCES
State of Decay (1980)

The Great Vampires should be extinct. According to the legends, in the ancient history of the Time Lords, the Great Vampires appeared from nowhere and swarmed across the universe. Each was as big as a medium-sized town and capable of singlehandedly sucking a planet dry. They resembled humanoid bats, with gnarled, goblin-like faces, pointed ears, sharp incisors and large fangs. They were so powerful that they were almost impossible to kill, as they could absorb any energy and use it to make themselves stronger.

The only way to kill one was discovered by the great Time Lord engineer, Rassilon. He ordered the construction of bow ships that could fire a bolt of steel to pierce a vampire through the heart. Only then would the vampire die. In those days, the Time Lords were equally corrupt and cruel; some accounts say that Rassilon was the cruellest Time Lord of all and the other Time Lords rebelled against him. But the war with the Great Vampires changed them; it was so bloody and terrible that the Time Lords renounced violence forever.

At the end of the war, however, the King Vampire, the mightiest of them all, vanished from time and space. Rassilon laid down a directive that any Time Lord who found the King must destroy him, even at the cost of their own life.

The King Vampire had, in fact, taken possession of the three officers of the exploration vessel *Hydrax* and escaped into the pocket universe of E-Space. There were few planets there to provide nourishment, so the King grew weak and entered a state of hibernation. He granted the officers some of his powers: they could live forever without ageing, and they would have a psychic familiarity with bats, being able to control them and see through them. All the officers had to do was provide the sleeping King with a supply of human blood until he was ready to arise. The three ruled over the descendants of the rest of the *Hydrax* crew for a thousand years, breeding them for obedience like cattle and selecting those with the most vigour for blood donation.

THE VAMPIRE MUTATION

Even when the vampires were gone, their legend lived on, in race memories, folk stories and myths on almost every inhabited planet. Their legacy also endured as a kind of primeval genetic template, giving rise to other vampiric forms, such as Haemovores and the Lazarus creature.

HAEMOVORES

Mutated future humans with an insatiable hunger for blood

Haemovores are, like the Dregs, a potential future form of the human race. One that may arise in a version of the Earth which has been poisoned by thousands of years of industrial pollution, where the surface is just a chemical slime. Under such circumstances, humans develop a vampiric infection and become cannibalistic, devouring each other, until only one is left.

That last remnant of life on Earth represented the ultimate, obscene mutation of humanity into a creature evolved to live beneath the surface, using gills to breathe and tentacles to feed. It watched its world die and waited for the end, but instead it became a pawn in the game of the ancient evil known as Fenric. It was sent in a time storm to ninth-century Transylvania to seek out and release Fenric, who was held in a flask. The flask was stolen by Vikings and transported to England, where the Haemovore attempted to regain the flask by sinking the Vikings' longboat and infecting them, but one escaped to the shore and buried the flask in an underground vault.

CREATED BY
Ian Briggs

APPEARANCES
The Curse of Fenric
(1989)

Over the centuries, the infected Vikings lured villagers into the waters and infected them too. A legend grew up regarding the nearby beach, Maiden's Point; it was said that you could hear the terrible lost cries of girls who went there and were never seen again.

The infected Vikings and villagers gradually transformed into Haemovores, creatures adapted to feed on blood. The first stage was a pallid appearance and extremely rapid and extensive fingernail growth. In time, their heads became a bloated, misshapen mass of sea-rotted flesh, their eyes empty sockets, their skin pale blue, covered in blisters and barnacles.

And, in the flask in the vault, Fenric waited. Waiting for the day it would be freed and could summon the Haemovores to live in a new version of Earth destroyed by chemical warfare.

ABILITIES AND WEAKNESSES

The Haemovore infection bestows its host with two other remarkable abilities. Firstly, the capacity to generate a strong electrical field with their hands powerful enough to weld metal. The Haemovores mostly use this power to create jewellery; discarded items may still retain a static charge. Secondly, they gain a form of telepathy. A Haemovore may destroy those it has infected by effort of will. This telepathy is also their great weakness; it renders them sensitive to displays of faith, which create a 'psychic barrier'.

HARMONY SHOAL

Disembodied brains that invade planets by stealth

The universe has bred some extraordinary creatures, and few are more extraordinary than the parasitic brains known as Harmony Shoal. Whether that is their real name or not remains a mystery, but for some reason whenever they are formulating plans of planetary conquest, they invariably do so under the cover of organisations calling themselves things like the Harmony Shoal Institute, Harmony Shoals Incorporated or even British Harmony Shoals.

This is because, being disembodied brains, they need bodies. Over the millennia their evolution paralleled that of the Morphoton brains of Marinus, as they outgrew their bodies and became independent life forms consisting of just brains with eyes living in jars. They quickly came to realise this was a huge evolutionary mistake and set about getting bodies back again. Fortunately they had advanced knowledge of open-head surgery and reengineered themselves so they could function as independent peripatetic central nervous systems. Or, to put it another way, so that they could scoop out the brains of their victims, pop in their own brains, and ride around inside them. Even if no brains were available, they could animate brainless bodies, as security drones.

They then began to migrate from planet to planet. They favoured humanoid life forms, as they required skulls that were a good fit and where the eyeholes were in the right place. Their nature lent itself to covert invasion as, rather than bombing a planet into submission, they could simply extract and replace the brains of key authority figures over a period of years. That way they could take over planets with the minimum of fuss and loss of assets; all it would take would be a little patience.

CREATED BY
Steven Moffat

APPEARANCES
The Husbands of River Song (2015)
The Return of Doctor Mysterio (2016)

UNANSWERED QUESTION

What became of Harmony Shoal after their failed invasion of Earth? The brain that had been inside Dr Sim took control of a UNIT soldier and quickly – and undetectably – rescued its fellow brains. Having given up on the Earth as a bad job, they kept a low profile until it was possible to leave and resume their interplanetary migration elsewhere. Three thousand, three hundred years later they had a new home planet and had built up an intergalactic crime syndicate, now called the Shoal of the Winter Harmony. Among other things, they operated the starship *Harmony and Redemption*. They were also loyal subjects of King Hydroflax – anticipating that, at some point in the future, they might be able to change his mind...

HATH

Militaristic humanoid fish engaged in a bitter war with humanity

The Hath are a fascinating example of a species adapting itself to a new environment. They are clearly descended from tropical fish, their bright colouring indicating that they come from a world of well-lit shallow waters. Yet they are also humanoid, with arms, hands and an approximately human skeleton, indicating that, on this world, they had evolved to walk on the seabed and manipulate their environment. They did this without adapting to live on land or breathe air, suggesting that this option was not available to them, and theirs was a world consisting entirely of oceans. It seems that, just as humans evolved from apes, the Hath evolved from creatures not unlike batfish, that also walk on the ocean floor.

They have since adapted to survive on land, using a mouth-mounted breathing apparatus. This apparatus enables them to respire as though underwater, the opposite equivalent of a diver wearing a breathing apparatus. That said, the device acts more as a filter, drawing in essential chemicals from the atmosphere, as it is unable to function if submerged — indeed, it shatters. Interestingly, the breathing device only fits over their mouth, suggesting that either they lack gills or the apparatus works for both inhalation and exhalation.

It also, conspicuously, works for communication, as the Hath speak by exhaling a stream of bubbles. Perhaps surprisingly this has enabled them to develop a language with as much scope for nuance as spoken English. Martha Jones, when she encountered the Hath on the planet Messaline, was able to understand the Hath perfectly. This is undoubtedly a testament to the translation skills of the TARDIS telepathic circuits, as the Hath's speech remained unfathomable to everyone else.

CREATED BY
Stephen Greenhorn

APPEARANCES
**The Doctor's Daughter
(2008)
The End of Time (2010)
The Magician's
Apprentice (2015)**

BUBBLE MEMORY

The fact that Hath communicate with bubbles is also what led to a breakdown between the human and Hath colonists when they first arrived on Messaline, with the humans believing the Hath wanted the world for themselves. Given its unsuitability for aquatic life, this seems unlikely, but if one party is communicating via a stream of bubbles it is easy to see how a misunderstanding may occur.

As a result, the humans declared war upon the Hath. Each side was forced to take up arms and to use progenation machines to create generations of new soldiers with no memory of the war's origins. Fortunately, the Doctor ended the week-long war between the humans and the Hath, and they agreed to share the newly terraformed world of Messaline.

HEAVENLY HOST

Robot servants programmed to provide tourist information and kill

INFORMATION: All robots have been programmed with a prime directive not to kill.
INFORMATION: Anything that can be programmed can also be reprogrammed.
INFORMATION: Robots can kill.

The Heavenly Host were designed to represent the ultimate in luxury. These were not just any robot servants. These were robot servants made of gold (well, gold-plated) and they could fly (for brief periods without recharging). They were quite deliberately designed to resemble statues of angels, complete with robes, halos and wings. They were given neutral, authoritative voices to instil confidence and, in a cursory attempt to avoid 'robophobia', jaws that would move in sync with their words. The only problem was the eyes: black, blank, unblinking. This was because these robots were built not just to serve, but to provide security. Eyes like security cameras would be an obvious reminder to people that they were being watched.

What nobody — apart from their creator — knew was that the Heavenly Host were also designed to kill. They had the strength of ten men and could break through solid metal with a karate chop. They were deadlock sealed to prevent sonic interference and could remove trapped limbs without injury. And, terrifyingly, their angelic halos could be removed and deployed as lethal, razor-bladed boomerangs.

The Host had only two vulnerabilities. Firstly, a powerful electromagnetic pulse could knock out their circuits, requiring them to perform a 60-second reboot. And secondly, being totally crushed.

The fact that the Heavenly Host on the interplanetary cruise liner *Titanic* were glitching should have raised suspicions that their programming had been interfered with. When one nearly broke the neck of a female passenger who had asked it to fix her necklace, it was a warning sign that should have been heeded. But it was not until the Host started killing everybody on sight that the crew finally realised that something was amiss.

CREATED BY
Russell T Davies

APPEARANCES
Voyage of the Damned (2007)

THE QUESTIONS QUESTION

The fact that the Heavenly Host will answer three questions under security protocol one is a little odd until you remember that they had originally been programmed to supply tourist information. Their command structure was, therefore, to prioritise answering questions over any other activity. The reason why only three questions were allowed was because it was thought that three questions would be enough for an engineer to diagnose a malfunction while precluding the possibility of someone preventing a Host from performing essential duties by asking it to help with the ship's quiz.

HOUSE

Sadistic thief with big green energy

House was the size of an asteroid. His exterior was rigid and his interior soft, which led the Doctor to describe him as 'like a sea urchin'. He sounded somewhat refined when speaking through others, using them as a speaker system, but his vocal tone had an edge of what can only be called 'growlspook'.

House had an unusual food source: rift energy, otherwise known as Artron energy. He eventually found a reliable source in TARDISes. He drew Time Lords to his surface in order to feed on the energy from their TARDIS core, but first he had to extract the Matrix from the TARDIS otherwise the TARDIS would destroy him.

A TARDIS consciousness could not be deleted after extraction; this would have blown a hole in the universe. Instead, the Matrix was simply deposited into any available living creature — a human, animal, alien. House's surface was littered with the remains of half-eaten TARDISes; a kind of junkyard.

House repaired two of his 'servants', Auntie and Uncle, using spare parts from the bodies of Time Lords. He enjoyed tormenting them. Nephew, an Ood, acted as another of House's mouthpieces, his eyes glowing as he spoke with the green light that was House's hallmark.

House was able to exploit distress signals as a lure for Gallifreyans and had a collection of Time Lord message boxes, or hypercubes, originally belonging to his victims. The Doctor, Amy and Rory were drawn to House by the hypercube of the Corsair, an old friend of the Doctor's, who retained a distinctive ouroboros tattoo even as they changed sex during the regeneration process. This tattoo marked the outside of the hypercube and was also visible on Auntie's arm.

The Doctor told House he was the last of the Time Lords, and therefore his TARDIS was also the last. House decided he had to take control of the TARDIS, having deposited her Matrix into the body of a young woman called Idris, and escape his own universe to find more sources of food. When House was in control, the TARDIS glowed green, and he played mind games on Amy and Rory for fun. The Doctor had to build a temporary TARDIS out of junk from the surface of House to pursue the monster and return his TARDIS Matrix to her rightful home from the dying human body of Idris. House reacted with fear and anger, but was expelled from the ship.

CREATED BY
Neil Gaiman

APPEARANCES
The Doctor's Wife (2011)

KING HYDROFLAX

A homicidal autocrat with a robotic body

King Hydroflax is a psychopathic tyrant without any redeeming features whatsoever. He has wiped out whole civilisations and entire solar systems before breakfast, and his breakfasts usually consist of several of his enemies, well-cooked but not necessarily dead. He rules by sheer terror, and any form of disobedience, incompetence or minor annoyance is punished with the perpetrator being flogged, flayed and burned until they are ready to be served up for lunch. He is responsible for numerous wars, at least four of which occurred because he 'felt like having a war now', and has stolen countless works of art from across the galaxy just so he could use them for target practice. His epithets include the Butcher of the Bone Meadows, the Pillager of the Hadron, and the Insanely Violent King.

As a bloodthirsty despot, Hydroflax has often been the target of well-meaning assassinations. Some have been more successful than others, as he is now a disembodied head reliant on a large, red, tank-like cyborg body. The cyborg body is powerful, heavily armoured and even more heavily armed, and has its own dedicated life-support computer, programmed to preserve Hydroflax's life at any cost. It is powered by a perpetually stabilised black hole which will destroy the surrounding solar system in the event of Hydroflax's death (this is a feature, not a fault). Just in case that isn't enough, Hydroflax is constantly guarded by warrior monks with sentient laser swords, genetically engineered anger problems and not enough to do.

All his efforts to protect his being turned out to be in vain, however, as he still had one weak spot — his brain. When he was leading a raid on the Halassi vaults (because he 'felt like doing a raid now'), the whole thing blew up in his face and he ended up with the most valuable diamond in the universe lodged inside his enormous head. Under normal circumstances such a wound would have been fatal, but Hydroflax's brain had the consistency of wet concrete. It would still kill him, though, unless he could find a surgeon willing to operate…

CREATED BY
Steven Moffat

APPEARANCES
The Husbands of
River Song (2015)

THE CYBORG

In the absence of Hydroflax's head, his body is able to continue functioning, homing in on a beacon implanted in the head for just such an eventuality. To gather intelligence, it can 'upload' new heads onto its body by a process of decapitating them and slotting them into the gap between its shoulders.

ICE LOPHIUS

A gigantic sea creature that absorbed heat and excreted fuel

'There are more things in heaven and earth ... than are dreamt of in your philosophy.' Shakespeare was mostly right when he wrote that, because some of the strangest creatures have evolved on Earth. There's the seaweed creature of the North Atlantic that can telepathically possess people and give them the power to exhale poisonous gas, as well as secreting enormous quantities of foam. And there is the creature that inhabited the River Thames for the three hundred years up to February 1814.

CREATED BY
Sarah Dollard

APPEARANCES
Thin Ice (2017)

The creature was indigenous to Earth, but its origin remains a mystery. It resembled a giant fish of the genus Lophius, better known as a monkfish. It was approximately one mile in length and under 60 feet in width (or it wouldn't have been able to fit into the Thames). Like a monkfish, it had glowing filaments on its head, which it used as lures, and frond-like appendages that resembled seaweed. It fed by burying itself in mud and sediment, waiting for its prey to swim within reach of its extremely large, wide mouth full of sharp teeth. Unlike a monkfish, it seemed to have been capable of communicating in a manner similar to whale song, emitting a mournful, plaintive cry.

It had developed a mutualistic relationship with another species of fish resembling blobfish but with the bioluminescent lures of anglerfish. These fish sensed vibrations from creatures moving about on the surface of the frozen Thames, sought out individuals on their own, then released a wave of heat sufficient to melt the ice beneath their feet. Once their victim was submerged, on their way to be consumed, the Lophius refroze the hole in the ice; it was naturally endothermic and had caused the Thames to freeze. In return for providing the Lophius with nourishment, the food-gathering 'blobfish' were rewarded with a belch of microbial nutrients.

The creature's most unusual feature, though, was the nature of its waste product; a black clay-like substance which could be used as an extremely powerful and long-lasting fuel. It burned at a temperature

higher than any instruments were capable of measuring; it was even hot enough to burn underwater, and lasted a thousand times longer than coal. Somehow the creature's digestive tract turned Londoners into a stable compound of metallic hydrogen, rocket fuel suitable for interstellar travel. Such a fuel could alter the entire course of human history.

ICE WARRIORS

A once-proud race of militaristic Martians

As the human race took form on Earth, another intelligent race was emerging across the gulf of space. At the time, Mars was a much warmer, wetter world of tropical rainforests and lagoons, the ideal circumstances for reptile life to become the dominant, intelligent species. These Martians were crocodilian humanoids, with the sharp teeth of carnivorous predators and red eyes adapted to the weak infrared frequencies of Martian light. They built a proud civilisation that was enlightened and peaceful.

Then Mars underwent catastrophic climate change. Its atmosphere thinned and it suddenly got a lot colder. The Martians found they could hardly breathe, developing a strained, wheezing manner. To survive the cold, they retreated into vast underground cities. The surface of Mars became a barren desert where no crops could grow, so the Martians faced extinction. When a strange illness known as the Flood emerged in the expanding ice caps, the Martians trapped it in the ice, but by then their society had already changed. The once peaceful Martians became ruthless and militaristic Ice Warriors. They gave themselves biomechanoid armour to enable them to survive the freezing cold, and they launched spaceships to colonise other planets. Nothing was ever heard of them again, so the Martians that remained on Mars retreated into their hives and placed themselves in cryogenic suspended animation. They slept, waiting for the colonists to return with tidings of a new Mars.

SURVIVAL ARMOUR

The main purpose of an Ice Warrior's armour was to help them withstand freezing temperatures. It even had a failsafe: if the occupant's temperature dropped below a certain point, the armour would keep them alive in suspended animation, ready to awaken when the thaw came. It also performed other life-support functions to such a degree that the Ice Warriors became completely reliant upon it. Outside its armour, the Martian creature was weak and vulnerable, so for any Martian to remove its armour was considered a grave dishonour.

CREATED BY
Brian Hayles

APPEARANCES
**The Ice Warriors (1967)
The Seeds of Death (1969)
The War Games (1969)
The Curse of Peladon (1972)
The Monster of Peladon (1974)
Cold War (2013)
Face the Raven (2015)
Empress of Mars (2017)**

As the Ice Warriors now spent all their time in their survival armour, they adapted to favour the cold environments where it functioned best. Sudden increases in temperature or intense light had a tendency to cause it to malfunction. Martian colonists not only retained their armour when they landed on new worlds, they also altered the environments to suit them. When they attempted to invade Earth in the twenty-first century, for instance, they deployed a fungus that would reduce the oxygen content of the atmosphere to make it like that of Mars.

As Warriors, their suits also had combat functions. The standard armour consisted of a helmet that revealed only the wearer's mouth, and a body armour of sections of thick carapace like a turtle shell, which could withstand most projectile weapons. They were fitted with sonic weapons that could kill their enemies either by resonating their brain tissue or by crushing them with concentrated frequencies. The neck section would sometimes also have a fur collar for extra insulation.

Martian Lords denoted their high rank by wearing capes and larger, bullet-shaped helmets that exposed the full chin. Martian Grand Marshalls had

helmets with reflective scales, while the most high-ranking Martian of all, the Queen Empress, had a scaled helmet designed to reflect her reptilian heritage.

THE NEW MARTIANS

As well as their unsuccessful invasion attempt, three more Martian expeditions ended up on Earth. They all crashed, having chosen particularly poor landing sites. One was buried in an avalanche and its crew became embedded in a glacier, while another ship's pilot, Skaldak, was frozen in the ice under the North Pole. The pilot of the third ship had more luck: after he crashed in South Africa, he was rescued by the British Army, who helped him return to Mars, where he revived Queen Empress Iraxxa. Her reign initiated a new Martian Age, as the Martians built a new spacefaring empire and were inducted into the Galactic Federation.

But some rogue Martians never forgot their heritage, and were determined to return to the days of death or glory...

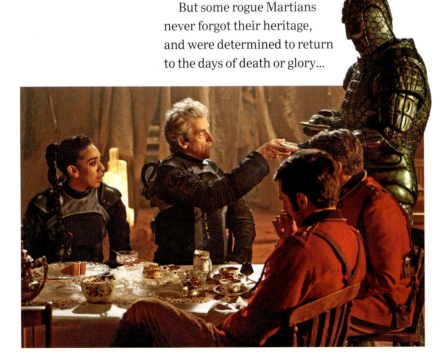

UNANSWERED QUESTION

The description 'ice warrior' was first given to the creatures by Walters, a member of Britannicus Base, and then adopted by the Doctor and his companions. So why do the Lord Azaxyr and the Queen Empress Iraxxa also refer to their race as Ice Warriors? Being reptiles, they have no affinity for ice! The reason is that 'Ice Warrior' is a name they gave themselves during the period when they were fighting the Flood, an infection that lived in the frozen waters in Mars. Unaware of its viral nature, they declared themselves to be at war with the ice itself; Ice Warriors. They now use the term for any soldier that honours their warmongering traditions. Their aversion towards water may also have caused them to overlook its effects on their oxygen-depleting fungus.

JAGAROTH

A vicious, callous warlike species that destroyed itself — almost

The Jagaroth were humanoid, but with bodies and heads covered in a mass of writhing dark green tentacles. Their faces consisted of a single eye and two gills, betraying their ancestry as creatures resembling sea anemones. They were the Medusa and the Cyclops rolled into one, and four hundred million years ago they dominated the area known as Mutter's Spiral or the Milky Way. With their advanced technology and sinister three-legged spider-ships they conquered and destroyed countless worlds. And yet they were great artists, scientists, engineers and philosophers, convinced of their own infinite superiority as they pillaged other worlds for their treasures in the name of civilisation. They reigned for a million years and then, almost in the blink of an eye, they were wiped out in a massive war. A war so devastating, so total, that history doesn't even record who it was with or whether it was a civil war amongst the Jagaroth.

CREATED BY
David Agnew

APPEARANCES
City of Death (1979)

All that is known is that no trace of the Jagaroth survived.

But one did survive. As the last Jagaroth spider-ship attempted warp thrust on a primeval world, it exploded, and its pilot, Scaroth, was thrown into the time vortex

and split into twelve different incarnations scattered throughout the planet's history. That planet was Earth, and Scaroth raised the human race up from nothing simply to gain the technology to build a time machine to travel back and avert his own destruction. To do this he utilised all his knowledge of Jagaroth technology, including micromeson scanners and prismatic beams, and all his knowledge of memetics to anticipate and manipulate human culture and guide his artistic and literary investments. But in the end, it all came to nothing, as the human race he'd shaped and cultivated came back and literally punched him in the face.

UNANSWERED QUESTIONS

The twelve incarnations of Scaroth all wore fleshy bodysuits to make them appear human, even in intimate situations. Notably, the faces of these bodysuits all looked like the same man. This was no accident, because the bodysuits were, in fact, skin-suits taken from humans using similar technology to that used by the family Slitheen, even incorporating compression fields. These suits were all from members of the same family, specifically raised through the generations by Scaroth to provide him with a suitable adult male skin-suit at the time of each incarnation. Scaroth was not Count Scarlioni; Scarlioni was the man who Scaroth bred and killed for his skin.

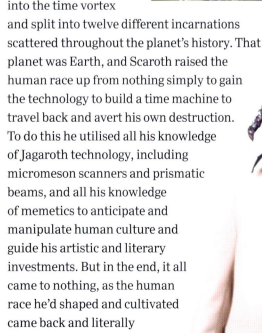

JAGRAFESS

A member of a merciless race of venture capitalists

The Jagrafess of the Holy Hadrojassic Maxarodenfoe is a member of a truly remarkable species. Physically, they are large, amorphous blobs, like quivering mountains of raw meat with barely developed eyes and mouths full of needle-like teeth. Which poses an evolutionary conundrum: why would creatures that can barely move need the teeth of predators?

The answer is more horrific than you may expect. This species originally lived in a world consisting of oceans of primeval ooze, absorbing nutrients through their skin like tapeworms. They had no natural predators but lived in constant, violent competition. Eventually this competition reached a point where they grew teeth to attack each

CREATED BY
Russell T Davies

APPEARANCES
The Long Game (2005)

other, which was closely followed by them acquiring a taste for their own flesh. This is a species that took competition to its ultimate conclusion — cannibalism.

As creatures adapted for merciless competition, this species soon came to the attention of the intergalactic banks. Surely such creatures, if properly trained and motivated, could be of some use in the financial sector? Maybe a creature that fed by stripping its rivals of their flesh could be equally adept at stripping companies of their assets?

By this point, the species had founded a religion dedicated to the worship of competition, the Holy Hadrojassic Maxarodenfoe (the Hadrojassic Maxarodenfoe translates as 'the ultimate winner'; the final member of their species that will be left alive after it has eaten all the others). And so this species started to find their way into boardrooms, consulting on hostile takeovers.

One highly successful and long-lived member of this species, known as the Jagrafess, was headhunted by an anonymous group to run the Fourth Great and Bountiful Human Empire. It was secretly installed on the top floor of the space station Satellite Five, which was dedicated to newsgathering. Over the next ninety years, the Jagrafess used the mainstream media to enslave humanity. The genius of it was, they wouldn't even realise it was happening. The Jagrafess would use the rolling news to maintain a climate of fear, keeping the population in a constant state of xenophobic anxiety. And soon the entire population of Earth, ninety-six billion people, were reduced to the status of cattle.

UNANSWERED QUESTION

How does the Jagrafess know all about the Time Lords? It can't have found out from Adam Mitchell because he was never told about them. The answer can only be that the Jagrafess was briefed by its secret masters... the Daleks!

JUDOON

Ruthless rhinoform space police force

The Judoon come from a world where the dominant species evolved from rhinoceroses and developed the ability to walk upright, speak and dispense justice against lesser species. They are distinguished by very thick, very tough, deeply furrowed grey hide, small, suspicious eyes and two horns formed from keratin. The Judoon consider their horns to be badges of honour, recalling a time when their ancient ancestors on the alluvial plains would literally lock horns in disputes over territory, primacy or legality, and there is no greater dishonour for a Judoon than to be deprived of one of its horns. Recently, some Judoon have taken to sporting a 'Mohawk'-style tuft of hair; it is not clear why they have done this, but knowing the Judoon, it is unlikely to be a sign of youthful rebellion.

CREATED BY
Russell T Davies

APPEARANCES
**Smith and Jones (2007)
The Stolen Earth (2008)
The End of Time (2010)
The Pandorica Opens (2010)
A Good Man Goes
to War (2011)
The Magician's
Apprentice (2015)
Face the Raven (2015)
Fugitive of the
Judoon (2020)
The Timeless Children
(2020)**

JUSTICE IS SWIFT

The question is, how did a race of humanoid rhinos end up becoming intergalactic mercenaries? They have been employed by bodies as eminent as the Shadow Proclamation, the Time Lords and the Eleventh Doctor, and as notorious as the Pandorica Alliance, the Mayor of Trap Street and the landlord of the Zaggit Zagoo bar, so what is it about Judoon that makes them ideally suited for law enforcement?

The answer is the Judoon are temperamentally suited to police work, being single-minded, stolid, logical and absolute sticklers for rules. They are both literally and figuratively thick-skinned and follow the letter of the law ruthlessly and without prejudice, acting as judge, jury, prosecuting counsel and executioner. The law itself may be unfair — condemning bystanders for unwittingly harbouring a fugitive, or imposing the death penalty for minor transgressions — but that is of no concern to the Judoon. They are paid to enforce the law, no matter what.

Because Judoon have undersized brains it has been said that they are 'thick' but this is not true; it's more a case that they are not paid to think and so they prefer not to. All that matters to them is fulfilling the terms of their contracts, getting results and delivering justice. Whilst they have been described by the Doctor as 'interplanetary thugs', they consider themselves to be a profoundly honourable species, and it is not wise to impugn the Judoon.

LANGUAGE ASSIMILATED

The Judoon have their own language, which consists entirely of single-syllable words ending in 'o', so they are reliant on technology to assimilate and translate other languages. This technology translates everything they hear into their tongue, so any strongly argued protestations of innocence sound to them like a small mouse squeaking, 'No no no no no no no'.

Their writing system is similarly terse, consisting of multiple rows of stamped quadrilateral shapes. It is believed to have originated because they really like stamping things.

CRIME-SCENE INVESTIGATION

Like all rhinoforms, the Judoon have extremely sensitive nasal membranes, approximately a million times more sensitive than those of human beings (or 25,000 times more sensitive than an Earth Bloodhound). They perceive the world in terms of smells, which makes them highly qualified for detective work, as they can arrive on a crime scene and immediately discern who has attended that spot over the past three months, what they had for lunch, the state of their personal hygiene and the state of their bowels. They are also able to detect even the slightest release of perspiration, meaning that they can literally smell guilt; the only problem is that when confronted with a heavily armed Judoon, almost everyone breaks into a sweat, meaning that the Judoon tend to believe that everyone they meet is probably guilty of something, they just have to find out what.

ALIEN TECH

As well as their natural abilities, the Judoon utilise specialised crime-fighting equipment, most notably a language assimilator, enabling them to communicate, interrogate suspects and pass sentences in any language, and a hand-held scanner which can be used to identify and categorise suspects by species, decrypt biological shielding, and detect magnetic activity and fusion energy. In the past Judoon have used permanent marker pens to brand eliminated suspects, but they have recently adopted electronic devices less likely to elicit mirth. Judoon are also armed with blasters that can instantly incinerate convicted felons or, occasionally, old ladies who are running away. However, the Judoon are not above the law and always carry compensation forms in case they make any entirely justifiable mistakes while going about their duties.

LAW ENFORCEMENT

The Judoon have their own spacecraft, known as Talwak freighters, which are easily recognised as they are large, cylindrical and tend to land with a heavy thud. But the Judoon are careful never to act outside their jurisdiction, which means they will either teleport their target's suspected hideaway to a neutral territory using an H_2O scoop or tractor beam, or secure the location with a zonal enforcement field, which prevents anyone from entering or leaving, and a temporal isolator, which freezes time.

THE GLOUCESTER INCIDENT

The Judoon were contracted to deliver – but to not kill – a Gallifreyan fugitive hiding on the planet Earth. Once they had locked down the general area, they located the fugitive's place of residence by tracking traces of chronotelluric alloy, not normally found on Earth.

The alien fugitive proved harder to find, as it was not only concealing its nature using a bio-shield, but had also used a Chameleon Arch to pass as human.

Nevertheless the Judoon soon found the fugitive's TARDIS and brought it on board their ship. And when they discovered that they had captured the fugitive known as the Doctor in not one but two incarnations, the Judoon took it in their stride. It just meant they could claim two payments!

KANTROFARRI

Psychic parasite crustaceans that induce a dream state

CREATED BY
Steven Moffat

APPEARANCES
Last Christmas (2014)

The only thing we know for sure about the Kantrofarri is that they are telepathic. We know this because anyone who has encountered them has had their perception altered by a telepathic field. This means they can no longer trust what that they see and hear, and the result is that accounts of these creatures tend to be somewhat garbled, as any account-giver finds it impossible to tell fantasy from reality and usually gets them muddled up with things they have recently watched on television.

They are known colloquially as 'Dream Crabs', and most descriptions of them are of large, pale blue crustaceans. Their bodies resemble hands with five claws instead of fingers and a gnarled shell on the back. They seem to be almost perfectly adapted to grip their victims' faces like a mask or a very effective limpet.

They don't require eyes or ears, as they can use their telepathic powers to 'hack' into the auditory and optic nerves of other beings, homing in on their own mental image. (According to legend, if you think about a Dream Crab it means that one is coming for you!)

Before it feeds, the Dream Crab places its victim in a dream state designed to be as realistic as possible; the victim must not be aware they are dreaming. The victim's only indication that something is amiss will be a gentle pain in the side of the forehead. This is where the Crab has parted their flesh and bone and inserted a thin, hollow dart or ovipostor into the soft tissue of their brain. It then regurgitates digestive fluid into the brain which causes it to liquefy, and the Crab drinks it up as though through a straw.

(Of course, none of this is known as a fact. The person who gave this account could have been watching a nature documentary recently.)

If the victim's conscious brain starts to fight back, the Crab will give its victim the sensation of waking and create another dreamscape for them. If they do awake, the Kantrofarri will immediately crumble away to nothing. This way, its victim will never be sure it wasn't all a dream.

NETWORKED DREAMS

It is believed that when several Kantrofarri attack, their victims will form a telepathic gestalt and experience a shared dreamscape. It is also thought that such gestalts can transcend space and time, but this could just be something somebody dreamed up.

KASAAVIN

Intelligence-gathering agents from another dimension

CREATED BY
Chris Chibnall

APPEARANCES
Spyfall (2020)

The Kasaavin are both creatures and cracks in the fabric of space-time leading back to their own universe. They appear as figures of glowing white light, detached from reality, as though outside the laws of our universe. much like the Cybermen did when they invaded Earth from from a parallel universe. Appearing at any time or place, they can walk through walls as though they are not there, and can even breach the outer defences of a TARDIS. An electromagnetic field can contain them, briefly, but they are otherwise impervious to all forms of attack. Although they have a humanoid shape it is not their true form; it is merely a shape they have adopted for their amusement, in mockery of humanity.

They are currently in the research and observation stage of a prospective invasion. They have embedded agents across the universe, gathering information in case they need to attack. But this could not come soon enough for the Master. He built a machine which would enable the Kasaavin to remain stable while on the Earth, and offered them an alliance. His plan was quite simple: to use human DNA as a form of data storage and turn the entire planet into the equivalent of a vast hard drive.

THE DANIEL BARTON CONSPIRACY

The Master's plan required him to enlist an ambitious business magnate, Daniel Barton, to secretly install an application on every piece of technology so that it would use Kasaavin energy, transmitted through the Master's machine, to erase the DNA of every human being. In order to understand human computer technology, the Kasaavin despatched an agent to the year 1834 to monitor the computer pioneer Ada Lovelace, even going so far as to transport her to the Kasaavin realm for analysis. (The Kasaavin realm is a forest of tree-like synapses suspended in an endless black void.)

The only problem was that some Earth intelligence agents became aware of the Kasaavin presence and began to investigate their connection with Daniel Barton. The Kasaavin, desperate to cover their tracks, killed the agents by erasing their DNA, which unfortunately only served to draw more attention to themselves.

KERBLAM! MEN

Delivery robots targeted as scapegoats by a human fanatic

There are, famously, three laws of robotics. Robots may not harm humans, robots must obey orders unless those orders are to harm humans, and robots must protect their own existence. There is, however, a fourth universal law, which is this: robots will eventually run amok and start killing people. Witness the Clockwork Robots, the Heavenly Host and the Voc Robots.

Which makes the Kerblam! Men an interesting exception. Because, despite being unduly sinister in appearance and manner, they didn't choose to kill anyone. If anything, they were the unwitting tools of a cruel plot to erode people's trust in automatons.

The Kerblam! Men were delivery robots utilised by the Kerblam! company. They were fitted with teleport circuits that enabled them to deliver to anywhere on the planet Kandoka (and even to dimensionally transcendental time machines). The first delivery robots were small tripods with domed heads containing a camera, known affectionately as 'Twirly', but over two hundred years the design evolved until the robots had a humanoid form. The marketing people thought that giving the robots a friendly face and uniforms reminiscent of nineteenth-century German 'postmen' would be good for business. They were proved right, as Kerblam! grew to become the biggest retailer in the galaxy, and Kandoka's moon was converted into a warehouse to store the company's six hundred million products.

The automation led to mass unemployment on Kandoka and a series of People Power protests. To quell unrest, the Kandokan government introducing a law that every company should employ organics for a least ten per cent of its workforce, at every level, so that even mindless, repetitive tasks more suited to robots would be done by humans. In response to this, Kerblam! introduced a new type of Kerblam! Men called TeamMates to supervise their human workers and give them helpful words of encouragement.

CREATED BY
Pete McTighe

APPEARANCES
Kerblam! (2018)

BUBBLE-WRAP

There were still radical groups on Kandoka opposed to the robots, and they managed to install one of their agents in Kerblam! as a mild-mannered maintenance man. His name was Charlie, an expert in cybernetics and explosives, and he had a plan. He would weaponise the bubble-wrap used in Kerblam!'s deliveries to explode in customers' faces, so that Kerblam!'s robots would be blamed. He would have got away with it, too, had he not tested the explosive on his co-workers and come to the attention of the System computer. Because, alas, you can't beat the System.

KRAALS

Belligerent pachyderms with a genius for building androids

The Kraals are, like the Judoon, humanoid rhinoforms, although their physiognomy has taken a more human form. They were originally herbivores like Earth rhinos but then evolved to become predators; their ears grew in size and their eyes moved to the front to give them depth perception, while their noses became vestigial and squat. They show signs of recent brain growth, as their forehead is visibly splitting under the pressure of an enlarging cranium.

The Kraals were once a warlike, brutish and impulsive race. They were also extremely intelligent and achieved a high level of technology, which, in a warlike, brutish and impulsive race, inevitably leads to extinction. Before they could wipe themselves out in a civil war, however, nature intervened. The level of naturally occurring radiation on their planet, Oseidon, began to increase very rapidly; the planet is unusual in having a core of sufficient heat and pressure to cause nuclear fusion. As their planet was turned into an uninhabitable wilderness and their population dwindled, the surviving Kraals devoted all their energies to science and formulated a plan to abandon Oseidon and conquer another world. They united in a chorus of 'It is a good idea, invasion!' and, when they rescued a mislaid Earth astronaut called Guy Crayford, they realised that his home planet would make an ideal target.

CREATED BY
Terry Nation

APPEARANCES
The Android Invasion
(1975)

They built an invasion fleet but, in facing an existential threat, the Kraals had now become a deeply cautious people. They were so few in number that they couldn't risk an all-out attack, so instead their chief scientist, Styggron, set to work creating android duplicates out of Crayford's memories and building a replica village to test them.

Styggron's plan was quite simple: Crayford's rocket would return to Earth with him on board; as the rocket entered the planet's atmosphere, it would release pod-like containers containing the android duplicates which would then disseminate a virus powerful enough to wipe out the human race in three weeks before burning itself out. Styggron would then signal the Kraal invasion fleet, which would arrive to find that they didn't actually need to invade because everyone was already dead.

UNANSWERED QUESTION

It turned out that Styggron's virus was not lethal to humans but was in fact lethal to Kraals. This is because he had been so busy with his androids and replica village that he accidentally tested it on a Kraal cell sample rather than a human one.

KRAFAYIS

A brutal, merciless species of scavengers with the power of invisibility

The Krafayis have a fearsome reputation. Even in the children's stories of the Time Lords, they are referred to as terrifying, indiscriminate killers. They have the ability to survive in space, travelling as a pack between the stars, seeking out easy pickings like galactic vultures. But, also like vultures, their ugly reputation turns out to be unwarranted. They are scavengers, not predators. They do not hunt for food. They do not kill deliberately. And when they are referred to as brutal and merciless, that refers to how they treat their own kind. Their species has a strict dominance hierarchy, which means that any Krafayis that is lame or injured gets left behind when the pack moves on to another world, abandoned forever with no hope of rescue. In the Time Lords' stories, all the Krafayis ever said were the words 'Fear me'. But they got it the wrong way around as, even for Time Lords, Krafayis are hard to understand; what it was actually saying was 'I am afraid'.

The Krafayis planet of origin is uncertain, although it has territories spanning several solar systems, favouring planets with oxygen and nitrogen-based atmospheres. They are large, bird-like creatures that are an amalgam of a parrot, a turkey, an iguana and an echidna, and they are effectively blind, sensing their surroundings with extremely powerful hearing.

Their most extraordinary attribute, though, is that they possess a form of invisibility. This is, of course, not something that the Krafayis are particularly aware of, being effectively blind. They would not notice if they were invisible or not. As they are scavengers, this ability can only have evolved as a defence mechanism, a type of camouflage, and it seems to be a kind of naturally occurring perception filter, like that possessed by the Tenza. It renders the creature invisible to most forms of life, save for exceptionally gifted impressionist artists.

CREATED BY
Richard Curtis

APPEARANCES
**Vincent and the Doctor
(2010)**

UNANSWERED QUESTION

Even the Doctor is unable to explain why Vincent van Gogh is able to see the Krafayis. One explanation is that Vincent's gift – and his mental illness – means he perceives the world in a way that defeats the creature's camouflage. But there is, perhaps, another reason. Vincent is also highly empathic, being able to sense that Amy is grieving when she herself is unaware of it. Perhaps he can see the Krafayis because of his empathy; because he shares its feelings of loneliness and persecution.

KRILLITANES

A composite race with ambitions of divinity

The Greek philosopher Plutarch famously posed the question of the paradox of Theseus' ship: after every part of it had been replaced, was it still the same ship? The same question could be asked of the Krillitanes. Like many races, they developed the science of genetic engineering and began to modify their own nature, but the Krillitanes took it further than most. They used a form of horizontal gene transfer to cherry-pick characteristics from other species. They believed that they could remodel themselves into the ultimate species, a race of gods. They swept across the galaxy, invading planets solely to harvest the indigenous species' genes. Then, once they had taken what they needed, they wiped each species out.

The end result, though, was that after a few centuries all of their Krillitane genes had been replaced. In genetic terms, they had made themselves extinct. What was now called a Krillitane was a composite race. And rather than producing the ultimate species, all the hybridisation had left them with various vulnerabilities. They became so allergic to their own body oil that exposure to it would cause them to spontaneously combust. Sensibly, they modified their forms so they no longer produced the oil, but they kept a supply of it because it worked as a mental conducting agent on other species; ingestion of the oil would temporarily increase their ability to learn and solve mathematical problems.

The Krillitanes' most recent form is that of a human-sized bat; they acquired their wings from the bat-like Bessan ten generations ago before destroying them. (Before this they had been more like humans, but with elongated necks.) Like bats they are carnivorous, eating rats out of necessity and human children by choice. They sleep hanging from ceilings and have extremely sensitive hearing, which is both a strength and a weakness. They have also acquired a form of natural perception filter, possibly from the Tenza or another species capable of morphic illusion, though some senior 'brothers' of their species do not need to use it as they are capable of shape-shifting.

CREATED BY
Toby Whithouse

APPEARANCES
School Reunion (2006)

THE SKASIS PARADIGM

The Krillitanes still believe their ultimate destiny is to become gods. They realised that the Logopolitans found a way to alter the structure of the universe through mathematics: now the Logopolitans are gone, the Krillitanes wish to take their place. But first they need to crack the fundamental code of the universe: the Skasis Paradigm.

KROTONS

Crystalline warmongers who enslaved the peace-loving Gonds

There comes a point in the evolution of any intelligent species where it outgrows the need for physical bodies. This point is known as the singularity — when a species has developed sufficiently advanced technology for it to upload its minds into an artificial 'cyberspace', only downloading them into specially constructed hosts when necessary to interact with its environment. Any such species would, in effect, become immortal, at least until somebody accidentally hits 'delete'.

CREATED BY
Robert Holmes

APPEARANCES
The Krotons (1968)

The Krotons are one such species. Due to the unique chemical composition of their home world, however, they adopted crystalline hosts rather than robotic or organic ones (other species, such as the Kastrians and the Xyloks, took a similar path). The Krotons' formidable, warlike

minds are stored as basic molecules within their spaceships, known as Dynotropes, which can function independently and indefinitely given a perpetual supply of mental energy (such as by enslaving a peaceful race and harvesting them for their brainpower, as with the Gonds). But, when presented with an opportunity or threat, the Dynotrope will automatically generate crystalline bodies for the Krotons within coffin-like vats using a process of electrolysis. These bodies, consisting mostly of tellurium, are entirely dependent upon the Dynotrope for lattice energy, without which they will revert to basic molecules. As the Krotons are prone to boast: 'We cannot die. We function permanently unless we exhaust.' It is, therefore, perhaps fortunate for the universe that Krotons tend to exhaust extremely quickly.

The Krotons' crystalline bodies are designed primarily to perform routine tasks within the confines of their Dynotropes, where they can easily be recharged with waist-mounted energy pipes. They are really not intended for extra-vehicular activity, as they are slow-moving, ungainly and so sensitive to light that they are effectively blind in daylight. They also have skirt-like lower sections which have been known to induce mirth; for this specific reason the Krotons always leave their ships armed with canister-like carbines which can eject a cloud of corrosive gas or a jet of superheated flame. Nobody mocks the Krotons and lives!

KRYNOIDS

Carnivorous vegetable parasites that are grotesque parodies of humans form

The Krynoid is an enormously successful parasitic plant organism that has spread throughout the cosmos. Its modus operandi is as straightforward as it is horrifying: on planets where the Krynoid gets established, the flora eats the fauna. The plant life reigns supreme, devouring all the animals to the point of extinction. And yet, paradoxically, the Krynoid is reliant upon animal life for its life cycle. It requires an animal host to provide it with the nutrients to grow, in the same way that other parasitic plants, such as mistletoe, require a tree or shrub.

The way it does this is particularly ghastly, as it doesn't merely attach itself to its host; instead, it transforms its host into a Krynoid whilst still alive. To begin with, it acts in the manner of an infection, the tendril of a Krynoid embryo pod or 'seed' stinging the flesh of its victim.

CREATED BY
Robert Banks Stewart

APPEARANCES
**The Seeds of Doom
(1976)**

Once it has done this, Krynoid schizophytes — single-celled plant bacteria — reproduce themselves within the bloodstream and then, in the manner of a virus, set to work altering the cells of the body, changing them from an animal phenotype to a plant one. If the victim is a human, after a transition of about twelve hours the victim's morphology will have transformed entirely, the face and limbs receding into a formless, seething mass of tendrils. Given sufficient food and sunlight, it will continue to grow until it is over a hundred metres in height, at which point it will germinate explosively in the manner of a dwarf mistletoe, ejecting thousands of pods over a wide area to infect more victims.

UNANSWERED QUESTIONS

Krynoids are rudimentarily telepathic, each having the ability to channel its power into other plants. It can make them animate, and it can use them as sensory proxies to hear and perceive things beyond its compass. This is why some humans feel a non-specific unease in the presence of a Krynoid pod as though it is 'alive'; they are sensing its telepathic aura.

As the Krynoid requires its hosts to be alive throughout this process, it also takes control of their minds. First the victim is consumed with feelings of fear and paranoia and then hunger and aggression, until all their mental processes are dominated by the Krynoid. The Krynoid will have access to all their memories and even their power of speech. They may still be conscious but they will no longer be in control.

LEANDRO

Duplicitious leonine invader

Leandro, of the Leonian species, had a mostly humanoid body, but both his head and his claws strongly resembled those of a large cat. His mane was part lion, part Barry Gibb of popular Earth beat combo the Bee Gees, and he topped it off with a flashy golden diadem. Leandro's eyes glowed red and he breathed fireballs at will.

Leandro came from the planet Delta Leonis, named after a white A-type star in the constellation of Leo that is larger (more than twice as big) than Earth's sun and 14–15 times as luminous. Leo is so called because the constellation is shaped like a lion, and Delta Leonis is located in the hip area of the lion's back. The star is otherwise known as Zosma, meaning 'girdle' or Duhr (an Arabic name meaning 'the lion's back') and is located 52 light years from Earth.

The Doctor first encountered Leandro when seeking to remove from circulation a dangerous purple amulet called the Eye of Hades, which required the sacrifice of a life to create a fracture in reality that would open a portal for travel in space and time. He accidentally interrupted a highway robbery by the immortal he had created via a Mire chip — Ashildr (at the time known as 'Me' or her outlaw name 'the Knightmare' because nobody remembered who she was). Ashildr was trying to steal the amulet. The Doctor met her new 'friend', Leandro, on their return to her manor house, and found out that they were planning to kill someone and use the amulet to escape Earth.

Ashildr was shocked by Leandro's treatment of the innocent townspeople. Leandro had told her and the Doctor that his wife and tribe were dead, his home planet was destroyed and he was the last of the Leonians, but he was an inveterate liar. This was revealed by Ashildr's use of the amulet on a jolly highwayman, Sam Swift, who was due to hang for his crimes. When a rift opened in the sky and spaceships were revealed, it became apparent that Leandro was happy for Ashildr to die so that the amulet, a 'door' which worked both ways, could enable the plentiful and very much alive Leonians to attack Earth. Ashildr neutralised the threat by using her spare Mire chip to save Sam Swift's life. This turned the amulet's light ray from purple (for death) to gold, and the rift closed. Leandro disintegrated.

CREATED BY
Catherine Tregenna

APPEARANCES
The Woman Who Lived
(2015)

MACRA

Giant crabs that forged an empire using brainwashed humans as slaves

The Macra present a fascinating opportunity to study the evolution of a single species over billions of years. At their height, they enslaved multiple human colonies, brainwashing the colonists into a happy docility — even if it meant working in dangerous mines extracting the poisonous gas upon which the Macra subsisted.

During this period, there were two distinct subspecies of Macra. Both of them were large, lumbering creatures resembling giant crabs with powerful claws and compound eyes on stalks. One variety, the black Macra, was adapted for life in near darkness, only emerging from its native caves onto the planet's surface at night to hunt animal life, which required only a rudimentary intelligence. The other variety, the albino or white Macra, could happily inhabit brightly lit areas, and had sufficient intelligence to operate a complex propaganda machine.

Such was the ingenuity of the white Macra that it spread its influence to other worlds, but then, like all empires, it fell. The Macra's total dependence on hydrogen chloride — a poisonous gas emitted by salt — was their great weakness, and soon the only Macra left were the primitive black kind. They retreated into the dark places beneath the human colonies, adapting to breathe the waste gases produced by human industry, specifically exhaust fumes. They still needed to feed, but on colonies such as New Earth there was always a plentiful supply of derelicts in the under city who would never be missed. And when they ran out, the Macra adapted to attack cars that ventured into the lower lanes of the motorways, using their powerful claws as tin-openers.

CREATED BY
Ian Stuart Black

APPEARANCES
The Moonbase (1967)
The Macra Terror (1967)
Gridlock (2007)

UNANSWERED QUESTIONS

How did the Macra enslave an Earth colony? The Doctor theorised that they are like germs or parasites, but that doesn't explain how a white Macra ended up in a control room operating a propaganda machine. However, we know that in the Colony the Doctor visited there was an old abandoned mineshaft, which was home to the Macra, and that they exuded a frothy foam when roused or hunting. This foam serves an evolutionary purpose: it contains a sweet-smelling soporific gas, the same gas which was piped into the Colony's sleep cubicles to brainwash the humans. So the explanation is that a prominent colonist - probably the one later enslaved as Controller - discovered the Macra when the mineshaft was being excavated, fell under their hypnotic thrall and installed the white Macra into a position of command.

THE MALUS

A living weapon of mass destruction

The diabolical Malus is a living being, reengineered as an instrument of war and a force of pure evil. It comes from the planet Hakol, where the people have harnessed psychic energy, and the Malus is programmed to gather this energy to fuel its campaign of destruction, by inciting fear and hatred wherever it goes. It can also use psychic energy as a weapon, by generating projections of beings from the past that are under its command. Given sufficient resources, it is even capable of causing a rift in the space-time continuum large enough for individuals to pass through, though this is more of a side effect of the Malus creating a psychic disturbance; when individuals do pass through the rifts it has unintentionally created, the Malus is often as surprised as they are.

The people of Hakol are notoriously belligerent, to such an extent that when sending out computer-controlled space probes they always put a Malus inside. Should it encounter intelligent life, it will immediately set about destroying it. Should it fail to discover intelligent life — for instance, when landing in prehistoric England — it is programmed to deactivate itself until intelligent life develops and wakes it from its slumber. At which point it will immediately set about destroying it.

CREATED BY
Eric Pringle

APPEARANCES
The Awakening (1984)

This is what occurred with the Malus despatched to Earth, which was reactivated during one of the battles of the English Civil War, where it woke to discover that a Norman church had been built on top of it. In order to produce more psychic energy, according to one witness it 'made the foightin' worse', convincing the occupants of the village of Little Hodcombe that they should burn their May Queen alive in the mistaken belief that it was a local tradition.

In its lust for destruction, the Malus induced the Parliamentarian and Royalist forces to wipe each other out, along with the entire village, cutting off its supply of psychic energy in the process. The Malus then deactivated, presumably feeling rather foolish.

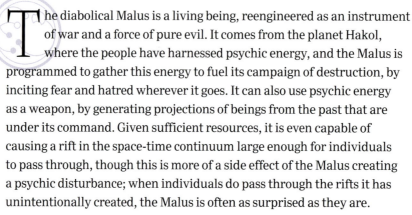

UNANSWERED QUESTIONS

The resemblance of the Malus to medieval depictions of the Devil would seem to be a massive coincidence – unless the Malus, with huge amounts of psychic energy at its disposal, modified its appearance to that of the Devil in order to prey upon the superstitions of the seventeenth-century villagers. Rather than the Little Hodcombe church carvings being based upon the Malus, the Malus based itself upon the carvings.

MANDRELS

Ferocious jungle predators that are hunted for their chemistry

CREATED BY
Dave Martin

APPEARANCES
Nightmare of Eden (1979)

Mandrels are a critically endangered species of mammal indigenous to the jungle planet Eden. While they are savage and indiscriminately carnivorous (they are happy to eat 'arms, legs and everything'), the reason they have been brought to the brink of extinction has nothing to do with their nature but is to do with their chemical structure. When subjected to a high voltage, Mandrels reduce to a fine white powder which happens to be a source of the extremely addictive narcotic xylophilin, also known as Vraxoin. As a consequence, they have been hunted, smuggled, traded and killed by drug dealers across the galaxy.

Aside from their residue, Mandrels have many striking features. Their bioluminescent eyes serve as headlights, their sinister glow enabling the creature to see its prey in the crepuscular jungles. When a Mandrel has located its prey, it has two methods of attack: it can stun its victim with a strike of its powerful claws, or crush the life out of them in its vice-like embrace. Its eye-lights also act as a lure, enticing iridescent jungle moths to fly into its snout-fronds which are coated in a sticky, paralysing venom. Mandrels have developed a natural immunity to the jungle moths' own tranquillising sting;

indeed, some scientists believe the reason Mandrels contain so much xylophilin is because they have absorbed it from the moths.

Perhaps surprisingly for such ruthless predators, Mandrels have no teeth, instead having a scoop like a duck-billed platypus and keratinised grinding plates. This way, they can mash up insects and small mammals as a main course and suck up the root sap of the carnivorous pitcher-plant as dessert.

Unusually for creatures of the tropics, Mandrels are covered in dense, black fur. Rather than being for warmth, the fur provides camouflage in the darkness, as Mandrels only come out to hunt at twilight. Being nocturnal and territorial, Mandrels can become extremely aggressive when in unfamiliar surroundings or subjected to a bright light.

UNANSWERED QUESTION

Although Mandrels have no visible ears, their hearing is nevertheless highly developed, enabling them to hear the distant roar of fellow Mandrels over the clamour of the jungle, and to locate one of their favourite morsels: a species of tree beetle that makes an extremely high-pitched clicking noise. They find its call almost irresistible. This is why they are attracted to K-9's dog whistle and the ticking noise of the Doctor's timing device.

THE MARA

A manifestation of evil that inhabits the dark places of the inside

The people of the planet Manussa were a highly civilised, technologically advanced civilisation. Their children had only one thing to fear: the snakes that lived up in the hills. They were poisonous, so the children's parents told them stories about the snakes being evil to keep them safe.

Years later, those children grew up and experimented with crystals that could transform thought into energy. In their hubris, they created a Great Crystal to combine their mental energies. They did not realise that the Great Crystal would absorb, amplify and reflect all their restlessness, hatred and greed and give it the form of the creature from their childhood fears, the snake. It created the Mara.

The Mara revelled in chaos and destruction. It reigned over Manussa for three centuries of barbarism, cruelty, degradation and superstition. The Manussan empire became the Sumaran empire.

But then a valiant man overcame temptations of fear, despair and greed to remove the Great Crystal from its place of power and the Mara was destroyed. Or at least that is what people presumed. Some legends said it had merely been banished to the dark places of the inside, and would one day return in a dream.

The legends were true. On a distant colony of the Manussan empire, the paradise planet of Deva Loka, the people had conducted similar experiments in telepathy. With the rise of the Mara, their civilisation descended into savagery, and when the Sumaran empire fell they remained as a primitive but peaceful tribespeople, the Kinda. They still had remnants of their technology: the wind chimes for collective dreaming, the box of Jhana used to heal psychic illness. But the rise and fall of the Mara had become the stuff of myth. And a prophecy of its return.

All it would take would be for someone to dream alone. Alone, in the dark places of the inside, where the Mara was waiting...

CREATED BY
Christopher Bailey

APPEARANCES
Kinda (1982)
Snakedance (1983)

UNANSWERED QUESTION

A human expedition to Deva Loka lost three members under mysterious circumstances, but their fate was unknown. The last member to go missing, Roberts, left his Total Survival Suit near the wind chimes. He must have fallen under their spell. But if he wasn't a suitable vehicle for the Mara's return – if it needed a strong-willed female – then it would have driven him out of his mind. So he and his predecessors must have forgotten who they were and joined the tribe of the Kinda.

MARSHMEN

Amphibious creatures with amazing powers of adaptation

CREATED BY
Andrew Smith

APPEARANCES
Full Circle (1980)

It is believed that evolution works in the same way wherever there is life. But that is not quite true. On the planet Alzarius, in the universe of E-Space, evolution follows different rules. Species do not change by a process of natural selection but by a process of inheriting acquired characteristics.

The world is abundant in vegetation but has little fauna. Every fifty years its orbit takes it away from its sun leading to an atmospheric cooling, known as 'mistfall'. At this point, eggs appear in riverfruit, heralding the arrival of animal life. Of course, there is no way those eggs can have been laid; instead they are the cells of the riverfruit adapting to an increase in nitrogen by becoming egg cells. These eggs then adapt into a form according to their location; if the riverfruit are in a cave, for instance, they will hatch into crab spiders with multiple eyes.

A similar process occurs in the marshes, with the 'marshmen'. When they are in the water they are adapted to breathe water; then, as they emerge onto the shore, they adapt to breathe air through their gills. They resemble amphibians, with bumpy anuran skin and frond camouflage, and yet their pocket-like lactation glands suggest they are already evolving into mammals.

They are adapting their behaviour to suit their environment, which in turn alters their physical form. A process which should take millions of years happens in a couple of hours.

The reason is that all the creatures of Alzarius share the same morphogenic DNA, which responds extremely rapidly to changes in the environment. And so, most remarkably of all, there are the creatures that descended from the marshmen. Creatures that spent so much time in a crashed spaceship — forty thousand years — that they transformed into humanoid beings resembling those that originally lived in the spaceship, learning to speak as them and to read their books. They still retained the rapid cellular adaptation of their marshmen ancestors, meaning that if they are hurt, the wound will heal itself almost immediately.

UNANSWERED QUESTION

The venom of the crab spiders seems to have the effect of 'infecting' or 'possessing' those bitten so that they help the marshmen. This is an odd thing for venom to do, until you realise that the venom also contains morphogenic DNA. It is adapting to its environment, and altruistically acting to assist other creatures with the same genes.

MEGLOS

A super-intelligent cactus with ambitions of galactic conquest

The Zolfa-Thurans are notable for being possibly the only instance, in an infinite universe, of intelligent cactuses. There are, of course, other cases of vegetable life gaining consciousness, but the Zolfa-Thurans are, as far as anyone knows, the first time cactuses have developed powers of cognition.

If you were to ask one why — and you could only ask one, as there is only one left — the remaining Zolfa-Thuran, Meglos, would reply, 'It is beyond your comprehension.' This is because Zolfa-Thurans are not only proud of being a unique combination of succulents and sapience, they also think that all other races are intellectually inferior.

What occurred on the planet Zolfa-Thura of the Prion planetary system is that the native xerophytes moved beyond photosynthesis and began to modulate themselves on other wavelengths of life. They found this gave them the ability to move by transforming into slithering green creatures. And when a race of humanoids arrived from the neighbouring planet of Tigella, the Zolfa-Thurans found that by modulating their wavelengths they could take over their bodies.

Once they had achieved this evolutionary leap, it was a relatively straightforward process for the Zolfa-Thurans to develop civilisation and technology, and to destroy themselves in a massive civil war. The war concerned the screens, which served to focus the energy of the extraordinary Zolfa-Thuran power source known as the Dodecahedron. Meglos thought the screens should be used to destroy other worlds as part of a campaign of galactic conquest. The other Zolfa-Thurans disagreed, so Meglos wiped them out and reduced the entire planet to a featureless desert.

Unfortunately this meant that, with no bodies available, Meglos was left trapped in his cactus form, with only a chronic hysteresis generator and interplanetary communication system at his disposal. As for the Dodecahedron, the final act of the other Zolfa-Thurans had been to convey it to the planet Tigella, where the inhabitants immediately began to worship it as a god, which if anything proved that they had been right about other species being thick all along.

CREATED BY
John Flanagan and Andrew McCulloch

APPEARANCES
Meglos (1980)

UNANSWERED QUESTION

It may seem strange that Meglos is aware of Time Lords and humans, and knows that an Earthling will provide him with a compatible body form. However, Meglos has had nothing to do but monitor interplanetary communications for ten thousand years, so it's not surprising he has picked up some gossip.

MENTORS

Sadistic mutated amphibians with a nose for business

CREATED BY
Philip Martin

APPEARANCES
**Vengeance on Varos
(1985)
The Trial of a
Time Lord (1986)**

The Mentors of Thoros-Beta were originally marine reptiles. They lived on seaweed and sea snakes, hunting their prey using their large, primeval stings. The sting also came in useful in disputes amongst the Mentors about who had failed to keep up their repayments of loans of seaweed. Because, even before they emerged onto the land, the Mentors were ardent capitalists.

Eventually they became amphibious and lived in islets, mires and marshes. Their diet now included delicacies such as young sand snakes and marsh minnows. Some Mentors remained in the sea as fishermen. Others turned their back on it, giving the oceans names born of contempt for their aquatic ancestry: the Sea of Turmoil, the Sea of Sorrows, the Sea of Despair and Longing.

Normally at this point there would be a gradual process of a species acquiring legs. The Mentors, however, were a species in a hurry and couldn't wait for evolution. Instead, they attempted to hasten their development with mutations and hybrids.

The results were not entirely successful. They vastly increased their brainpower, but this meant that their brains now barely fitted inside their thick, rigid craniums and they were highly sensitive to loud noises. They remained unadapted for life outside the ocean, requiring constant moisturising, finding normal levels of gravity excessive, and needing servants to bear them. Fortunately there was a humanoid race on Thoros-Alpha that could be easily enslaved.

The Mentors' appearance reveals their hybrid nature, as they have humanoid faces and torsos and short, stubby tails. Their physiognomy varies according to their branch of mutation, and their skin colour changes as they age: they start off brown but turn green after a century or so. They have a ridged head-crest, originally used for heat regulation but now mostly used for display because Mentors are, on the whole, a very vain species. They are also avaricious, sadistic and petulant.

Despite this, or perhaps because of this, they have proved highly successful in finance. They are happy to trade in anything from weapons to slaves, but their favourite type of venture is just the grinding exploitation of the masses.

LANGUAGE TRANSPOSITION

Mentors use personal language transposers which convert their speech impulses into vocalisations in other tongues. These transposers are often unreliable, creating odd phrasing and syntax, and converting the Mentors' inner thoughts into speech so they appear to be giving Shakespearean asides.

METEBELIS SPIDERS

Giant arachnids with formidable psychic powers

Metebelis Three, the famous blue planet of the Acteon group, is a harsh and uninviting place. It's also not actually blue; it only appears blue at night due to reflection of the moonlight. And it's at night, when it's a world of howling winds and blistering snowstorms, that its most deadly creatures emerge to hunt: giant snakes, giant birds, and hoofed, trumpeting beasts.

But there are no giant spiders on Metebelis Three. Or there weren't, until a starship from Earth came out of time-jump and crashed. The survivors eked out an existence through sheep farming, unaware that some spiders from their ship had been blown into a crystal cave in the mountains.

Those spiders were a form of giant house spider, so they were already quite large and fearsome. Over a period of decades, the crystals in the cave caused generations of the spiders to grow larger and caused their brains to expand; they not only became intelligent, they also developed psychic powers. These spiders were telepathic, they could fire lethal bolts of energy, they could conceal themselves with a form of perception filter, by combining their powers they could teleport through time and space, and they could possess humans by leaping onto their backs. If it was feeling generous, a spider could allow its host to retain independent thought and give them instructions through a mind-link. If they dared to disobey, the spider could always cause them agonising pain.

The 'eight-legs' evolved an all-female monarchy with a ruling council and soon enslaved the weak-willed 'two-legs' (which they considered something of a delicacy). One spider, however, remained within the crystal cave. The crystal rays had caused this spider, the Great One, to grow to the size of a house while a crystal web amplified its thought patterns. If the web was complete, its mind would dominate the entire universe. Fortunately the web was incomplete, as an acquisitive Time Lord had stolen one essential crystal as a souvenir. So the Great One had to get it back…

CREATED BY
Robert Sloman

APPEARANCES
Planet of the Spiders (1974)

OH, WHAT A TANGLE

While the Great One intended to rule the universe, the spider council had a different plan: to return to their rightful home, Earth, and becomes its rulers. They had, though, established a link through time to Earth in the twentieth century, so the success of their plan would have resulted in the spiders changing their own past. This did not concern the spiders, as the thought of weaving a new Web of Time rather appealed to them.

THE MINOTAUR

A creature of legend that feeds on faith

Throughout the cosmos, there are myths of the minotaur. A creature, half-man and half-bull, trapped in a labyrinth. The source of these myths is unlikely to be the Nimon, as they destroy every planet in their wake, but rather their distant cousins, the Minotaurs.

The Minotaurs have a similar but subtly different modus operandi. They seek out worlds occupied by civilisations that are likely to be easily intimidated by the Minotaurs' fearsome appearance. They have evolved to exploit the most primal fears, and as a result they have seven thick golden horns, wield powerful claws and wear a kilt.

They don't just want to provoke terror for its own sake, though; they want to be worshipped as gods. This is not an exercise in vanity but in sustenance, as they feed on faith. They are psychic parasites that require a very particular, very strong form of emotional energy. They need to be praised.

Unfortunately the faith-extraction process is fatal for the worshipper, so the Minotaur requires a constant supply of fresh converts. This, in turn, tends to mean that on planets where the Minotaur has set itself up as a god, a sense of religious scepticism begins to set in, followed by very indignant secularism.

At this point Minotaurs usually try to leave the planet before they get lynched, but in some cases they are not quick enough. One planet decided that death would not be a sufficient punishment for the Minotaur's crimes, so they placed it in an automated prison which they set to drift through space. The prison was programmed to locate individuals with strong belief systems (both religious and nonreligious) and teleport them into a holographic maze. The maze took the appearance of a place familiar and yet unnerving to the victim, and contained rooms designed to play on their deepest fears, thus forcing them to fall back on their faith. At which point the prison would convert their faith into worship for the Minotaur, enabling the creature to feed.

CREATED BY
Toby Whithouse

APPEARANCES
The God Complex (2011)

THE MINOTAUR OF ATLANTIS

A Minotaur attempted to install itself as the deity of the ancient city of Atlantis, only to find itself supplanted by another alien posing as a god, the Chronovore Kronos. However, the legend of the Minotaur was so persistent that, when Kronos needed a guardian for its crystal of power, it transformed a man into a creature that was half-bull in order to exploit the Minotaur myth.

MIRE

Adrenalin-seeking lampreys that rely on intimidation tactics

The Mire have a fearsome reputation. They are one of the deadliest warrior races in the entire galaxy, up there with the Sontarans, the Ice Warriors and the Stenza. Whole planets have been laid waste by the mighty armies of the Mire. The Mire are brutal, sadistic and have never been defeated. They think nothing of firing upon armed civilians. Any race that dares to surrender to them will be executed for cowardice. They exult in all forms of war and destruction.

Of course, none of this is actually true. The Mire are a second-rate bunch of thugs who have got their hands on some advanced technology and used it to create a fearsome reputation. Because a fearsome reputation is all they've got. They're not actually very brutal and haven't actually conquered any planets. If a race surrendered to them, they wouldn't know what to do. If a race possessed superior might or technology, they would run away. They are cowards.

Their modus operandi, therefore, is a mixture of pillaging and bullying. They will select a primitive, out-of-the-way settlement and pose as one of the local deities using a holographic sky projector. The Mire leader will continue to use a personal hologram to maintain the illusion, while his warriors will don heavy metal battle armour and teleport down to the settlement to collect the finest warriors, ostensibly to dine with their deity as a reward for their valour. The Mire's armour is equipped with wrist-activated teleports, guns and augmented reality scanners, so they can select their 'guests' based on health, strength and age. Because what the Mire really want are the bodily juices of the valiant, specifically adrenalin and testosterone. Not for any reason except that they like the taste.

The Mire's armour is designed to induce shock and terror, which is ironic because their genuine appearance would be far more effective. They are creatures that evolved from lampreys, where evolution only got as far as the neck before giving up. The Mire are therefore humanoid but with yellow exoskulls containing a large, permanently open mouth with three rows of jagged teeth.

CREATED BY
Jamie Mathieson and Steven Moffat

APPEARANCES
The Girl Who Died (2015)

REGENERATION TECHNOLOGY

Mire helmets are also equipped with a remarkable piece of battlefield medical kit stolen from a more advanced race: an implant that can repair the cells of any living being indefinitely.
In effect, this means the Mire are immortal, barring accidents. But they have a lot of accidents.

MONKS

Sinister corpse-like figures that enslave worlds by brainwashing

The Monks are, by accident or design, an enigma. They do not have a home planet or a history. This is why they seek to occupy other worlds; they want somewhere to belong. Because, uniquely, they are not interested in ruling by coercion. They want to be invited. Then, when they take over a planet, they write themselves into its history and culture, so the population won't question the Monks' right to rule, because as far as they are concerned the Monks have always been in charge and always will be.

Their process of taking over planets has evolved over thousands of years and thousands of attempts, successful and unsuccessful. First, they use a sophisticated simulation machine to evaluate a planet's strengths and weaknesses. They then use the machine to identify a crisis point in the planet's future; a point where the planet will suffer an extinction-level catastrophe. A catastrophe that the Monks can prevent — but only if they are asked. The offer is, the Monks will save the planet on condition that it will henceforth come under their 'protection'.

But the request has to be made out of pure motives. Requests made out of fear or strategy are not acceptable. The request must be made out of love.

The individual who makes the request will then become the anchor that keeps the Monks in power. Their consent is channelled, amplified and transmitted by statues of the Monks so the population will believe what the Monks tell them; for instance, that the Monks' numbers are far greater than in reality. When the anchor grows old, they are replaced by their offspring, so the link is passed down through the generations. The only thing that can weaken the Monks' grip on a world is if the anchor dies without passing on the link.

The irony is, if the Monks wished to invade by force they probably could. They can teleport at will, read minds, access computer systems, drag submarines out of the ocean and reduce their victims to ash with a single touch. But they don't want to conquer. They want to be wanted.

CREATED BY
Steven Moffat

APPEARANCES
Extremis (2017)
The Pyramid at the End of the World (2017)
The Lie of the Land (2017)

ROTTEN CHOICE

For their invasion of Earth, the Monks chose to take on the form of decomposing corpses because, they said, that is what humans looked like to them. This is because the Monks view humans four-dimensionally and have averaged out what they look like over a period of a thousand years.

MONOIDS

One-eyed reptile slaves of humanity

CREATED BY
**Paul Erickson
and Lesley Scott**

APPEARANCES
The Ark (1966)

Monoids are humanoid reptiles, with three unusual characteristics. Firstly, they only have one eye. Secondly, they are unable to hear or talk without artificial assistance. And thirdly, they have large 'mop-tops' of hair.

Their origin is obscure; all we know is that in the distant future they came to Earth and offered humanity their assistance on board their interstellar ark in return for passage, with thousands more Monoids preserved as micro-cells, ready to be reconstituted when the ark reached its destination. Earth was about to be swallowed up by its sun, and the Monoids claimed their own world had met a similar fate. The ark does not contain any other examples of non-terrestrial life, so presumably the Monoid refugees did not bring any of their native species with them.

The Monoids' appearance suggests a strange evolution. Although they have webbed hands, they have opposable thumbs, like humans, and have a similar level of intelligence and scientific knowledge (if not slightly greater). They are highly susceptible to pathogens, indicating that, just like the humans of the far future, their immune systems have been diminished by a sterile environment. The fact that they only have one eye means they have never needed depth perception, so they must have evolved on a world without predators or prey. They do need food and drink, which they ingest through a well-concealed orifice.

Like snakes, they haven't any ears, and instead communicate using a complicated sign language (although after seven centuries on the ark they developed collar-mounted voice synthesizers and hearing aids). But, also like snakes, they can detect low-frequency sounds by vibration, which is why their funeral rites consist of a repeated drumbeat.

(The Monoids with hearing aids were still unaccustomed to the process of how sound carries, which could account for their unfortunate tendency to state their secret plans out loud without realising they might be overheard.)

Their hair gives another clue to their evolution. Their ancestors were once ectotherms, cold-blooded reptiles, but due to a change in their environment they became endotherms, growing thick head fur in order to retain heat. As such, they have more in common with birds than reptiles. This heat-loss did not seem to be an issue for the Monoids on the interstellar ark, though, who spent the whole time completely naked (aside from their fetching collars).

ENCORE PERFORMANCE

Although the Doctor only encountered the Monoids once, the adventure clearly left a lasting impression on him — many years later on Trenzalore, he staged a lively puppet show which depicted his present incarnation defeating one.

MORAX

An army reduced to sentient mud intent on occupying human corpses

CREATED BY
Joy Wilkinson

APPEARANCES
The Witchfinders (2018)

Billions of years ago, the Morax army was the scourge of our galaxy. Their name was a byword for mindless brutality. So when they were ultimately defeated and rounded up, they stood trial for atrocities too great to number. Their prosecutors — whose identity is long since lost to the pages of history — did not wish to lose the moral high ground by executing them. Instead, they found an unremarkable uninhabited planet on one of the outer spiral arms and buried the Morax there. They would remain alive and conscious but with their bodies scrambled down to a primordial ooze. Their liquefied state would be maintained by a highly advanced biomechanical security system, which resembled a tree.

And there the Morax would have remained, had it not been for life evolving on that unremarkable planet. After several billion years, a woman called Becka Savage chose to chop down the tree that wasn't a tree because it was spoiling the view.

The security system was damaged but still partly functional. Part of the Queen of the Morax managed to ooze herself out and infect Becka Savage, but Becka resisted her control, seeking refuge in her faith. She thought that her malaise and the blight on the land were caused by witchcraft and set about persecuting likely suspects. But the Morax soldiers were making their way up through the ground beneath Pendle Hill. They could extrude mud tentacles in search of bodies for bodies to occupy, but then it turned out they didn't need to, because Becka had done them a favour. By executing thirty-six women, she had provided them with very good hosts.

Once they had taken over the corpses, the Morax began to regain some of their powers, being able to kill with a blast of energy. But they remained limited by their hosts' forms, so were slow-moving and vulnerable to burning torches made from the security system tree. What they needed was their King...

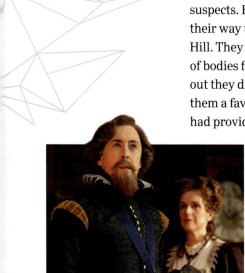

UNANSWERED QUESTION

It may seem odd that the security system tree was indistinguishable from the other trees in the Pendle Hill wood, unless, of course, the evolution of those trees was influenced by the security system tree. It seems likely that it made the other trees look like it in order to avoid drawing attention to itself, because then, as the saying nearly goes, people wouldn't be able to see the tree for the trees.

MOVELLANS

Sophisticated humanoid robots dedicated to pure logic

Only one race has matched the Daleks for cunning and firepower. Not the Cybermen, not the Sontarans, not even the Time Lords. A race of humanoid robots called the Movellans.

How they came into existence is not known. Perhaps they were the creations of a species with ambitions of conquest. Perhaps they were the result of organic creatures becoming cybernetic. All that is known is that they originated in the star system 4X Alpha 4 and immediately began a campaign of galactic conquest. They converted whole worlds into factories dedicated to the production of battle cruisers, weapons and more Movellans. The reason for their campaign is also a subject of conjecture: was it a question of survival or simply a question of abstract logic?

The Movellans were, in most respects, formidable warriors. Their spacecraft could bury themselves for camouflage and defence. They carried hand weapons that could stun or kill and possessed great strength and resilience. They could self-repair, upload memories to their computer, and could not be killed except through massive circuitry disturbance. They created a Nova device that could destroy a planet by changing the molecular structure of its atmosphere to become flammable. They were experts in biological warfare. They had autonomous reasoning, and no qualms about sacrificing themselves for the Movellan cause.

But they had two great weaknesses. They carried their power packs in their belts; if these packs were removed, they immediately became inanimate. And, secondly, their brains were vulnerable to high-frequency sounds and could be scrambled by a toot on a dog whistle.

Neither of these weaknesses was any use to the Daleks. When they assembled a battle fleet to destroy the Movellans, the Movellans simply matched them, spaceship for spaceship. When the fleets met, both their battle computers took over. As soon as one fleet positioned itself for an attack, the other countermanoeuvred to anticipate it. The result was a total logical impasse and the longest period of peace the universe has ever seen.

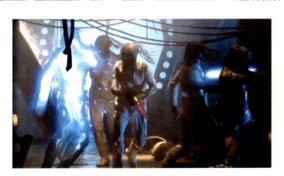

CREATED BY
Terry Nation

APPEARANCES
Destiny of the Daleks (1979)
The Pilot (2017)

UNANSWERED QUESTION

For beings dedicated to pure logic, the Movellans' appearance may seem strangely non-utilitarian, as they resemble attractive men and women with metallic braiding for hair and white spandex uniforms. But in fact it has a purpose. Movellans may be required to perform covert intelligence-gathering operations and, as such, conceal their strength and artificial nature. They need to pass as unthreatening organic beings, and what could be less threatening than looking a little bit disco.

NIMON

Nomadic planetary parasites that prey on the selfish and gullible

CREATED BY
Anthony Read

APPEARANCES
**The Horns of Nimon
(1979)**

A Nimon is a large, powerfully built, humanoid creature, with a head that resembles that of a bull. This head is effectively a machine, with the power to shoot lethal energy rays from its two golden horns. Nimons are therefore unique in that they are the only cyborg species known to have retained their organic bodies and disposed of their heads; it is usually the other way around.

Being cyborgs, Nimons do not feed in the traditional sense, but instead ingest binding energy drained from organic compounds, such as flesh.

This requires a dedicated apparatus resembling a sacrificial slab. The Nimons then extract the energy, leaving their victim a desiccated husk.

The Nimons are highly advanced scientifically, and their migration cycle — or 'the great journey of life', as they call it — is one reliant on a specialised combination of astrophysics and gullibility. So specialised, in fact, that it is something of a surprise how successful it is. What the Nimons do is they send a single Nimon to a world ripe for conquest; that Nimon will find someone in a position of authority and promise them technology, peace, prosperity — anything at all, in fact — in return for the construction of a power complex and the fuel to power it. It then uses the power complex to pump out a gravity beam, creating a black hole. This hole is linked through hyperspace to a black hole near the planet of origin, and more Nimons are transmatted through it. The Nimons initially exploit the fact that they are virtually identical to disguise their numbers until they reach a point where they have built enough transmats to migrate exponentially. This is why worlds that have fallen to the Nimons all send out the same valedictory warning: 'How many Nimons have you seen today?'

This process has been likened to that of a plague of locusts, if locusts relied on people being gullible enough to build large locust transport networks for them.

The Nimons do have some weaknesses. They are vulnerable to energy weapons using Jasonite for their electromagnetic charge, and they have very limited peripheral vision; it is said the best way to hide from a Nimon is to stand beside it.

HIDDEN DEPTHS

The machine heads of the Nimons are deliberately designed to look artificial, oversized and masklike, to make their superstitious, power-hungry dupes believe that the face of the being concealed inside resembles that of their own kind.

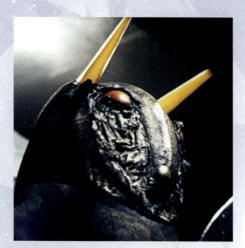

NUCLEUS OF THE SWARM

A megalomaniacal microbe with delusions of grandeur

For thousands of years the swarm had lain dormant, drifting in the wastes of space near the asteroid belt. It was an oily, diaphanous cloud, flashing with electrical energy, waiting for a suitable carrier to come within reach. It was both a virus and a colonial organism with a single guiding intelligence. Rather like the queen of an insect hive, it consisted of a nucleus which was capable of reproduction, protected by a mass of subordinate viral 'drones'. As a virus, it required hosts, which it selected for intelligence as it possessed them mentally: those of lower intelligence it would use as hosts for the drones, while a host of higher intelligence would be reserved for the nucleus. As it consisted of electrical impulses, the swarm could also infect artificial life forms, such as a mobile computer dog.

The virus of the nucleus took over each host by entering through the eyes and ascending through the optic nerve to the brain, where its first instruction would be for the host to announce that 'Contact has been made.' It would then take control of the host's mental activity. It was noetic, meaning that its hold became stronger when the brain was active than when it was idling. In most cases, the mind of the host was then effectively dead and beyond recovery; only the mind of a Time Lord or a mobile computer dog could endure possession. The 'infection' was initially asymptomatic but would gradually lead to the growth of silver scales and coarse metallic hair on the face and hands. When the nucleus was active (i.e. when its host was awake) it was able to telepathically commune with its viral 'drones'; when it was inactive they had to resort to verbal communication.

CREATED BY
**Bob Baker
and Dave Martin**

APPEARANCES
**The Invisible Enemy
(1977)**

THE AGE OF THE VIRUS

At first the nucleus only wanted to find a place in which to breed and multiply. But its ambitions became more grandiose after it possessed the Doctor's mind. It would dominate not just the microcosm but the macrocosm as well. And not just the macrocosm, but time as well. It would become the new master of time, space and the cosmos.

And so it vastly increased its dimensions and emerged into the macrocosm in the form of a large, heavily pregnant, prawn-like crustacean. This was, it turned out, a mistake. As a microbe, it had been invulnerable; in the macro world it couldn't even move without assistance.

OGRI

Standing stones that are hungry for blood

It would be incorrect to say that the Ogri resemble large, rugged standing stones because they *are* large, rugged standing stones. To be precise, they are a silicon-based life form from the swamp planet of Ogros that 'feed' by absorbing amino acids from the marshes. Ogros is unusual in that it has seen the emergence of both silicon-based and carbon-based life, not just in parallel but on the same food chain. Ogri

CREATED BY
David Fisher

APPEARANCES
The Stones of Blood (1978)

have some similarities to diatoms, if diatoms were not microscopic but were two metres high and weighed several tons; an Ogri can be considered a single-cell organism with an extremely thick but porous shell. The Ogri's resemblance to a big rock is accidental, rather than camouflage, as it has neither predators nor prey. It is thought that Ogri can live for thousands of years because virtually the only thing that can kill them is being smashed to pieces by heavy industrial machinery.

As befits a creature that has evolved to spend its time in a bog absorbing protein, the Ogri is of limited

intelligence, although its instincts may be harnessed to make it serve as a kind of guard dog. It will 'sit' in certain places if it knows it is going to get fed, and can be made to perform simple errands in return for treats. If it is not fed, however, it is liable to go hunting for food, and if there isn't a protein-rich swamp nearby this means hunting for any source of protein, such as blood. Should it make physical contact with a living creature, its absorbent force is enough to bind the creature to it, reducing its victim to a skeleton within seconds. You are therefore well advised not to touch any megaliths that turn up unexpectedly on your doorstep.

When feeding, Ogri emit a pulsing glow. This is a by-product of its digestive processes and not an indication that it has a heart. Ogri are heartless, they do not have hearts of stone.

UNANSWERED QUESTION

Given that the Ogri have no visible means of propulsion, how do they move? The answer is that they move like all stones, by sliding. What happens is that the Ogri's underside becomes endothermic, freezing any ambient moisture so the resulting ice fractionally elevates its rear, causing it to slide forward. This is why once an Ogri has built up speed it finds it very, very difficult to stop.

OGRONS

Slow-witted space mercenaries employed by the Daleks

Ogrons are regarded as a form of higher anthropoid, somewhere between humans and gorillas. Their skin is dark and leathery, and their deep-set eyes peer out from beneath a beetling brow. Straggly tufts of horsetail-like hair grow from the corners of their mouths and the rear of their heads. They are about two metres tall, heavily built and extremely strong. Their stamina is such that they can perform demanding manual tasks for several days without fatigue. They are extremely well coordinated and proficient in the use of projectile weapons. Temperamentally, they are subservient, fearless, loyal and honest. They are also extremely stupid.

They weren't always like this, though. They once had sufficient intelligence to reach a level of civilisation equivalent to that of medieval Earth. But then their planet suffered a disaster which made much of

CREATED BY
Louis Marks

APPEARANCES
Day of the Daleks (1972)
Carnival of Monsters (1973)
Frontier in Space (1973)

its surface a barren wilderness. The Ogrons physically retreated to scattered communities in underground cities, and intellectually retreated to superstition and barbarism. They blamed all their misfortunes upon science and technology and pursued a life of primitive simplicity, their minds atrophying through lack of stimulus even as their bodies grew more resilient. Everything had to be simple or they did not trust it. Their philosophy could be summed up in two words: 'No complications'.

THE OGRON EATER

The Ogrons only fear two things: their Dalek masters, which is understandable; and the one creature that can survive on the surface of their planet – a large, amorphous, orange blob somewhere between a sponge and a sea cucumber. This creature has evolved to prey exclusively on Ogrons, so they have, in their simplemindedness, decided to worship it as a god. It is not a particularly edifying god but it is one that they have found they can keep happy by giving it plenty of heretics to feed on.

Eventually they came to the attention of more sophisticated spacefaring species, which swiftly recognised the Ogrons' potential as mercenaries and labourers. Their steadfast adherence to rules meant they made excellent policemen, while they were, with training, even capable of piloting spacecraft. Their main use, though, was as foot soldiers, as their physical strength and unquestioning obedience more than compensated for the slowness of their lumbering gait. They could be sent into battle secure in the knowledge that if they were captured and interrogated by the enemy they would be too stupid to know the answers to any of the questions.

OOD

When they are silent, they are screaming

The Ood-Sphere is an ice and snow-covered moon of a ringed planet in the Horsehead Nebula. It is located in the same star system as the Sense-Sphere — home to the Sensorites, with whom the Ood share some characteristics. The Ood have large, pale, cephalopod heads and humanoid bodies. The upper part of their facial structure resembles that of an African elephant: wise and heavily lined with hooded eyes. The lower part of the face is dominated by long red tentacles, dangling down to their sternums.

The Ood have no vocal cords; they communicate with each other via telepathy. Their eye colour is determined by their level of telepathic activity: red when connected to their hive mind, white when disconnected. The species have two brains. Processing of basic sensory information, telepathic communication, movement and everyday thought takes place in the forebrain, located in the head. Memory, emotions and values are lateralised to the hindbrain, which is held in the hand and joined to the chin via a structure akin to an umbilical cord. If the hindbrain is damaged — or removed and replaced with a translator ball, enabling them to 'speak' aloud to humans — Oodkind are able to survive, but with less mental and emotional capacity and control. This treatment functions as a form of lobotomy.

Their telepathy is centralised in the giant Ood Brain, located on the Ood-Sphere, and disruption of this signal has terrible consequences. The Ood's low-level passive telepathy and gentle nature allows them to be controlled by bad actors with stronger telepathic powers, with limited resistance. The Beast was able to possess the Sanctuary Base 6 Ood, while a damaged solo Ood, Nephew, was possessed by House. When the Ood were possessed by the Beast, the usual basic 5 level of their telepathy register went up to basic 30. This felt like screaming in their heads. The Ood attacked crew members, via the Beast, and spread his messages. That telepathic connection between the Beast and the Ood was eventually disrupted by sending a signal from the Ood Habitation zone and the Beast was sent into a black hole. When the base was breached, all non-essential Ood were confined, and the human crew decided to initiate Strategy 9: open the airlocks and release the Ood into the vacuum to die.

CREATED BY
Russell T Davies

APPEARANCES
The Impossible Planet/
The Satan Pit (2006)
Planet of the Ood (2008)
The Waters of Mars
(2009)
The End of Time (2009)
The Doctor's Wife (2011)
The Magician's
Apprentice (2015)
Face the Raven (2015)
Hell Bent (2015)

SLAVERY

Future humans act very much the same as past and present humans in the face of less powerful people that they can exploit: they enslave them, put them to work and trade in their lives. The Ood were enslaved by humans over hundreds of years. Danny Bartock, of the Sanctuary Base 6 Ethics Committee, irony in his job title noted, called them a 'basic slave race'; saying that they were 'useful' and 'born for it'. He even falsely claimed that Ood pine to death if they are not given orders. Klineman Halpen, CEO of the slave traders Ood Corporation, clearly viewed Oodkind as chattels. He spoke of them as lowly animals, rather than citizens worthy of respect and full rights. Groups such as Friends of the Ood had tried to help the Ood in the past, and Rose was mocked by the Sanctuary Base 6 crew for showing concern for the Ood's welfare. Danny Bartock described them as 'like cattle'.

The first time he met them, on Sanctuary Base 6, the Doctor had never thought to ask if the Ood were servants or slaves. In 4126, however, he encountered the Ood Corporation at the height of the Second Great and Bountiful Human Empire. Having taken over the Ood-Sphere, the Corporation marketed the Ood like the latest technology and couriered them across the three galaxies of the empire via a network of distribution centres. Two centuries after humans had first found and enslaved the Ood, nearly every human had an Ood servant. Donna was horrified, realising that their hindbrains had been cut off and replaced with translator balls, and their connection to the Ood Brain suppressed. Ood Operations had covered this up and lied when they told everyone that the Ood loved orders and offered themselves up for service.

The Ood liberated themselves via their own actions, especially those of Ood Sigma, but the Doctor asked if he could have the honour of flicking the switch that finally freed them — an unfortunate move. As well as telepathy, the Ood are a dab hand at prophecy. They accurately described the motivations of Sanctuary Base 6 crew and predicted the futures of Rose, and later the Doctor and Donna — the DoctorDonna, who they loved.

'Our children will sing of the DoctorDonna, and our children's children, and the wind and the ice and the snow will carry your names forever.'

SONGS OF CAPTIVITY AND FREEDOM

The Ood sing collective songs as a way of telling and preserving their own story. The lyrics are translated by the TARDIS into Latin, as they are in a high classical language of their own. The lyrics appropriately reference Cicero, Seneca and Petronius. Classical scholar Katherine McDonald has translated and annotated the lyrics:

cum tacent, clamant. — *When they are silent, they are screaming. (Cicero)*
cum tacent, clamant. — *When they are silent, they are screaming. (Cicero)*
serva me; servabo te. — *Save me; I will save you. (Petronius)*
serva me; servabo te. — *Save me; I will save you. (Petronius)*
dum inter homines sumus, colamus humanitatem. — *While we are among humans, we should look after humankind. (Seneca)*
cum tacent, clamant. — *When they are silent, they are screaming. (Cicero)*

OOD SIGMA AND THE OODITIES

The history of Oodkind is full of those who stood out from the hive crowd. The Ood Elder had a visibly larger, external forebrain. Einstein once visited the TARDIS and accidentally turned himself into an Ood via one of his own experiments. Delta 50, who killed Mr Bartle with his translation sphere, was shot to death but was remembered as a 'he', not an 'it'.

Most important of all, Ood Sigma was the assistant to Klineman Halpen and wore a prominent sigma symbol on his uniform. He had secretly been working for the liberation of the Ood as a representative of the Ood Brain. His connection to the Ood Brain made him able to function as an individual and he adulterated Halpen's hair tonic with Ood graft, transforming him into an Ood. Sigma maintained his connection with the Doctor until the end of the Tenth Doctor's life, easing his regeneration by showing him that his story would not end with his song.

PIPE PEOPLE

The indigenous people of Terra Alpha forced to scavenge in the syrup pipes

CREATED BY
Graeme Curry

APPEARANCES
**The Happiness Patrol
(1988)**

Before the humans came, Terra Alpha was a paradise. A temperate climate, no particularly savage predators, and vast, rolling fields of sugar beet. It grew everywhere, and as a result formed the staple diet of the native inhabitants: short, wizened, goblin-like folk with pinched features, pointed ears and large, black eyes adapted for hunting at night. They had limited culture, as they had very limited language, being quite unable to string more than two words together. But they never needed to develop complex speech, because they never had anything particularly complex to discuss.

But then Terra Alpha was designated a human colony world and everything changed. The humans identified a natural resource and immediately set about exploiting it. They built massive sugar beet farms, processing plants and factories. Despite being given names like 'Nirvana' and 'Shangri-La', the workers suffered terrible conditions and were at the mercy of the guards. Outside the factories, with every square centimetre of the planet dedicated to sugar production, the planet's ecosystem was destroyed and all the indigenous life was either wiped out or forced to scavenge in the cities.

The native people concealed themselves within the pipes beneath the main city. They lived on syrup that had crystallised in clogged pipes but were occasionally forced to venture onto the surface at night to forage for food. There, they were glimpsed by colonists and became known, in hushed whispers, as 'the Pipe People'.

The Pipe People didn't notice as the world above them changed for the worse. Thousands more factories were being built and the people who worked in them and on the flatlands were being ever more harshly oppressed. Being oppressed made them depressed, but rather than try to improve their lot, the ruler of the colony decided that they needed cheering up. Brighter colours, happier music. Fun and games. Sweets galore courtesy of the Kandyman, the state's psychopathic confectioner-in-chief. And instead of guards, there would be women with rouged cheeks to weed out the killjoys. The era of the Happiness Patrol had begun...

... while down below, the Pipe People were close to starvation. Something had to give.

STIGORAX

The ruler of Terra Alpha, Helen A, only had feelings for one living thing: Fifi, her pet Stigorax. A ruthless, intelligent predator, it was halfway between a wolf and a rat with the redeeming features of neither. It was not indigenous to Terra Alpha but in fact evolved in the disused canals of twenty-fifth-century Birmingham.

PLASMAVORES

Solitary, vampiric creatures that feed on the blood of children

Bloodsucking is not uncommon throughout the universe. There are the Great Vampires of antiquity and the Haemovores of the far future. And blood is a convenient and delicious source of plasma, as Androgums, Ogri and Saturnyns can all attest. But one race has such an appetite for blood that it has been named after it. The Plasmavore.

CREATED BY
Russell T Davies

APPEARANCES
Smith and Jones (2007)

Plasmavores are, to the untrained eye, indistinguishable from human beings. The only tell-tale sign is that they may exhibit symptoms of salt deficiency because they require it in greater quantities than humans. And, while a diet of blood may confer immortality on some species, Plasmavores do visibly age, albeit at a vastly reduced rate. A Plasmavore that may appear to be a frail, little old lady of seventy could well be over a thousand years old.

But the Plasmavores are unquestionably alien. On their world, the dominant, intelligent, humanoid species that emerged was strictly carnivorous in diet. An evolutionary 'arms race' then ensued, as the creatures upon which the Plasmavores preyed developed flesh that was both repellent and toxic to their predators. In response, the Plasmavores adapted to subsist exclusively on their quarry's blood.

And the Plasmavores would have lived in peaceful butchery, had they not come to the attention of other species. Because when they saw the Plasmavores, they mistook them for the vampires of legend. As a result, the Plasmavores were persecuted throughout the galaxy and forced to hide in the desolate outer worlds. And there, in hunger and adversity, the Plasmavores' resentment at their treatment turned to thoughts of revenge. 'If they think us vampires... then vampires we shall be!'

The Plasmavores then emerged from hiding. They acted alone, keeping to the shadows, selecting their victims for maximum cruelty, favouring children born to privilege, such as the Child Princess of Padrivole Regency Nine. In extremis, they were prepared to kill millions simply to make their escape and cover their tracks. As a result, the Plasmavores became even more persecuted, with the Judoon being hired down to hunt them down across the galaxy.

STRAW MEN

In order to remain undetected, the Plasmavore use special straws designed to let them feed without leaving a puncture mark. They also engage the services of Slabs, faceless, unthinking slave drones made of solid leather. Slabs have no blood, which means the Plasmavores won't accidentally be tempted to feed on them.

PRAXEUS

An alien bacteria that feeds on plastic waste and turns seabirds into killers

On a world much like Earth, a species much like the human race had a problem. They had filled most of their world with plastic, even ingesting it into their bodies, but then a bacteria emerged that fed on plastic — and on the people that had ingested it. Accounts differ whether it was the result of a mutation or was created in a laboratory with the intention of it cleaning up the planet. Either way, it quickly spread out of control. Every part of the ecosystem was infected, which manifested itself as a growth of crystal-like shards over the skin before it devoured its host completely. The bacteria was given the scientific name Praxeus, meaning 'plastic eaters'.

CREATED BY
Pete McTighe and Chris Chibnall

APPEARANCES
Praxeus (2020)

The planet was devastated and most of its inhabitants were killed. The survivors were assigned to laboratory ships to search for an antidote, each carrying a large sample of the Praxeus bacteria. Their mission was to seek out worlds with an abundance of plastic to use as a living laboratory, the equivalent of a giant Petri dish. After crossing three galaxies, one of the laboratory ships found such a world: the Earth. Its crew intended to use the Indian Ocean plastic waste gyre, but they lost control of their ship and crashed. The ship sank to the ocean floor and released the Praxeus sample, infecting the crew. The bacteria quickly spread, pulling down plastic from the waste gyre to surround the crashed laboratory ship as though forming a nest. In response to its change of environment, it was beginning to develop intelligence.

UNANSWERED QUESTION

Praxeus has evolved to alter its hosts' behaviour as a means of proliferation. Firstly, any infected host will develop the urge to travel in search of plastic – which is why the birds that ate the plastic in the Indian Ocean flew as far as Peru. Secondly, they will become highly aggressive and attack creatures with a high plastic content. The unconscious urge to travel may also explain why the alien scientists researching it decided to have labs in two different continents.

Plastic infected with Praxeus was then eaten by seabirds, which became aggressive and passed on the infection to humans. The rate of cellular mutation was very fast in humans, meaning people could become infected, show symptoms and then disintegrate into dust in a matter of minutes. The laboratory ship's crew set to work finding a cure... but it was a race against time.

PRISONER ZERO

A fugitive inter-dimensional multi-form

In its true form — when it thinks no one is looking — Prisoner Zero is a very large, long, snake-like creature with translucent skin and a head consisting of two beady eyes and an oversized mouth crammed with needle-sharp fangs.

Because it consists solely of a face and a tendril, its species is sometimes referred to as Face Tendril, but physically it more closely resembles an Earth viperfish, a creature which uses light-emitting glands to disguise itself. Prisoner Zero also has a means of camouflage, as it can adopt the forms of other beings at will; it is what is known as a multi-form. To do so it needs to maintain a psychic link with a living but dormant mind to provide a body pattern. In effect, this means that it can take people or animals from the dreams of coma victims and wear them as disguises. The only problem with this is that Prisoner Zero habitually disguises itself as more than one creature at a time and loses track of which voice comes out of which mouth. It is also unable to disguise its needle-sharp fangs, which tend to be another giveaway.

Prisoner Zero also possesses another means of concealment. It can extrude a perception filter and place it around its nest, enabling it to hide in buildings for extended periods without their occupants' knowledge. Occasionally, though, when lying low in the Pond residence, it liked to slip out for walks around the village in different bodies and go and feed the ducks, to itself.

CREATED BY
Steven Moffat

APPEARANCES
**The Eleventh Hour
(2010)**

THE ATRAXI

Prisoner Zero was a prisoner of the Atraxi, who could be forgiven for not anticipating that a crack in time would appear in the wall of Prisoner Zero's cell enabling it to escape. Having discovered this, the Atraxi attempted to follow the fugitive through the crack, but it was closed by an interfering Time Lord. The Atraxi then tracked down that Time Lord, hoping that he would lead them to Prisoner Zero which, fortunately, he did, because the Atraxi stop at nothing when it comes to recapturing prisoners; they would rather send a battle fleet to destroy the planet the prisoner is hiding on than allow them to escape justice.

Beyond this, little is known about the Atraxi save for the fact that they consist of a giant quivering eyeball embedded in a crystalline snowflake. But you should always be wary before confronting them, because the Atraxi never blink first.

PTING

Indestructible parasites that feed on energy and can eat through metal

Hard as it may be to believe, the Pting were once a perfectly ordinary species living on a perfectly ordinary, temperate planet. They were hairless bipeds with opposable digits, and were well on the way to evolving reasoning intelligence, but then disaster struck. Their planet's orbit began to decay, moving closer to its sun. The Pting had to adapt or die, and so they adapted. They became tolerant of extreme temperatures and a lack of oxygen. They began to feed on molten ore. They became extremophiles, surviving as all other forms of life on their world perished.

After a period of about ten million years or so, things got even worse as their planet began to crack and crumble due to extreme gravitational forces. The Pting evolved to subsist in a vacuum. They adapted to life in zero gravity, becoming extremely fast and powerful, with eyes that could penetrate the darkness of space and withstand the unfiltered light of a sun. They were virtually indestructible, barring accidents. In terms of diet they could not only eat solid rock, they could instantly convert it into energy through a process of digestive nuclear fission (giving onlookers the impression that they could eat objects larger than themselves). But by preference they ingested highly radioactive minerals, as particle radiation was their equivalent of chocolate pudding.

They were now what scientists begrudgingly classed 'extreme extremophiles'. Then their planet broke up completely, leaving the Pting to scavenge in the asteroid belt made of its rubble. They now had the ability to sense sources of energy. Electromagnetic, quantum, antimatter... they could sniff them out like sharks.

CREATED BY
Tim Price

APPEARANCES
The Tsuranga Conundrum (2018)

Astrobiologists studying the Pting — now categorised as 'very extreme extremophiles' — observed that the Pting were non-carnivorous and made the error of thinking they were harmless. This was a mistake they rapidly reassessed as the Pting tore through their ship, eating through solid metal and devouring the anti-matter drive. Any attempt to capture them failed as they could eat through any cage and their touch was lethally toxic. The Pting then spread across the galaxy, consuming an entire Neuro fleet before infesting the Seffilun junk worlds.

UNANSWERED QUESTION

It is often wondered how the Pting got their name. It is thought to come from the last communication made by the astrobiology team that was studying them: a scream of 'No stop! Stop eating! Stohhhhh pee-ting!'

PYROVILES

Creatures of lava and stone with the power of prophecy

The planet Pyrovillia would not normally have been considered habitable. A world of magma seas and infernal volcanoes had none of the normal conditions for life. But life will find a way, and it emerged in the swirling crucible of molten rock. This would be a new form of life: instead of skin and bone, it would have a carapace of stone; instead of blood, it would have lava. The Pyroviles were born.

They built great cities on their world, cities of obsidian temples and palaces on cliffs of basalt. Some would call it a vision of hell, but to the Pyroviles it was a heaven.

Perhaps as a product of the turmoil of their birth, the Pyroviles possessed the ability to see into the future. When they saw their world being lost in the flames of time, they launched ships to colonise other worlds. To turn them into new Pyrovillias.

One ship came to Earth, falling so fast that the ship and its crew were shattered into dust. Only a few survived in an escape pod which was buried in the ground. After sleeping for thousands of years, they were awoken by an earthquake and reconstituted themselves in the magma chamber of a volcano. They were visited by humans from the nearby town, soothsayers and sibylline priestesses. The humans thought the Pyroviles were gods of the Underworld. And the Pyroviles saw that they could use them to build a new empire on Earth.

They infected the soothsayers and priestesses with their rock dust, granting them the gift of second sight even as their bodies transformed into Pyroviles. They instructed the priestesses to act as their eyes and to encourage girls with latent psychic powers to inhale their rock dust from the hypocaust, seeding their bodies so that they too would become Pyroviles. And they ordered the soothsayers to provide them with the materials to construct an energy converter. They would use the power of the volcano to create a fusion matrix and transform the entire human race into their own kind.

The only thing that could prevent this would be if the volcano erupted. Its name was Vesuvius. And the name of the nearby town was Pompeii...

CREATED BY
James Moran

APPEARANCES
**The Fires of Pompeii
(2008)**

PYROVILLIA RESTORED

Pyrovillia was not, in fact, destroyed, but was returned to its own space and time intact. When the Pyroviles realised their mistake, they resolved never to pay attention to doomsday forecasters ever again.

QUARKS

The deadly robotic servants of the cruel Dominators

The Dominators are a race superficially similar to humans, but with superior intelligence and physical strength. Their uniforms consist of a carapace with scale-covered arms and legs, designed to give the impression that they are turtle-like while protecting the vulnerable wearer. The uniforms also, unintentionally, encapsulate the dual nature of the Dominator psyche: they are essentially belligerent, callous beings, motivated by an insatiable appetite for mindless destruction, but constrained within a rigid social structure that channels their savage desires towards more productive ends.

Dominators are expected to demonstrate self-discipline and ruthless emotional detachment, to obey their society's strict hierarchy of command without question, and to exercise asceticism; they must not indulge in self-gratification or wastefulness of any kind. And it is this credo — 'That which threatens us, we destroy, that which is too weak to harm us, we ignore' — that has enabled them to become Masters of the Ten Galaxies (although it should be noted that 'galaxies' are what Dominators call solar systems, and that seven of them were uninhabited).

They have been aided on their war mission by mechanical beings called Quarks. Quarks are short, metallic and cuboid, with a sphere on top with five radiating sensors which permit them to perceive their surroundings within a hexagonal aperture (its lens is even equipped with a 'zoom' function). Each Quark has two arm-like appendages which it can extend when it needs to manipulate its surroundings, draw power, supply power, or use its inbuilt weaponry. It usually keeps these arms enfolded to conserve energy. It has two types of weapon: it can emit a molecular force which fuses its victim to the nearest vertical surface, and it can fire a molecular ray capable of dissolving organic matter and destroying buildings. This ray has only a limited range so it requires precise targeting, which risks depleting the Quark's limited power supply. Unfortunately, Quarks are not the most mobile of machines and when subjected to violence have a tendency to go berserk and explode.

CREATED BY
Norman Ashby

APPEARANCES
The Dominators (1968)
The War Games (1969)

UNANSWERED QUESTION

Because they require the Quarks for galactic dominion, the Dominators have plans to replace them with slave labour on their own planet. But if the Quarks are robots, why don't the Dominators just build some more? The answer can only be that the Quarks aren't quite robots, and their diminutive size, their gleeful delight in destruction, and their childlike voices betray an altogether more sinister origin...

RACNOSS

Carnivorous space-faring giant spiders from the Dark Times

CREATED BY
Russell T Davies

APPEARANCES
The Runaway Bride
(2006)

The Racnoss are extremely large arachnids, resembling hybrids of a red widow spider and a human being. Their heads and torsos are broadly humanoid, except they have crown-like crests with six eyes and multiple fangs. Instead of hands, they have narrow pedipalp claws. Their bodies are adapted for the vacuum of space, where they spin impressive webstar ships with their own silk and, just as some spiders decorate their webs to improve their efficiency, the Racnoss like to furnish their webstars with technology and weaponry pillaged from vanquished species.

The Racnoss emerged during the universe's primeval Dark Times and quickly spread across the stars, devouring whole planets. Their breeding cycle evolved to work on a literally astronomical scale, as they would weave special webstars to house their eggs and form the core or 'secret heart' of newborn planets. The Racnoss would take care to place these new worlds within orbits conducive to life, so that when their spiderlings hatched millions of years later they would have a ready source of food (Racnoss are born starving). The Racnoss utilised Huon energy, inimical to most forms of life, to fuel their webstars and to trigger the hatching process.

Unfortunately for the Racnoss, they were almost entirely wiped out by the Fledgling Empires, and all the Huon energy in the universe was harvested by the ancient Time Lords to use in their TARDISes. With no power source, the last nest of Racnoss spiderlings never hatched, and their last surviving Empress went into hibernation at the edge of the universe waiting for the Huon energy of the secret heart to be released. Over billions of years, life on the planet that formed around that nest, the Earth, evolved to a point where it had sufficient intelligence and means to drill down to the core and send a wake-up burst of Huon energy across the stars to the Racnoss Empress. Then she returned and set in motion a plan to create enough Huon energy to act as a key to unlock the secret heart and rouse her young from their sleep. All she wanted was to wake up her babies.

UNANSWERED QUESTION

As they have evolved to live in zero gravity, the Racnoss may appear to be ungainly and sedentary if encountered on a planet's surface. This is why they like to travel individually by teleport rather than landing their webstars on the ground.

RILLS

Peace-loving, ammonia-breathing creatures from Galaxy Four

The Rills are terrifying. They are quite aware of this. Indeed, they expect other species to by shocked by their appearance, so they hide themselves away in their spaceships, cloaked by clouds of ammonia gas, safe behind glass partitions. They cannot even speak, possessing no vocal cords; if they wish to communicate with another race, they transmit their thoughts through their robot servants known as Chumbleys. Chumbleys are capable of deciphering any language they encounter, and they speak in a plummy, reassuring tone. They consist of a stack of concentric domes that they can raise or lower telescopically. Their wobbling, bobbling mode of travel and the fact that they are blind may make them appear whimsical and harmless, but they are formidable machines, able to sense their surroundings through heat and sound waves, and armed with flamethrowers and ammonia bombs. This is because, while the Rills themselves are agreeable, benevolent creatures, they have learned that not all species they might meet are quite as forthcoming.

The Rills resemble a cross between a deep-sea viperfish and a walrus, having scaly skin, long tusks, and large, plate-like eyes. The size of their eyes, and the fact that they have built robots with no visual sense, suggests that they are creatures of the pitch dark, which is why there has been no evolutionary incentive for them to become more attractive. They have instead gained intelligence, empathy and telepathy, suggesting that cooperation rather than competition informed their development. They have now transcended their stygian origins and travel the stars in spacecraft powered by solar and geothermal energy.

The other notable thing about the Rills is that they breathe ammonia rather than oxygen. This means that their evolution took place in a unique set of circumstances, where life evolved to use nitrification to gain energy, like a bacteria, rather than respiration. Again, if they originated as extremophiles of the deep, this would also explain why they value life so highly: they know how precarious it is.

CREATED BY
William Emms

APPEARANCES
Galaxy 4 (1965)

UNANSWERED QUESTION

Given that the Rills are so altruistic, it's a surprise that they haven't been wiped out. There is one uncomfortable explanation, which is that the Rills have only been pretending to be nice, and in fact the Drahvins were telling the truth all along; when their spaceships met in space, the Rills fired first.

RUTANS

Metamorphic hydrozoans that live and die for the glory of their empire

Rutans are the universe's most successful colonial organism. They have little concept of individuality, seeing themselves as 'the Rutan', the all-conquering mother race. Because all Rutans are female. Or at least, the only Rutans that anyone has encountered have been female, as only female, medusoid Rutans are assigned as Rutan Scouts. And even then they are rarely seen in their true form — a green, semi-transparent, gelatinous mass with stinging tentacles, not unlike a box jellyfish — because Scouts are trained in metamorphosis techniques, and can take on the physical appearance of any other creature (within limits of size and density). Indeed, they are such masters of mimicry that, it is said, they are incapable of recognising a fellow Rutan in disguise.

Of course, this could just be war propaganda. Because the most well-known fact about Rutans is that they have been at war with the Sontarans for so long that both sides have forgotten who started it. Over the course of such a long conflict so many grievances have built up that both sides are mainly fighting to avenge earlier slights and because after such a long time it would be humiliating to lose.

Rutans originated in the oceans beneath the ice crust of Ruta Three. They evolved bioluminescence in order to see in the abyssal gloom, but even then their vision was limited to black and white. They communicated by emitting shrill ululations and killed their prey by discharging an electric current through their tentacles. They dwelt mostly in the upper parts of the ocean away from the planet's hydrothermal vents, as they find heat intensely painful.

Rutans were originally individual organisms, which is why they still think and act as individuals; it is a source of endless frustration to them that they are not one of those organisms that forms a gestalt or a hive mind. Nevertheless, becoming a social colony enabled them to emerge from the ice and develop space travel; their spaceships are as amorphous as their pilots, appearing as fiery vortexes despite their crystalline infrastructure.

CREATED BY
Terrance Dicks and Robert Holmes

APPEARANCES
Horror of Fang Rock (1977)

UNANSWERED QUESTION

Why did the Rutans give up on Earth after their Rutan Scout was defeated at Fang Rock lighthouse in the early twentieth century? Was the loss of a Rutan mothership really enough to deter them? No. The answer is that, in the ever-changing theatre of war, Earth lost its 'strategic importance' as suddenly as it had gained it, as the battlefront moved to a less remote part of the galaxy.

SATURNYNS

Hideous creatures of the deep that pass themselves off as vampires

Saturnyne is one of the forgotten casualties of the Time War. It was once a water world, its seas brimming with life, but then a shockwave of temporal disruption from the conflict hit the planet and caused life to transform according to no natural laws of evolution. The strange-looking creatures adapted to life in the darkest depths suddenly became semi-humanoid, sentient and able to survive on dry land. They were hideous, unnatural abominations, and when they saw what they had become they cursed those who had created them.

CREATED BY
Toby Whithouse

APPEARANCES
**The Vampires of Venice
(2010)**

And so Saturnyns have the unusual distinction of having developed perception filters before space travel. Before they could make contact with other species, they had to disguise their natures. Every Saturnyn was equipped with a device that manipulated the brainwaves of the beholder so that they would appear to them as they desired.

That wasn't the end of Saturnyne's bad luck, as its population watched as cracks appeared in the heavens, through which they could see other worlds. These cracks threatened to tear the planet apart, so one Saturnyn female fled with her male offspring through a crack to another world of oceans. The crack then closed behind them, and Saturnyne was lost forever to the silence.

The Saturnyns had escaped to Earth; the lagoons of Venice, to be precise. The Saturnyn female adopted the identity of a noblewoman, Rosanna Calvieri, and established herself in a position of power. Her problem, though, was that, without any Saturnyn females, her species would die out. The only solution was to use the primitive technology available to her to surgically alter human females into compatible 'wives' for her children . Then, once she had sunk Venice beneath the waves, it could be repopulated with her grandchildren.

So Rosanna started a school for young women. The genetic conversion process would make them extremely photosensitive, like all creatures evolved for the depths, and not even a perception filter could prevent people seeing their elongated fangs, although it would prevent them from being seen in mirrors. They would be mistaken for vampires... and, given vampires' fearsome reputation, that suited Rosanna just fine.

UNANSWERED QUESTION

When Rosanna sacrifices herself, she appears to remove some of her clothing, even though her clothes are an illusion created by her perception filter. You can, however, do anything with illusory clothes, even remove ones that aren't there; that is kind of the point.

SEA DEVILS

Warriors of the deep

The Sea Devils are a subspecies of Silurian that adapted to life underwater. This was during a period of tectonic upheaval, when conditions on the land deteriorated and Silurians had to spend more time feeding and breeding in the sea until it become their sole habitat. They followed a similar evolutionary path to turtles, developing

CREATED BY
Malcolm Hulke

APPEARANCES
The Sea Devils (1972)
**Warriors of the Deep
(1984)**

beaks and nostrils to breathe out of the water, while their Silurian crests became, through a process of exaptation, gill arches situated at the rear of the head. Their eyes shifted to the sides of their heads as another aquatic adaptation, while their claws became dexterous webbed hands. While they could, with some effort, communicate verbally,

they were much more efficient at communicating underwater using a form of ultrasound. They were, therefore, extremely sensitive to intense sounds outside of the water.

The Sea Devils also entered hibernation when their astronomers predicted a catastrophe would end all life on the Earth. As their hibernation colonies were based underwater, they were less vulnerable to geological activity. To maximise their chances of survival, the Sea Devils hid these colonies in every ocean of the world. Only those who knew of their location could find them, and each contained thousands of Sea Devils in suspended animation. The only drawback with the Sea Devils' colonies was that the trigger mechanisms of their reactivation units tended to deteriorate over time and become faulty, meaning the Sea Devils were sometimes not woken up as they had planned in the first place.

The Sea Devils gained a reputation as fearsome warriors, noted for their agility both in and out of the water (although ones that had been recently revived tended to be slow-moving and mildly disorientated). The nature of their mission also determined their clothing: loose netting for fast, amphibious missions and ceremonial armour for martial combat.

THE MYRKA

The Sea Devils shared the depths with the Myrka, a large creature adapted to the abyssal depths. The Silurians biologically reengineered it so that it could survive out of the water, albeit in a very ungainly fashion, and it remained mortally sensitive to ultraviolet light. The Silurians used it as a living weapon, as it electrocuted upon touch and could knock down steel walls as if they were made of foam rubber. The cruel irony of this was that the Myrka was by nature a placid and playful creature which never meant anybody any harm.

SENSORITES

A timid, highly civilised and peaceful species that has developed telepathy

CREATED BY
Peter R Newman

APPEARANCES
The Sensorites (1964)

At first glance, the Sensorites could be mistaken for wizened old men. They have bald, bulbous heads, whispery whiskers and sunken eyes with no lids. On closer inspection they are more alien, as their feet are flat, round pads, and their hearts are in the centres of their chests.

Perhaps the most extraordinary thing about the Sensorites is that they are altruistic to a fault. Usually evolution favours behaviour that transmits an individual's own genes, prioritising their own descendants or close relatives. But the Sensorites, while they still retain 'family groups', only think in terms of a 'Sensorite Nation'. They have no names and are incapable of telling each other apart, being 'contented with their similarity'. It is only in order to function as a society that they have devised a caste system, denoted by sashes of position: Elders think and rule, Warriors fight, and other castes work and play. This is a system based entirely on trust; it would never occur to a Sensorite to impersonate another.

Another reason the Sensorites can't tell each other apart is because they have extremely poor eyesight, a weakness stemming from the fact that their home planet, the Sense-Sphere, is in perpetual daylight from its two suns. They consequently have a congenital fear of the dark. On the other hand, their hearing is very sensitive. This has also developed an evolutionary defect, as loud noises can stun their brains and paralyse their nerves. This is why the Sensorites' severest punishment is banishment to the desert wastes where there are dark caves and raucous animals.

With their poor eyesight and oversensitive hearing, it is perhaps no surprise that the Sensorites use a different form of communication — telepathy. The Sense-Sphere is abundant in high frequencies that make thought transference possible using disc-like devices called mind transmitters. These enable

a Sensorite to project speech into other minds; two-way communication requires both parties to use mind transmitters. These devices also grant Sensorites a limited amount of control over humans: they can wipe people's memories, or place them into a state of suspended animation. They are very reluctant to do this, though, as it sometimes accidentally drives the person insane.

UNANSWERED QUESTIONS

If the Sensorites are so peace-loving, why do they even have a Warrior caste and weapons in the first place? The answer is, of course, that these things were only introduced in response to the arrival of humans.

THE SILENCE

Nightmarish, memory-proof agents of the Papal Mainframe

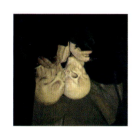

The Silence are a humanoid species, taller than the average human with hairless, grey skull-like heads with large craniums and sunken eyes. They do possess mouths, but they are not used for speech and are only visible when the Silence are absorbing electrical energy. When they do speak, their voices are deep, raspy and punctuated with insect-like clicks and hideous death-rattles. Their hands have only three elongated fingers and a stubby thumb, while their toes have a powerful grip as they like to sleep hanging upside-down from the ceiling like bats.

Little is known about the origins of this species. What is known is that they were recruited by the Church of the Papal Mainframe to serve as confessional priests and genetically engineered to be memory proof, so that anyone who looked at them would forget all about them the moment they looked away, the idea being that penitents would forget everything they had confessed. The obvious flaw with this idea being that the penitents would also forget they had spoken to the confessor, and go and confess to them again.

CREATED BY
Steven Moffat

APPEARANCES
The Impossible Astronaut/
Day of the Moon (2011)
A Good Man Goes
to War (2011)
Let's Kill Hitler (2011)
Closing Time (2011)
The Wedding of
River Song (2011)
The Time of the Doctor
(2013)

INSTANTLY FORGETTABLE

Unless, that is, the Silence are able to control the memory-wipes. There is some evidence for this: they have been known to use memory-wipes to brainwash unsuspecting victims (such as the unfortunate Dr Renfrew of the Greystark Hall Orphanage) and it would make sense for a confessional priest not only to absolve the confessor of their sins but also to take away their memory of committing them.

In this, it seems the ability is similar to that of the perception filter of the Tenza. The difference being that it affects only the short-term memory and does not replace memories with alternative events; it

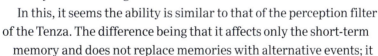

simply edits out the section in which it appeared. Nor does it require a conscious effort on the part of the Silent, as the memory loss still occurs if the Silent is being unknowingly observed, or is even just a hologram. When someone is looking at a Silent, however, it is able to implant hypnotic instructions which the person will then follow without being conscious of it; the only drawback with this is that anyone else can also implant post-hypnotic instructions in someone while they are looking at a Silent.

SILENT BUT DEADLY

Silence are powerful but rarely find it necessary to resort to physical force when in battle. Instead, they can draw in the electrical energy from their surroundings; one of the tell-tale signs of the presence of the Silence is flickering or dimming lights. They can then discharge this electricity in the form of a lightning bolt. If they wish, this bolt can vaporise their unlucky victim, or merely electrocute them. It has been theorised that a Silent submerged in liquid would be insulated and therefore defenceless; however, Silence can survive perfectly well without electricity, as they demonstrated in all the centuries before electricity was discovered.

SILENT ASSASSINS

The Silence have successfully lived clandestinely on Earth for thousands of years. They have effectively been ruling the world since the first use of fire, an invisible hand guiding the course of human history. Sometimes a human may glimpse a Silent out of the corner of their eye, only to immediately forget all about it.

UNANSWERED QUESTION

One of the most incongruous things about the Silence is that they favour formal attire. Whenever they are glimpsed, they are always wearing black suits and usually a tie. There is a reason for this. The Silence are actually naked but are using hologram shells developed by the Church of the Papal Mainframe, programmed to project an image that suggests authority. As for why the Silence don't appear naked, there are some things that even their memory-wipes cannot erase, and the sight of a Silent in the nude is one of them.

The reason why they have been guiding human history is that the Silence on Earth are a breakaway faction of the Church of the Papal Mainframe that is determined, for complicated reasons, to ensure that a prophecy of the Doctor being killed at Lake Silencio in 2011 comes true. The prophecy stipulates that the Doctor is killed by River Song wearing a spacesuit, so the Silence's mission is to make sure that human technology has reached a point where there will be spacesuits and that River Song is trained and conditioned to kill the Doctor. In this, they are largely successful, even going so far as to put the young River Song in the spacesuit for practice.

It might be asked why the Silence go to all this trouble just to get a spacesuit; the answer is that they are, by their very nature, technological parasites. They have never learned how to make things for themselves because they have always been able to get other life forms to do it for them. They are the ultimate puppeteers, manipulating events from the shadows.

SILURIANS

Highly civilised humanoid lizards from the Dawn of Time

Long before the existence of humanity, Earth was home to another race of intelligent bipeds. These had evolved not from apes but from cold-blooded reptiles similar to iguanas. They first emerged about 350 million years ago, when the Earth was warmer than it is now, a world of carboniferous tropical jungles and swamps. The early Silurians were herbivores but developed intelligence and language as they became carnivorous predators. They built a great civilisation and achieved an extremely advanced level of biotechnology; for instance, they could use bio-programming to alter the internal molecular structure of plants so they could be used in engineering and construction. Their laws forbade any unprovoked aggression, and they lived in peace for thousands of years. Individual Silurians could live for several centuries.

The evolutionary history of the Silurians is a little confusing, as they appear to have existed on Earth in periods 300 million years ago, 200 million years ago when Jurassic Earth was one continent, 65 million years ago at the time of Cretaceous dinosaurs such as Tyrannosaurus rex, 40 million years ago during the Eocene and about 20 million years ago when the first apes walked on the Earth.

They were also present when what they mistakenly believed to be a small planet was approaching the Earth, threatening to destroy all life. They placed themselves in suspended animation to avert the disaster, unaware that the 'planet' would be drawn into Earth's orbit as a moon (even though, technically, it wasn't a moon; it was an egg).

But this wasn't the first or the last time this had happened.

The reason the Silurians' occupation of the Earth spans so many different eras is because they repeatedly placed themselves in hibernation to sit out natural disasters (such as infestations of the red leech) and periods of global cooling, setting their 'alarm clocks' to wake them up whenever the climate had returned to normal.

CREATED BY
Malcolm Hulke

APPEARANCES
Doctor Who and the Silurians (1970)
Warriors of the Deep (1984)
The Hungry Earth/ Cold Blood (2010)
The Pandorica Opens (2010)
A Good Man Goes to War (2011)
The Wedding of River Song (2011)
Dinosaurs on a Spaceship (2012)
The Snowmen (2012)
The Crimson Horror (2013)
The Name of the Doctor (2013)
Deep Breath (2014)
Face the Raven (2015)

UNANSWERED QUESTION

Both the Silurians and the Sea Devils were given their names by humans – so why do they sometimes refer to themselves and each other by those names? The answer is, of course, that those are their proper names and the humans who used them did so because they retained them as ancient race memories.

SILURIAN SUBSPECIES

This also explains why the Silurian species has diverged into at least four distinct subspecies. While one Silurian tribe or 'triad' might place itself in cryogenic suspension, another tribe might continue living for hundreds of thousands of years, evolving into a different form, before placing itself in suspension somewhere else on the planet. These two species of Silurian might then wake up at the same time and discover they were sharing the planet with 'cousins' who looked quite different to them.

The most dramatic divergence is, of course, the Silurians that adapted to life underwater and became known as Sea Devils. (They have their own entry.) Of the Silurians that continued to live on the surface, there are three known varieties:

EARLY SILURIANS

The earliest Silurians were, ironically, the most physically advanced. While they were perhaps the most iguana-like in colour, skin and form, they possessed a form of telekinetic projection through the third eyes in their foreheads. They could, if they wished, produce a force capable of killing an ape (or each other), or simply use it to unlock doors. These Silurians are distinguished by having three-clawed hands and feet, and large, ear-like fins for heat regulation. When they lived side by side with apes they found them a nuisance, so they developed a bacterial infection to control their numbers. This was enough to instil in the apes a mortal fear of Silurians that would endure as a race memory.

MIDDLE SILURIANS

The Silurians then adapted to a more desert-like environment, gaining a large carapace like a tortoise shell. Their colouring became lighter and more sand-coloured and their claws were now hands with opposable thumbs. Most significantly, the Silurians' third eye was now used solely for communication; as the creatures were now virtually identical, they used it to indicate who was speaking. As their society had become more technology-based, developing computer manipulators and powerful cutting devices, their telekinetic abilities had atrophied through lack of use.

LATE SILURIANS

The late Silurians would appear to be an example of parallel evolution because, while they retain the green, scaly skin and crests of their predecessors, facially and vocally they are broadly human, having lost their third eye completely. These are creatures that evolved to hunt apes; they are the only Silurians to have noses to scent their prey, and they are equipped with extremely long, elastic tongues, like chameleons, which can deliver a highly venomous sting. Their warriors still wear their ceremonial hunting masks, and apes — or their descendants — remain their dish of choice. Like the other subspecies, Silurians of the same gene-chain are virtually identical save for skin markings.

SKITHRA

Scorpion-like scavengers with a superiority complex

CREATED BY
Nina Métivier

APPEARANCES
Nikola Tesla's
Night of Terror (2020)

Shooting red bolts of electricity from their hands and shrouding themselves in dark hooded robes, the Skithra's cool cloak and the ability to project unlimited human disguises based on real people hides a beastly exoskeleton.

Asserting their superior intelligence, the Skithra regularly steal technology from other species rather than developing their own. They believe they are entitled to it and, when the technology breaks down, the brightest and the best from other planets are taken by force in order to repair and improve it. The Skithra wanted to kidnap genius inventor Nikola Tesla to work for them as an engineer.

Tesla, the Doctor and her fam were chased by a Skithra shooting green laser beams at them with a Silurian blaster. The scavengers were trying to get hold of another stolen piece of alien tech, a repurposed Orb of Thassor that had turned in Tesla's Niagara Generator. The Doctor was fascinated by the Skithra's adaptations, making an elegant information-sharing sphere into a noisy energy-emitting scanner.

The Skithra's stolen human disguise is marked by glowing red eyes and the ability to shoot red electricity, reflecting the red glow of their scorpion-like tails beneath the projection and their Queen's humanoid upper body and electric stinger. Their faces can warp, blur and become unconvincing as their real appearance is revealed and their voices are scraping and horrible.

THE QUEEN OF THE SKITHRA

The Skithra's Queen is much larger and more monstrous than her subjects. As the Skithra are a hive species, the Queen is key to their survival — if she is destroyed, they too will die. While her hind quarters are insectoid and scorpion-like, akin to her subjects, her torso resembles that of a human. Her tail is enormous and vicious, her face is skull-like and rises into giant horns, and her eyes are dark and sharp.

The Queen accused the Doctor of trespassing on her ship but, like the rest of Skithra technology, it was stolen and cobbled together from interesting parts. The Doctor identified it as Venusian spaceship containing a Klendov warp drive and Durillian resonator, which infuriated her as the Skithra are more than capable of thinking of and building their own devices instead of looting them and murdering obstacles. But the Queen did not consider Tesla to be special, just a good engineer who had stumbled upon their signal. She mocked the Doctor for being unarmed, and threatened to kill her personally, but was undermined by Tesla's inventions and the unwillingness of her species to evolve.

The Queen died as her subjects teleported away using the warp drive.

SKOVOX BLITZER

A robot programmed to fight in a long-forgotten war

The Skovox Blitzer is one of the deadliest killing machines ever created. It consists of a metal torso and head attached to a central dome unit that ambulates on four crab-like legs. It is literally 'armed' with two different but extremely lethal laser weapons: a triple-barrelled precision incinerator and a single-barrelled short-range mortar cannon. Each Blitzer carries enough explosive in its armoury to destroy an Earth-sized planet. It is equipped with binocular thermal imaging eyes and has long-range sensors that can detect most types of energised particle. Its programming is fairly straightforward, consisting of an instruction to locate targets and destroy them. When it is faced with any problem not covered by its programming, it is instructed that the solution is to destroy whatever is causing the problem.

CREATED BY
**Gareth Roberts and
Steven Moffat**

APPEARANCES
The Caretaker (2014)

THE SKOVOX-HELICON WAR

The Blitzers were originally created by the Skovox, a highly advanced and belligerent species, for use in their interplanetary war against their arch rivals, the Helicon, a highly advanced and easily annoyed species. The two species preferred to conduct their battles by proxy, using robots on innocent planets located between their two systems, which would end up as either radioactive wastelands or previously uncharted asteroid fields.

The intention was for the Blitzers to deliver a decisive victory. They proved successful against the Helicon, homing in on their tell-tale particles, until the Helicon found a way to convince the Blitzers that they were their superior officers and that they should attack the Skovox, homing in on their tell-tale Artron emissions. Unfortunately, they neglected to include the word 'instead' in the instruction, and the Blitzers turned their fire on both the Skovox and the Helicon. During the resulting chaos, all the Skovox who knew the shutdown codes for the Blitzers were lost, and whenever the Skovox or the Helicon tried to command the Blitzers to shut down they self-destructed with catastrophic consequences, as each carried enough explosive to destroy a planet.

The final result of the conflict was a large empty patch in the galaxy where their two solar systems used to be. Most of the Blitzers were destroyed but a few survive, drifting through space awaiting new orders. They continue to scan for Helicon and Artron emissions in the hope of finding new targets. It is believed over eight hundred Blitzers are still fighting the Skovox-Helicon war.

THE FAMILY SLITHEEN

Criminal clan using stolen technology in pursuit of get-rich-quick schemes

CREATED BY
Russell T Davies

APPEARANCES
Aliens of London/
World War Three (2005)
Boom Town (2005)
The End of Time (2009)

Raxacoricofallapatorius has a bad reputation. It's largely undeserved, as its indigenous species are mostly intelligent, cultured, law-abiding citizens. Indeed, it served as a model for the other worlds in the Raxas Alliance: Clom, Plix and Raxacoricovarlonpatorius. The problem is that one clan, the family Slitheen, have criminal ambitions.

Admittedly, in some ways all Raxacoricofallapatorians are a little harsh. They are creatures that have evolved to hunt, possessing large, powerful claws, night-adapted eyes and an extremely strong sense of smell. Under the stewardship of the family Blathereen, they largely put such savagery behind them, although Raxacoricofallapatorius does still retain the death penalty, and in a very inhumane form. Raxacoricofallapatorians are calcium-based life-forms, and convicted felons are publicly executed by being slowly lowered into a cauldron of dilute acetic acid and boiled alive until they form a kind of soup. Still alive, still screaming.

If life under the Blathereen was severe, it was even worse after the family Slitheen bribed their way into power. The Slitheen family embraced their species' bloodthirsty inheritance. They lived to hunt, elevating it to a ritual sport in the belief that it purified their blood. All their young were raised to revel in their bloodlust from the moment they emerged from the egg in the family Slitheen hatchery. At the age of thirteen they were made to carry out their first kill; if they showed the slightest reluctance, they would be fed to the hunting pack venom grubs. What they actually hunted is unknown; their original prey, the Baaraddelskelliumfatrexius beasts, were hunted to extinction centuries ago.

The family Slitheen were cruel and decadent, with a childish disposition, and ruined the planet's economy. The population rose up against them and the family Slitheen were deposed and fled. In their absence, the new Grand Council found them guilty of crimes against the Raxas Alliance and condemned the entire family to death.

The exiled family set out on a career as organised criminals, intent on amassing sufficient wealth to buy a fleet of battle cruisers and take revenge upon their home planet's government. They scavenged and stole technology from other races to use in their get-rich-quick schemes, most of which revolved around trying to acquire assets to sell on the galactic market, reducing planets to radioactive molten slag to sell as spaceship fuel, draining energy from suns and planets, and harvesting telekinetic energy from psychic species.

As their schemes often go wrong, Slitheen are always prepared to make a quick getaway, using personal teleports and a supply of stolen tribophysical waveform macro-kinetic extrapolators (also known as pan-dimensional surfboards). The family Slitheen's nefarious days could be numbered, however, if the Judoon are assigned to hunt them out and bring them to justice, once and for all.

OFFENSIVE ABILITIES

In extreme circumstances, female Raxacoricofallapatorians can extrude poisonous spines in their fingers and fire them like darts. The excess poison can also be secreted as a powder to slip into drinks or exhaled as a gas, though it can be easily neutralised with a breath spray. In their natural form, Raxacoricofallapatorians can move extremely rapidly; indeed, when they are in motion they may appear quite physically different to when they are at rest.

SKIN-SUITS

Lacking numbers and military might, the family Slitheen's favoured tactic is to infiltrate a planet by hiding in the skins of the dominant native species. The process of acquiring the skins from a victim is brutal but mercifully swift. As Raxacoricofallapatorians are eight feet tall and usually quite tubby, they use compression fields to fit themselves inside the skins of smaller species. This requires an opening to be created in the head which, once the suit is occupied, can be sealed with a zip embedded in the skin hidden in an undetectable fold. The compression field is generated by a device worn around the neck, which also acts as a voice synthesizer and translator. When a subject unzips their forehead and decompresses, the release of electrical energy tends to play havoc with any light fittings, causing them to flicker.

Being compressed inside a tight skin-suit is very uncomfortable and causes Raxacoricofallapatorians to suffer 'gas exchange'. The gas they emit smells of calcium decay and can cause the suit occupant to suffocate so, whenever possible, Raxacoricofallapatorians prefer to be naked.

UNANSWERED QUESTION

The question with any species that uses a skin-suit as a disguise is how can they see out? The answer is that the Slitheen skin-suits retain the human eyeballs. Their neck devices create a short-range interface between the retinas of the human eyeballs and their own optic nerve, so they are effectively seeing through the eyes of the dead. This is why they always close their eyes before taking the suits off, so the eyeballs don't fall out.

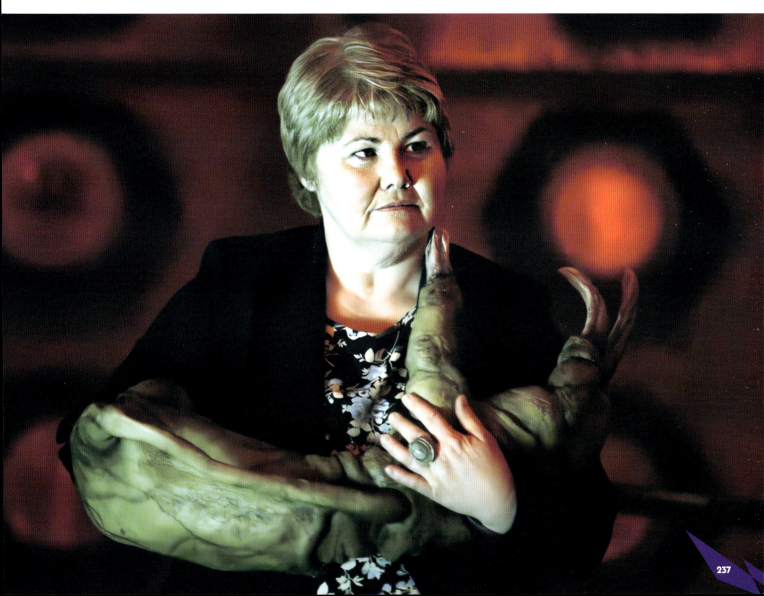

SOLITRACT & ANTIZONE CREATURES

A conscious universe banished to its own dimension

CREATED BY
Ed Hime

APPEARANCES
It Takes You Away (2018)

The Solitract is part of the Time Lords' creation myth, a tale passed down through the generations. In the story, after the Big Bang, all the fundamental elements of the universe existed but couldn't resolve into a consistent set of laws because of the destabilising presence of the Solitract. The Solitract was a consciousness formed of pure energy but its very existence was an anathema to the rest of creation. And so the elemental forces of the universe combined to banish the Solitract into a separate plane of existence where it would remain alone for eternity.

For the Time Lords, the Solitract was meant as a cautionary tale, a reminder that one person's prosperity comes at the cost of another person's freedom. They had no way of telling whether or not it was actually true. But it was.

The Solitract knew that it could never return to the universe but it yearned for companionship. It tried to establish a portal linking to the universe but instead created an Antizone, a kind of 'buffer zone' of lightless tunnels with portals at both ends. Creatures began to enter the Antizone, by accident or design, only to end up caught in the space between worlds.

Eventually the Solitract portal attached itself to a mirror in an isolated house in Norway. The house was occupied by a grieving widower, Erik, who entered the mirror and passed through the Antizone to emerge into a mirror-copy of his home where his wife Trina was still alive. The Solitract had taken her form to ensure that he would never want to leave... and when Graham O'Brien entered the Solitract plane, it recreated his late wife, Grace, before taking the form of a frog as a tribute to her.

The Flesh Moths were the first creatures to be lured into the Antizone, quite literally like moths to a flame. They are piranha-like predators and a swarm can strip the flesh from the bone in seconds.

RIBBONS

This species of demonic scavengers were rejected by the Solitract but remained in the Antizone, acting as traders to others who had entered the zone — before eating them. Eventually only one of them was left, Ribbons of the Seven Stomachs, who thought of the Antizone as his home. As for exactly why his forebears were rejected by the Solitract, the answer is simple; they smelt very strongly of urine.

SOLONIAN MUTANTS

A premature mutation of a metamorphic species

CREATED BY
Bob Baker and
Dave Martin

APPEARANCES
The Mutants (1972)
Frontier in Space (1973)
The Brain of Morbius
(1976)

The planet Solos has one of the strangest ecosystems in the universe. Its orbit of two thousand Earth years is highly elliptical, resulting in four seasons of five hundred years each: a spring as it approaches its sun; a summer during the closest quarter; autumn as it moves away; and winter during the furthest quarter. In each system, the planet's flora and fauna adapts. In fact, it has evolved to change its very nature in response to the changing seasons. Every creature and plant undergoes genetic regulation, switching on latent genes and switching off others so that it becomes almost a different species. This way, it is always perfectly adapted to the dramatically changing environment.

We know the most about the transition from spring to summer. In spring, Solos has a temperature similar to that of Earth and its dominant species are creatures very similar to humans that have reached the hunter-gatherer level of civilisation.

As the planet enters summer, it increases significantly in temperature, becoming much too hot for human-type life to exist. The native humanoids undergo a process similar to metamorphosis (but technically not metamorphosis, as it is not part of their life cycle, but an adaption to climate change). To complete the genetic reconfiguration they require a high level of background radiation (preferably thaesium) and a crystalline catalyst, both of which occur naturally in the caves of Solos. They then adopt their 'summer' form: a luminescent humanoid, composed of pure energy. In this eidolic form they are capable of flight, thought transference, passing through solid matter and emitting an energy beam sufficient to vaporise matter.

When, during the thirtieth century, they were deprived of the radiation and the catalyst, they became insectoid creatures with claws, mandibles and thick exoskeletons, referred to as 'Mutts'. In this form they were creatures of instinct, highly territorial and aggressive. It was not so much an intermediate stage as a false turning or atavism. It was mainly the result of outside intervention in Solos's atmosphere, leading to premature, accelerated mutations. Unfortunately, the Solonians were unaware of the nature of their life cycle and believed they were undergoing mutation caused by pollution.

SEASONAL TRENDS

The Solonians' historical tablets are rather obscure as to their autumnal and winter forms. As far as can be gathered, their autumn forms are glowing hexagonal eggs; their winter forms are represented by a grid of snail-curls.

SONTARANS

A ruthless, disciplined race dedicated to perpetual war

The Sontarans are the finest soldiers in the galaxy, a species whose entire existence is devoted to warfare. Originally, they were a broadly humanoid species, albeit a nasty, brutish and short one, as their size and proportions were an adaptation to the high gravity of their home world Sontar. On Sontar, a Sontaran weighs the equivalent of several tonnes, so Sontarans have great load-bearing strength and find Earth-gravity worlds awkwardly buoyant.

CREATED BY
Robert Holmes

APPEARANCES
The Time Warrior (1973)
**The Sontaran
Experiment (1975)**
**The Invasion of Time
(1978)**
The Two Doctors (1985)
**The Sontaran Stratagem/
The Poison Sky (2008)**
The End of Time (2010)
**The Pandorica Opens
(2010)**
**A Good Man Goes
to War (2011)**
The Snowmen (2012)
**The Crimson Horror
(2013)**
**The Name of
the Doctor (2013)**
Deep Breath (2014)
Face the Raven (2015)

CLONE WARRIORS

In response to the outbreak of hostilities with the Rutan, and the massive casualties they suffered, the Sontarans genetically reengineered themselves as a race. Rather than relying on an inefficient reproductive cycle based around two genders, they would now be clones, grown in vats of clonefeed in batches of a million or more. Whole planets became hatcheries or 'clone worlds', delivering millions of speed-grown warriors for the Sontaran Military Academy muster parades. As a result, most Sontaran warriors are only a few years old and, given the high mortality rate of their war with the Rutan, a Sontaran that is more than twelve years old is regarded as a battle veteran. The high mortality rate also means that it is rare for a Sontaran to live long enough to be promoted, so instead the various Sontaran ranks of Group Marshal, Commander, Field Major and so forth are allocated at gestation.

The Sontarans also altered their biology so they would no longer require food and drink for sustenance; instead they could be fed with pure energy through probic vents at the backs of their necks. This was their one vulnerability, since a blow to the vent could stun a Sontaran warrior, but Sontaran propagandists decided to make a virtue of this weakness because it meant that a Sontaran would always have to face their enemies. Indeed, for greater honour a Sontaran will face them bare-faced ('open-skinned') too. 'We stare into the face of death!'

BRED FOR WAR

Sontaran culture is entirely dedicated to war. There is only one greater honour than participating in a battle and that is to die in it for the glory of the Sontaran Empire. Sontarans would rather be court-martialed than show fear or pain, which are court-martial offences. They are ruthlessly dedicated to observing military protocol, utterly methodical and fastidious. They are also obsessed with time efficiency, often giving their missions arbitrary and impractically short deadlines. In battle they give no warnings and take no prisoners. Disputes between Sontarans are traditionally resolved with a duel to the death, while disputes between Sontarans and other races are traditionally resolved by destroying them with scalpel mines and acid.

Sontaran society is arranged on strictly martial terms. The highest authority is the Sontaran High Command, followed by the Grand Strategic Council overseeing the various battle fleets, battle groups, battle survey teams and other battle-related divisions.

BATTLE TECHNOLOGY

Sontarans are never seen without their space armour and rarely without their large, dome-shaped helmets. As well as protection, the helmets are designed to conceal their appearance, usually so they can reserve the moment of revealing their true nature for when they need to instil shock and terror. Sontaran warriors in the field carry a variety of equipment, including personal translators (for ordering primitives), fear inducers (for frightening primitives), hypnotisers (for interrogating and controlling primitives), and a large number of laser weapons and grenades (for destroying primitives).

TIME-TRAVEL AMBITIONS

The Sontarans have long wanted to possess 'time-dimensional' technology but have only managed to achieve very limited time transference using frequency modulation. They can visit the not-too-distant future using an osmic projector and even kidnap people and materials using a matter transmitter but that is as far as it goes. They have attempted to steal time-travel technology from other species (it is a longstanding Sontaran protocol that any TARDISes should be captured) and once even attempted to invade Gallifrey (their military intelligence mistakenly believed that the Time Lords lacked the moral strength to withstand a determined assault). It remains a point of great irritation to Sontarans that they were 'not allowed' to be part of the Great Time War. As for why they want to travel back in time, it is so they can find out how their war against the Rutan started; not so they can avert it, but so they can enjoy it all over again.

UNANSWERED QUESTION

It has occasionally been noted that, somewhat ironically for a clone species, no two Sontarans look alike. Indeed, there have been remarkable variations in the species in terms of height, colour, facial hair and the number of fingers. The explanation is, of course, that Sontarans are always tweaking the settings of their hatchery vats, duplicating particularly successful warriors and doing their best not to reproduce unsuccessful ones. Even fully grown Sontarans may be gene-spliced for certain tasks, such as Sontaran nurses having the ability to produce magnificent quantities of lactic fluid.

STAR WHALE

The last of a species of intelligent, spacefaring leviathans

The twenty-ninth century was the United Kingdom's darkest hour. The Earth was being scorched by solar flares, and every other nation had fled into the depths of space. There was no hope. The children cried.

And then, like a miracle, a star whale appeared in the skies. The star whales were thought to have lived in the depths of space and this was the last of its kind. Her Majesty's Government saw their chance and trapped the creature. They surgically implanted feeder tubes into its gullet and bolted a carapace-like shell onto its back. On this shell they built a city: *Starship UK*. The lowest part of *Starship UK* was built into the whale's head, exposing the pain centre of its brain. When it was time to leave, a powerful electrical charge was sent into its brain and it began to accelerate away to safety.

The star whale itself was extraordinary. Over fifty miles long, it was a composite of creatures of the deep. Like a whale it had pectoral fins, for steering in the solar winds and cooling itself when basking in the sun. Like an angler fish it had a bioluminescent lure to catch spacefaring prey. And like a squid it had eight undulating tentacles which it used to create propulsive gravity waves so gentle they would not cause the water to ripple in a glass. Its spongy, space-weathered skin was mauve and speckled with bioluminescent dots; these could be used both for camouflage in the star-flecked darkness of space and to signal to other whales. The glowing tendrils beneath its mouth served another purpose, as a courtship display.

But the human race should have remembered the legends about star whales guiding early space travellers through the asteroid belt. The star whales were benign and empathic. This whale had come to Earth for just one reason — because it couldn't bear to watch the children cry.

CREATED BY
Steven Moffat

APPEARANCES
The Beast Below (2010)

UNANSWERED QUESTION

***Starship UK*'s authoritarian regime would send protestors and citizens of limited value down feeding tubes into the star whale's mouth, but the whale would always spare the children. Why did it do this? Because it was trying to make the population of *Starship UK* realise it wanted to help. They didn't even know they were riding on the back of a star whale, they had all chosen to forget. That's why it forced its roots up into the city. To remind them of the truth.**

STENZA

A ruthless race of interplanetary trophy-hunters

The Stenza are a humanoid, pale blue race that evolved to live at temperatures far below zero. They are, quite literally, cold-hearted killers. They consider themselves a 'warrior race' but think nothing of slaughtering innocent, defenceless species in their beds.

Their social system is based upon the accumulation of hunting trophies; these are normally their victims' teeth, which they embed into their faces. Their leaders are selected through a hunting ritual: to locate and capture a randomly designated human with no weapons or assistance. If a Stenza faced with this challenge returns home with their human trophy, they can then ascend to leadership. If they fail, they are ignominiously decapitated. As for the trophy, they are locked into a stasis chamber to remain on the cusp of life and death for eternity. It is the dream of the Stenza to one day hold whole civilisations in stasis.

The Stenza have idiosyncratic ideas about honour. Before a planet can be used as a hunting ground they must have consent from one of its inhabitants, even if it is given unwittingly.

The Stenza claim to be the conquerors of the Nine Systems, one of which contains the planet Desolation. The Stenza wiped out most of the indigenous population, save for the scientists, who were put to work creating new poisons, weapons and killing machines, turning the planet into a toxic, scorched wilderness. The scientists' final act of defiance was to attempt to destroy all their creations. They failed. Even after thousands of years, their SniperBots and Remnants still roamed the planet. As a result, long after the fall of the Stenza the planet was selected as a venue for the final Rally of the Twelve Galaxies.

CREATED BY
Chris Chibnall

APPEARANCES
The Woman Who
Fell to Earth (2018)
The Battle of Ranskoor
Av Kolos (2018)

REMNANTS

The most sinister creations of the scientists of Desolation are the Remnants. They are snake-like strips of cloth or bandage that can float and smother their victims. They are also telepathic, able to demoralise and distract their prey by taunting them with their darkest fears and secrets.

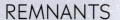

GATHERING COIL

When the Stenza warrior Tzim-Sha (or, as he was renamed by the Doctor, Tim Shaw) came to Earth for his challenge, he decided to improve his odds by breaking the rules and using a Gathering Coil to locate his human target. A Gathering Coil is a biotechnological device, half-organic, half-machine, resembling a seething mass of tentacles, each of which is an information-gathering creature. As well as tracking, the Gathering Coil can be used to implant DNA bombs in any inconvenient witnesses.

SUTEKH & THE OSIRIANS

The godlike race whose wars inspired Egyptian mythology

Seven thousand years ago there existed a race of immense power. They enjoyed vast mental resources, which enabled them to project their minds across the gulfs of space and to read and control the minds of lesser species. No being possessed the willpower to resist them. They were all-powerful. Their planet was Phaester Osiris, and they were the Osirians.

CREATED BY
Stephen Harris

APPEARANCES
Pyramids of Mars (1975)

The Osirians were a peaceful, benevolent race. They believed in kinship with all life. All of them but one. One Osirian refuted this creed. His name was Sutekh and he revelled in destruction. All life was his enemy. Evil was his good.

While the Osirians were broadly humanoid, with high, dome-shaped heads enclosing their enlarged spiral cerebellums, Sutekh altered his appearance to that of a creature somewhere between a wild ass and a jackal, known as the Typhonian Beast. In this form, he destroyed Phaester Osiris and left a trail of havoc across the galaxy. His other names — Set, Satan, Sadok — became bywords for evil on every civilised world.

Eventually the seven hundred and forty other Osirians, led by Horus (who had altered his appearance to that of a falcon), confronted and defeated him in ancient Egypt during the First Dynasty of the Pharaohs. The resulting battle formed the basis of Egyptian mythology.

The Egyptians believed that Sutekh was killed by Horus, but execution was in fact against the Osirian code. Instead they imprisoned him for eternity in a burial chamber beneath a pyramid in Saqqara, unable to project his mind, his body paralysed by a force field generated on Mars. And there he would have remained, were it not for an incautious Egyptologist called Marcus Scarman...

UNANSWERED QUESTION

It does seem odd that the only security Horus and the Osirians put in place around the power source on Mars was a series of puzzles and brainteasers that even a child could solve. But that was the whole point: to torture Sutekh for eternity with the knowledge that his freedom was only a few 'childish stratagems' away.

ROBOT MUMMIES

For routine tasks, Osirians employed service robots, machines consisting of armourflex skeletons covered in chemically impregnated bindings to protect them against corrosion, controlled via a cytronic induction point at the back of the frame. Their resemblance to Egyptian mummies was not a coincidence; they inspired the ancient Egyptians to begin the practice of mummification, in the belief that it would enable them to serve their gods after death.

SYCORAX

Interplanetary scavengers and slave-traders

When most species achieve interstellar space travel, it is usually because they have reached a high level of civilisation. The Sycorax are the exception. They have managed to build an empire based entirely on savagery. Everything they possess has been stolen or scavenged or won with the proceeds of slavery. They wear masks made from the skulls of an equine race, they wear necklaces made from the bones of their enemies, and even their spaceships are built into the shells of spacefaring Triton snails.

The ironic thing is that it is all just for show. What stolen 'foreign machinery' the Sycorax possess is unreliable and outdated, such as blood control, and largely beyond their understanding. They are more like a cargo cult, practising what they believe to be witchcraft, 'forbidden arts' and 'the lost rites of Atrophia'. Their social structure is essentially medieval and, though they claim to observe 'sanctified rules of combat', they tend not to follow them very much.

As the Sycorax aren't very powerful, they rely on their powers of intimidation to subjugate other races. Their greatest weapon is fear. This is why they wear skull helmets and half-masks. Why they flay their skin until it is raw and why they sharpen their teeth. Why they only speak in their own guttural tongue. And why they communicate only in terms of threats and demands, commanding races to surrender while boasting of their own strength and the fact that they 'rock'.

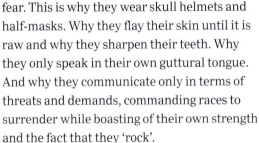

But it's all a bluff, because they are never in a position to carry out their threats. They may claim to have an armada, but nobody has ever seen it. Instead, for all their bluster, they are careful not to overplay their hand. They only ask for one-third of a species' population, along with minerals and precious stones (and, sometimes, women, though this may be a mistranslation).

The best way to defeat the Sycorax, then, is to call their bluff. Because like all bullies, they are cowards at heart. Just show them you're not scared and let them run away.

CREATED BY
Russell T Davies

APPEARANCES
The Christmas Invasion (2005)
The End of Time (2009)
The Pandorica Opens (2010)
The Magician's Apprentice (2015)

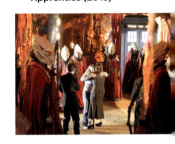

SYCORAX SIGHTINGS
Sycorax can be found in disreputable drinking establishments across the cosmos, trying either to hawk their ill-gotten gains or to intimidate someone into buying them a drink. They joined the alliance to imprison the Eleventh Doctor in the Pandorica though, conspicuously, they stood at the back and let the other species do all the talking.

THE TELLER

Super-sensitive scanner in a straitjacket

CREATED BY
**Steven Moffat and
Steve Thompson**

APPEARANCES
Time Heist (2014)

The Teller and his female partner have flat noses and wriggling eyestalks arcing around each side of their heads like a cross between horns and antennae. They are the last of their species and bear a close resemblance to each other. The crown of the Teller's large and swollen head is concave, showing the characteristic indentations of the brain's structure, and his mouth is wide. His eye ridges are prominent and light pink, in contrast to his greyish, scaly hide. Each arm ends in a pair of long claws, and his tail is short and ribbed in texture.

The Teller is telepathic and can particularly sense guilt when scanning others' minds. His reptilian exoskeleton glistens, and his eyestalks sharply point themselves towards the person or creature whose thoughts he is trying to examine.

When the Teller discovers guilty thoughts, his eyestalks bristle and join to form a circular aperture. This is followed by a piercing whistling sound as a circular wave of shimmering air locks his brain to that of his object of study, who is immediately paralysed by an invisible telekinetic grip.

Everything around them will shake and shudder. As the Teller burrows, the mind of the guilty is wiped and then liquidised — turning the brain tissues into 'soup' and leaving the skull deflated.

The Teller's telepathy and powers of destruction were exploited by the Bank of Karabraxos for an innovative form of security. Madame Karabraxos and her clone Ms Delphox forced the Teller to work for the Bank; he was trapped in an orange straitjacket to prevent his escape, with his partner held hostage and howling as a kind of insurance policy. Guilt was fatal in the Bank, and when there the Doctor and Clara and their new friends Psi and Saibra had to wipe their own minds regularly using memory worms. The more they knew about why they were at the Bank — to steal items important to each individual from the vaults — the stronger the guilty signal to the Teller and the more of a target they became.

The Doctor knew that the Teller was not really a villain, and that he must constantly have felt tortured by the secrets and emotions of others. The Doctor and Clara's reason for being part of the Bank heist was to free the Teller and his partner and take them to a tranquil wilderness planet, where no other creatures or noisy thoughts could hurt them.

TERILEPTILS

War-obsessed beauty-loving reptiles

The Terileptils are intelligent, humanoid reptiles evolved from iguana-like lizards. Although they are now bipedal, they retain two key characteristics: distinctive bright colouring and razor-sharp teeth. These two characteristics are fundamental to their nature.

Firstly, their colourful appearance. They have long, scaled cloak-like backs and multiple dewlaps, almost like Elizabethan ruffles. Both their backs and necks are used for display, as a way of indicating territory, as a visual dominance signal, and to attract a mate. Even though they are a technologically advanced race, Terileptils still prefer to remain unclothed in order to show off their vibrant colours. They are a very vain species.

The importance of colour in their evolution has also led Terileptils to become great aesthetes, highly sensitive to and appreciative of beauty in all forms. This is reflected in their culture, as even the most functional item, such as a control bracelet or android, is designed to be an object of beauty. Terileptils have also achieved advanced forms of holographic energy projection and subtle lighting effects using Vintaric crystals.

CREATED BY
Eric Saward

APPEARANCES
**The Visitation (1982)
Time-Flight (1982)**

THOUGHT CONTROL

One notable Terileptil technical achievement is the polygrite bracelets used to restrain difficult prisoners on their prison planets. These essentially enable them to direct another being by remote control. They can transmit images and instructions directly into their subjects' brains; if the person wearing the bracelet concentrates, they can send back their thoughts. These bracelets would mean that escape from a Terileptil prison was impossible, were it not for the inconvenient fact that they don't work on Terileptils.

It follows, then, that the severest punishment for a Terileptil is to be deprived of their own beauty. This is why the most notorious Terileptil criminals are sentenced to work in the Tinclavic mines on the prison planet of Raaga. Tinclavic has a corrosive effect on Terileptil skin, resulting in carbuncle-like growths. This further serves to reinforce their belief that appearance is a reflection of moral worth.

Secondly, their piranha-like teeth indicate that they are, by preference, carnivores. And so, even though they are a species of art lovers, they are also extremely cruel, callous and warlike. Indeed, it could be said they are obsessed with war, considering it 'honourable' in all forms; there is no more noble death than to die fighting. This innate tendency for violence is perhaps why there are so many Terileptil criminals and why their chief export is Tinclavic.

TETRAPS

Humanoid vampire bats turned galactic mercenaries

CREATED BY
Pip and Jane Baker

APPEARANCES
Time and the Rani (1987)

You only have to look at a Tetrap to realise they must have extraordinary evolutionary origins. They resemble large bipedal bats with prehensile claws and vestigial wings. These are creatures that were once capable of flight — or at least gliding from treetops — but which have adapted to life on the ground, although they still sleep hanging upside-down in caves or eyries. Their thick shaggy fur also suggests a change of environment, from arid desert and tropical rainforest to extreme cold.

But it is their heads which tell the most striking story. They possess four ears — two facing forward, two facing backward — and four eyes — facing forward, left, right and behind. These are creatures designed to be able to detect an attack coming from any direction (apart from above or below, again indicating an adaptation to living on the ground in open spaces). Their quadro-visual eyes are also designed for night vision, as evidenced by their vertical, cat-like pupils.

This is because the Tetraps' home world was one of the most inhospitable worlds in the galaxy, a planet of both environmental extremes and extremely rich natural resources. This resulted in a form of hyper-competitive evolution, with every species vying for dominance in the fight for survival. Literally everything was trying to kill and eat everything else, every minute of the day and night. As the world is called Tetrapyriarbus, we know that the Tetraps finally reigned supreme. They have the abilities of both predator and parasite: they can immobilise their prey with a venom secreted by their long, forked tongues before feeding by puncturing their skin and sucking up their blood.

Sadistically, they like to keep their victims alive for as long as possible, hanging them upside-down in their nests to maintain the blood flow, like carcasses in an abattoir.

These are creatures that have evolved as merciless killing machines, which is why they have gained employment as mercenaries and henchmen — notably for the Rani, who used them as her enforcers when she took over the planet Lakertya. However, just as they are highly adapted to detect predators, they are also congenitally predisposed to anticipate other forms of attack too. Tetraps are deeply paranoid creatures that constantly suspect betrayal. You would be advised not to get on a Tetrap's wrong side, but being able to see in all directions, Tetraps don't have a right side.

UNANSWERED QUESTION

The Rani's killer insects are also from Tetrapyriarbus. This is why the Tetraps don't fear the insects; they are impervious to the insects' bite.

THARILS

Time-sensitive leonine humanoids trafficked as slaves

The Tharils were once the most powerful beings in the universe. Before there were Time Lords, Tharils were the only species to acquire sensitivity to time. They could see into the future, they could cross the striations of the continuum of time to observe the past, and they could withstand the ageing effects of the time winds. They could place themselves out of phase with time. No shackle could hold them, except one made out of dwarf star alloy, 'the only substance dense enough to pin down a dream'.

How they came into being is the stuff of legend. Their species was forged in the aftershocks of the Big Bang when time was in flux. Their planet was exposed to the time winds, and its indigenous species of leonine humanoids evolved, first to become time-resistant, then to become sensitive to time's shifts and patterns. They could cast their minds into the future, into multiple potential futures, and select the course of events that would lead to their desired outcome.

With this ability, they quickly built an empire that spanned the early universe. The vastness of space was no obstacle, as they built a mighty palace at a gateway outside time itself that could lead to any world they desired. It was as if they descended from the sky as kings. But they were greedy and cruel kings and abused their power.

CREATED BY
Stephen Gallagher

APPEARANCES
Warriors' Gate (1981)

They plundered worlds of their riches and enslaved their people.

Then their slaves found a way to defeat them. They built robots, Gundans, that could withstand the time winds and enter the Tharils' domain. The Tharils were forced to flee through their gateway, and the Gundans reduced their mighty palace to little more than a single archway.

When they ran their empire, the Tharils believed the weak enslaved themselves. Now they were the weak and they became enslaved, hunted down and used as time-sensitive navigators for warp ships. A few tried to hide on the planet Chapir, but they too were enslaved.

Yet the Tharils could still see into the future. They could see a course of events that would lead to their liberation...

UNANSWERED QUESTION

If Tharils can see into the future, how did the creators of the Gundans manage to surprise them? The answer lies in the nature of the Gundans: robots that could pass through the fiercest time winds, where the future is obscure even to Tharils.

THIJARIANS

Ancient assassins now on a mission to bear witness to the dead

Back when the universe was less than half its present size, the planet Thijar was home to a sophisticated feudal society. Their various hive states were locked in constant territorial and succession disputes, and a kind of arms race developed as they vied to train the best spies and assassins. As their technology improved, they genetically engineered themselves and accelerated their evolution. The result was a race of perfect assassins, the deadliest killers in the known universe. They were as silent as death; they communicated by telepathy; they used personal transmats to enter establishments without detection. They became mercenaries, hired by other species to murderously settle scores, and soon became figures of legend and folklore. It was said that the Assassins of Thijar could kill someone without disturbing the fall of a feather; that they were so swift that their victims died without feeling even a whisper of pain.

But then, while the assassins hunted across the stars, their home world was destroyed. Some say they destroyed themselves; other legends say they were destroyed by the Great Vampires or the Osirian Sutekh. All that is known is that when the assassins returned they found nothing but dust.

This changed the Thijarians profoundly. It wasn't just that they had lost everything; it was the thought that all their people, all their ancestors, had died unwitnessed and unmourned. They had died without being honoured. So the Thijarians renounced killing and spent a hundred generations in remembrance of their lost dead. But that wasn't enough. They turned their technology to a new mission; they would travel the stars, through time and space, to bear witness to all those who died alone and unacknowledged, to honour them and commemorate them by adding them to their memorial hive.

While the Thijarians can travel in time, they consider it entirely deterministic; they believe that time is a fixed force that cannot be changed, because if the dead could be saved, grief would have no meaning. They can only follow the timewaves and witness events, they cannot change them.

CREATED BY
Vinay Patel

APPEARANCES
**Demons of the Punjab
(2018)**

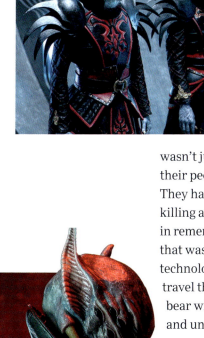

TIVOLIANS

A sly and aggressive race of unscrupulous cowards

Tivoli is a very grey world full of very grey people. Its indigenous species, the Tivolians, evolved from creatures similar to naked mole-rats, and they retain some of their characteristics: prominent incisors, pale, hairless skin, underdeveloped ears, pinched features and beady eyes. And, also like mole-rats, they possess an unusual talent for longevity, having one of the most enduring civilisations in the galaxy. This can be attributed to their dominant genetic trait — cowardice.

Tivolians' first and only concern is self-preservation. They have a pathological compulsion to surrender (indeed, they often use 'I surrender' as a greeting). If they are threatened, their first instinct is to hide behind the nearest small child, their own offspring if necessary. If accused of anything, they will usually claim to be their own identical twin. They are automatically sympathetic to any would-be oppressor and would happily turn in their own mothers if they thought it might gain favour.

Tivoli is the most invaded planet in the galaxy, and the entire Tivolian culture is dedicated to displays of obeisance to potential invaders. They have fifty-six different words for surrender, and their anthem is 'Glory To Insert Name Here'; their schools have mottos like 'Resistance is exhausting', and their capital city has a sign saying, 'If you occupied us, you'd be home by now.' Their streets are even planned for the comfort and convenience of invading forces.

But their cowardice is not quaint or whimsical. It is sly and aggressive. Tivolians are cunning, deceitful and opportunistic, without mercy or shame. Above all, they are highly irritating. This is quite deliberate, as it means any invading force will tend to leave their planet at the first opportunity, often contacting other races to ask them to occupy it instead. In Tivolians' experience, they only have to wait and someone will come along either to liberate them or enslave them, and given the choice, they'd prefer to be enslaved.

THE ARCATEENIAN OCCUPATION

The Tivolians were gratefully enslaved by the Fisher King, only to be liberated — and then enslaved — by the Arcateenians. But the Fisher King wasn't defeated in battle. Rather, the Arcateenians simply raised the planet's sea level, flooding the cities and putting the population into immense slave ships. The Fisher King and his army could only survive on arid and barren worlds, and so the Fisher King pretended to be dead just to get off the planet.

CREATED BY
Toby Whithouse

APPEARANCES
The God Complex (2011)
Under the Lake/
Before the Flood (2015)

TOCLAFANE

Humanity's ultimate future – disembodied heads with the minds of children

CREATED BY
Russell T Davies

APPEARANCES
The Sound of Drums/
Last of the Time Lords
(2007)

Humanity has many potential futures. We may become Cybermen. We may become mixed with other species, with the Lady Cassandra the last remaining 'pure' human. We may become Dregs or Haemovores. We may become the scavenging savages of the Futurekind. But our most awful possible fate is to become the Toclafane.

When the last humans at the end of the universe set forth for Utopia, they thought it would be a haven. They even dreamed it would have skies made of diamonds. Instead the Utopia Project was a last, desperate attempt to find a way for humanity to survive the end of reality.

The solution was to lose their humanity. To cannibalise themselves until they were just heads, magnetically clamped inside metal spheres the size of footballs. The spheres kept them alive and were covered in sensors to replace the human senses. They could move by teleporting or by hovering and even had their own defences: inbuilt spikes, extendable knives and disintegration lasers. They were designed to be both elegant and deadly.

The most horrifying part of the Toclafane, though, was what the scientists did to the brains of those selected for conversion. They regressed them to childhood in the hope that childlike minds would be the best equipped to survive because of their innate adaptability and imagination. In the process something went terribly wrong. They linked the Toclafanes' minds and memories together, so they lost any sense of individuality, and accentuated the worst childhood traits of cruelty and petulance. The result were monsters that killed just for fun.

THE MASTER'S FRIENDS

Of course, 'Toclafane' wasn't their real name. It was merely the appellation given to them by the Master, who thought they should be named after creatures from Gallifreyan fairy tales as a joke. When he visited Utopia, the last of humanity were living in terror of the coming darkness. He offered them a way out: an escape into the past to build a new empire across all of space and time. He could only bring a few of them back with him to the twenty-first century but promised to open up a tear in the fabric of reality to enable the other six billion to evacuate. They could alter their own past, even murder their own ancestors with impunity, as everything would be sustained by the Master converting the Doctor's TARDIS into a paradox machine.

TRACTATORS

Burrowing crustaceans with the power to control gravity

At first look, the Tractators broadly resemble Earth woodlice, particularly those of the family *Trachelipodidae*. They possess the unusual capacity to manipulate gravity using their upper flippers and antennae. They evolved this ability as a defence mechanism — they could use it to immobilise any aggressor and bombard it with rocks or heavy nuts while they retreated to their tunnels and concealed themselves in specially created cavities.

Tractators existed for thousands, if not millions of years, as harmless burrowing creatures. Then their species developed an extreme caste polymorphism, with each colony having the equivalent of a termite king, known as a 'Gravis'. Gravis Tractators differ not only in their green skins but also by being vastly more intelligent, capable of both speech and telepathic control over the drones. Nevertheless, just like a Queen Bee, a Gravis is utterly dependent upon its subjects; deprived of the telepathic support of the colony, a Gravis is reduced to the docile status of a normal Tractator.

CREATED BY
Christopher H Bidmead

APPEARANCES
Frontios (1984)

A wild aberration of natural selection over the centuries made the caste polymorphism more and more pronounced, until the Gravis Tractators had such highly refined powers of abstract reasoning they could arrange their tunnels to form wave guides for their gravity beams. Their ambitions did not end there. They also constructed machines to smooth the walls of their tunnels to concentrate their powers further. These machines required a captive mind to act as a motive force, so the Tractators enslaved the native humanoid species of

their own world, acquiring the ability to steer it through space under the power of gravity. As they ran out of excavation machine drivers, they moved on to other worlds, insidiously growing and breeding beneath the surface before acquiring fresh victims — selecting the weak and injured to avoid detection — by dragging them underground.

Soon they spread their scourge across the galaxy, infesting inhabited planets only to leave them as lifeless husks. The primal inhabitants of the planet Trion would have been wiped out, had the Time Lords not covertly intervened to end the blight. Some Tractators escaped, however, taking refuge in the distant worlds of the Veruna system...

UNANSWERED QUESTION

Like all woodlice, Tractators require large amounts of moisture, as they constantly excrete water through their cuticles. This is why the surface of the planet Frontios is so barren, as the Tractators have dehydrated most of the soil.

TRITOVORES & WORMHOLE RAYS

Humanoid flies that feed on detritus and intergalactic locusts

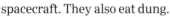

The Tritovores are humanoid flies. They have two arms, two legs, two prehensile claws, two antennae, two maxillary palps, two labial palps and two very large, compound eyes. They are covered in wiry, black hair. They use their palps for communication, making a high-frequency chirping, chirruping, clicking sound. They are scientifically advanced; their technological achievements include personal translators (essential if you communicate by making a high-frequency chirping, chirruping, clicking sound) and stylish interstellar spacecraft. They also eat dung.

The Tritovores are not ashamed of this fact. They consider themselves fortunate to have a source of nourishment which is both abundant in supply and whose swift removal is highly desirable. It is a form of mutually beneficial cleaning symbiosis. The fact that they depend on what other species leave behind has given them a cordial, philosophical outlook on life and made them very ecologically aware. They don't regard themselves as detritivores; they regard themselves as recyclers, travelling the universe gathering waste in lucrative trade deals.

CREATED BY
Russell T Davies and Gareth Roberts

APPEARANCES
Planet of the Dead (2009)

TRITOVORE EVOLUTION

The Tritovores' development was strange and unique. Their ancestors lived on a low-gravity world, enabling its species to achieve gigantism, but then their environment changed quite drastically. An ice giant in their solar system disintegrated and huge fragments of ice fell onto the Tritovore world, greatly increasing its size and mass. Over a period of ten thousand years, the gravity increased until it was about the same as that of Earth. Most of the planet's species became extinct, but the flies adapted: their wings atrophied while their hind legs thickened to enable them to stand upright.

WORMHOLE RAYS

When the Tritovores came to the planet San Helios, they found it had been devastated by wormhole rays, flying creatures analogous to Earth

stingrays. The rays have two notable characteristics. Firstly, they eat practically anything, absorbing all nutrients and minerals, extruding metal to form their exoskeletons. They can reduce a planet to a lifeless desert in under a year.econdly, after they have stripped a planet bare, they congregate into swarms a billion strong which sweep around a planet until the combination of their speed, numbers and size generates a wormhole in space; a wormhole leading to their next destination.

VASHTA NERADA

Swarms of microscopic predators that conceal themselves as shadows

The Vashta Nerada are the stuff of nightmares. One of the most efficient predators ever to exist, they are known as 'the piranhas of the air', while their name translates literally as 'the shadows that melt the flesh'. Because that is what they appear to be: shadows. Individually, they are barely visible, though they may be glimpsed as motes of dust. When gathered in swarms, they manifest themselves as regions of total, inky blackness. And they hunt by stealth. They may make it look as though someone has turned out the lights, or they may take the guise of an innocuous shadow. Should someone enter that shadow, the Vashta Nerada will devour them in an instant. They can eat through any material, even a spacesuit mesh, but they usually leave the bones behind.

The Vashta Nerada exist on most planets, and are the reason why most intelligent species have an instinctive, but entirely rational, fear of the dark. On inhabited planets they tend to exist only in small clusters to avoid detection, but on forest worlds they are abundant, favouring the twilight of the forest floor, building nests inside the trees and hunting the animal life. They are a form of microsporidia, reproducing by releasing microspores which remain inert until they enter their hatching cycle, at which point they emerge to form a very aggressive, and very hungry, swarm.

When swarming, the Vashta Nerada develops a kind of hive mind. They will form a shadow attached to their prey, like parasitic infection, to ensure that they can feed on it while it is still alive, and when it is dead they can make its skeletal remains walk. They can also communicate and learn: if linked to a spacesuit neural relay containing the remnants of a human mind, the 'data ghost' gives voice to the swarm intelligence.

While the Vashta Nerada appear as shadows, they cannot conceal themselves inside existing shadows, so they can be spotted as a shadow without a light source or as an extraneous second shadow. They can also be tricked – a Vashta Nerada swarm may be fooled into thinking an area of darkness is another swarm and leave it alone. So ironically, if you think there is a swarm nearby, the best thing to do might be to turn out the lights. Because the one place where there aren't any shadows is in the dark…

CREATED BY
Steven Moffat

APPEARANCES
**Silence in the Library/
Forest of the Dead
(2008)**

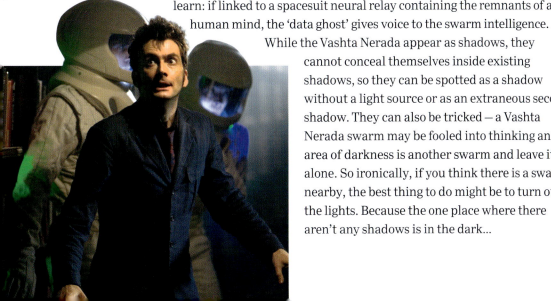

VERVOIDS

The results of an obscene scientific experiment in creating plant slaves

The Vervoids are an entirely artificial form of intelligent, bipedal plant life. Although they have a humanoid shape, they have waxy, veined leaves instead of skin, and heads that resemble tropical carnivorous plants. Instead of eyes and noses they have a pink bud with furrowed, brain-like sepals and a brushy Venus fly-trap mouth, and instead of fingers they have opposable tendrils and a thorn containing quick-acting poison. They do not need to breathe, instead photosynthesising using chloroplasts like all plants, but should the need arise they are capable of exhaling lethal marsh gas.

By accident or design, they are equipped with an assortment of deadly defences and the innate belief that all animal-kind is their enemy. They are also slaves to instinct; the Vervoids being transported on the *Hyperion III* compulsively piled their victims' corpses onto a compost heap.

But the Vervoids weren't created simply as a perverse exercise in horticulture. Professor Sarah Lasky and her assistants Doland, Bruchner, and Ruth Baxter created them to serve as a slave labour force on Earth, to run the factories and farms in return for only water and sunlight. In their turn, the Vervoids came to the conclusion that, since they were the only examples of their species, they would only be able to secure their continued existence if they eliminated the human race. Peaceful coexistence was impossible because, at some stage or other, directly or indirectly, all animal life consumes plant life — or vice versa.

Fortunately for humanity, the Vervoids did have one weakness: their life cycle was governed by light. They were in a dormant state inside their pods until they were accidentally exposed to high-spectrum light, and the Doctor realised that exposing them to more intense light and carbon dioxide would accelerate their life cycle so that they would pass through spring, summer and autumn within a matter of seconds. His plan succeeded, and all that remained of the Vervoids was a pile of rotting leaves.

CREATED BY
Pip and Jane Baker

APPEARANCES
**The Trial of a Time Lord
(1986)**

UNANSWERED QUESTION

Ruth Baxter transformed into something approximating a Vervoid after getting a speck of Vervoid pollen in a scratch on her thumb, so it seems likely that the other Vervoids were the results of experiments in transforming humans into plants. This explains why they had the ability to speak, why they all spoke English, and why one of them had a pronounced Liverpool accent.

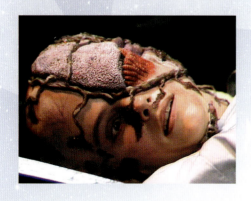

VESPIFORM

Giant shape-changing wasps with a thirst for knowledge

CREATED BY
Gareth Roberts

APPEARANCES
The Unicorn and the Wasp (2008)

I t has been noted elsewhere that parallel evolution is a constant throughout the universe. Lots of planets have species that are humanoid and almost indistinguishable from humans. Other planets have horses, rats, bats and cats, so it should be no surprise that lots of planets have wasps.

The Vespiform are one such species. They are 'social' wasps, living in colonies and creating vast hives in worlds in the Silfrax galaxy. They are adapted to worlds with much lower gravities than Earth, leading to comparative gigantism. A Vespiform male drone is about three metres tall and his main functions are reproduction and defence of the Queen, for which he is equipped with very large and venomous stingers. Although Vespiform, like bees, lose their stingers when they sting, they are capable of regrowing them almost immediately.

Their evolution took an unusual path, as they developed a form of metamorphism which enabled them to mimic other species for short periods. This, in turn, led to the Vespiform becoming more advanced as they were exposed to other species' ideas. Indeed, the Vespiform could be regarded as parasites, as all their knowledge and technology derives from other species.

The Vespiform developed a hunger for knowledge, and despatched agents to the stars in search of new cultures and concepts. At last they had something else to use the drones for! These agents were equipped with telepathic recorders in order to gather and retain as much information as possible and to pass more convincingly as other life forms.

One such agent was sent to Earth to learn about humans. And then something either very romantic or very unfortunate happened, depending on how you look at it. The Vespiform drone fell in love with a human woman called Clemency. In the heat of the moment, and the heat of a Delhi night, he revealed his true nature and fulfilled his main evolutionary function. Reproduction.

THE VESPIFORM-HUMAN HYBRID

It turned out that humans and Vespiform were sufficiently biologically compatible for Clemency to give the Vespiform a son. A son that appeared to be completely human. Clemency returned to her life in England, with the Vespiform's telepathic recorder as a keepsake, and her son grew up, unaware of his alien heritage. Until he became angry in the vicinity of the recorder and it beamed details of his true identity into his brain... along with the plot of an Agatha Christie novel.

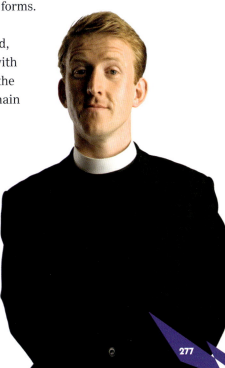

THE VIGIL

Ruthless cyborgs dedicated to ensuring the sacrifice of an innocent child

CREATED BY
Neil Cross

APPEARANCES
The Rings of Akhaten
(2013)

The planet Akhaten is alive. It may even be sentient. Initially it was little more than a vast amoeba that had grown a crusty shell, absorbing electromagnetic energy from space. But it evolved a symbiotic parasitic relationship with the creatures that lived on the worlds of its double-ring system. As they developed intelligence, the planet developed the ability to feed on the psychometric energy of objects imprinted with emotional and historical value. It feasted in cycles, setting back the progress of civilisation each time it did so. And then, when it was sated, it slept. But it made sure that one priest was kept alive in a pyramid on the rings of Akhaten to act as its 'alarm clock'.

The people of the rings devised a scheme to prevent Akhaten ever waking again. They realised that if they sang lullabies the priest would remain unconscious; the equivalent of jamming down the 'snooze' button on the alarm clock. They locked him within a glass case — all they had to do was ensure that the lullaby continued uninterrupted. This was the responsibility of the Sun Singers of Akhat: Choristers trained to sing the lullaby, handing the song over from Chorister to Chorister down the generations.

THE QUEEN OF YEARS

For a million years, the Long Song continued. The reason for the song became obscured in myth and tradition, as the encased priest became mummified and Akhaten became known as the Old God and 'Grandfather'. Akhaten still threatened to wake every thousand years or so, so every thousand years the Choristers selected a female baby to become the Queen of Years. She was raised to sing at the Festival of Offerings but really they had another purpose in mind to her. She was to be offered to Akhaten as a living source of psychometric energy; it would feed on her soul. Her sacrifice would return Akhaten to sleep and save the rest of their civilisation.

The first Choristers feared that the purpose of the Queen of Years could become forgotten in the gaps between Festivals so they converted some of their number into cyborgs known as the Vigil. The Vigil were effectively immortal, locked within armour that kept their minds alive even as their flesh decayed. They were equipped with personal teleports and force-field generators to enable them to carry out their sole purpose: to feed the Queen of Years to Grandfather.

VOC ROBOTS

Impassive machines programmed to kill all humans

Robots cannot kill humans. That is their prime directive. It is the first program that is laid into every robot's brain, from the simplest Dum to the most complex Super Voc. Every robot has over a million multi-level constrainers in its command circuit. For a robot to even harm a human, all of them would have to malfunction at once. Such a thing is impossible. But circuits can be bypassed and commands can be reprogrammed. Robots can be made to kill.

This is what happened on Storm Mine 4. Like all sandminers, its small crew of humans was augmented by humanoid robots. The robots were designed to be the perfect servants, sleek and unhurried in their motions, like walking Greek statues. The robots that could speak, the Vocs and the single Super Voc, SV-7, had voices synthesised to suggest calm, deference and efficiency. They and the mute Dums performed all the routine tasks, leaving the crew to spend most of their time at leisure. Only when the robots detected a mineral-rich dust storm were the crew roused from their indolence.

Even before the robots turned, people were never at ease in their company. Perhaps this is why, despite all the assurances of the robots' unassailability, every sandminer was fitted with a deactivator switch that could turn them all off, and a final deactivator which would cause their brain circuits to explode.

The robots induced fear in some humans due to their uncanny lack of non-verbal signals, triggering hysterical, self-destructive episodes of 'robophobia'. Those affected compared the robots to the walking dead, and they weren't the only ones; in the construction centres when a robot was deactivated it was marked with a red deactivation disc called a 'corpse marker' as a black joke. The robots' disposal was covered by a strict code to avoid causing them suffering — but if they were capable of suffering, that meant they were not mindless objects; it meant they were actually slaves.

And so a brilliant scientist, who had been raised from childhood with only robots for company, decided it was time for his brothers to live as free beings…

CREATED BY
Chris Boucher

APPEARANCES
The Robots of Death
(1977)

SUPERIOR BEINGS

Robots are clever enough to be unbeatable at chess and strong enough to twist a man's arm off. They can outrun any human, never tire and cannot easily be harmed. Knives bounce off them, and if one catches its hand in a door the detached hand will keep moving.

VOORD & CREATURES OF MARINUS

Sinister amphibian cyborgs seeking control of the Conscience Machine

The Doctor once observed that, wherever there are people, the same pattern repeats itself: the people become Cybermen.

Take the planet Marinus, for example. A water-world of isolated archipelagos, each of which gave rise to its own civilisation, each of which took the first steps to automation. There was the island, home to the Conscience Machine; a computer created by the people of Marinus to do their thinking for them, to decide what was right and wrong. Which resulted in eliminating not just criminality, but personal freedom too.

Then there was the city of Morphoton, secretly ruled by disembodied brains that 'outgrew' their bodies. They mentally conditioned human slaves to work for them, to act as their machines; once again, they used technology to eliminate freedom.

Or consider the work of the scientist Darrius. Obsessed with tampering with the forces of creation. Working away in his laboratory, guarded by automatons resembling suits of armour.

There were similar automatons in the mountains, standing sentinel over one of the keys to the Conscience Machine. Were they robots — or men converted into cyborgs? The fact that they were activated by heat suggests they were men, trapped inside metal, conditioned to obey.

And finally there were the Voord. Humanoid beings, sealed within synthetic rubber bodysuits. Their faces were featureless; they didn't need to breathe, as their bodies had been surgically altered to perform amphibian missions; and they didn't need to see or hear, because they had been fitted with sensor antennae which could also receive instructions. (Each Voord had a unique antennae shape; one, final concession to individuality.) No wonder the Voord wanted to reactivate the Conscience Machine — they were designed to serve it.

Most significantly of all, their headpieces had handlebar-like attachments. Their function is obvious; they were part of a cooling system designed to prevent the organic brain inside the casing from overheating.

When the Doctor visited Marinus, he defeated the Voord, and destroyed the Conscience Machine. But did he prevent the inevitable rise of the Cybermen, or merely delay it?

CREATED BY
Terry Nation

APPEARANCES
The Keys of Marinus
(1964)

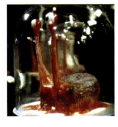

UNANSWERED QUESTION

As Arbitan was growing older, he was also on the path to Cyber-conversion, prolonging his life by occasionally wearing a Voord-like head-case and a hooded cloak. This is why, when Arbitan's daughter Sabetha returned to his island, she was fooled when Yartek the Voord pretended to be Arbitan by wearing a hooded cloak.

WEEPING ANGELS

Malevolent living statues that feed on time energy

The Weeping Angels are the most deadly predators ever to have evolved. Which means they are also the hardest to research, as anyone investigating them tends to end up dead. They are believed to be nearly as old as the universe, and on some worlds, their existence has passed into myth. But on worlds where the Angels have brought fear and dread, they are spoken of with hushed tones...

CREATED BY
Steven Moffat

APPEARANCES
Blink (2007)
The Time of Angels/
Flesh and Stone (2010)
The God Complex (2011)
The Angels Take
Manhattan (2012)
The Time of the Doctor
(2013)
Hell Bent (2015)

TIME PREDATORS

The Angels feed on all kinds of energy — radiation, gravity, light, electricity — but preferably time energy, and preferably potential time energy. Rather than killing its victims, an Angel sends them back in time, with just a single touch, so it can consume the energy of all the days of the life they might have lived.

The Angels live on unfulfilled potential. As they usually hunt covertly, they tend to displace one victim at a time and select people who are unlikely to be missed (the Angels used to be known as 'the lonely assassins', which was thought to refer to their solitary nature but which could equally well refer to the fact that they frequently target the lonely). They have, however, been known to create 'battery farms', in which they feed on the same victims repeatedly. The existence of these farms suggests that the Angels themselves are capable of a form of time travel, but this has never been directly observed, so whether this is by touching themselves or by touching each other is a secret known only to the Angels.

It should be made clear that by feeding they don't literally 'eat' time energy. Rather, they absorb it, using it to restore themselves, repairing any damage or decay by simply undoing the time that has passed. A 'starving' Angel is one that has become malformed due to corrosion, losing its features and its wings.

Similarly, a well-nourished Angel looks like a freshly carved statue; no one has ever encountered a fat Weeping Angel.

There is, possibly, a link between nourishment and reproduction. It's not known whether Weeping Angels are as female as they seem, but their young have been observed, and they resemble stone cherubs. They tend to be found in Weeping Angel strongholds, such as graveyards, gothic cathedrals and garden centres.

DEFENCE MECHANISM

The Weeping Angels have survived for so long because they have evolved the most perfect defence system: they are 'quantum-locked'. This means that, following the Copenhagen interpretation of quantum theory, observation of an entity will lock it down into a state of either being a particle or a wave, so any observation of an Angel causes it to turn to stone. The moment it is seen by another living being — or another Angel — it will, effectively, become a statue.

THEIR IMAGE IS THEIR POWER

Another, less well-known ability of the Weeping Angels is to utilise copies of their image. Just as observation affects their state of being, so observation of images of Weeping Angels enables them to come into being.

Whether it is in a video recording or a photograph, an Angel can use its image to project itself into other places, as a means of spreading its image further, because merely looking at the eyes of an image of a Weeping Angel will allow it to get inside your head through your eyes. And once it's inside the vision centres of your brain, it can alter your perceptions for its own sadistic amusement and kill you.

This also explains why sculptures not made of stone (such as the Statue of Liberty) may become Weeping Angels; anything that looks a bit like an Angel may become an Angel!

It is uncertain whether this is because it is a fact of their biology or an instinct; appropriately enough, it can be either of these two things until it is observed and locked down into being one or the other. Either way, this is the reason they cover their eyes: they are not weeping, they are avoiding making eye contact with other Angels.

The Angels can only move when they are unobserved; usually they are content to walk but they are capable of flight if there is no alternative (they are reluctant to fly in public places because the last thing an Angel wants to do is to attract attention in mid-air).

Their immobility raises another question; how do they communicate? Angels cannot speak — though they have been known to use others as mouthpieces — but they have been heard to laugh (a sound rather like pigs being tortured). Possibly they communicate telepathically or through energy waves, but one thing is for sure — it's not via sign language.

ONE FINAL WARNING

'That which holds the image of an angel becomes itself an angel.'

Which includes these very pages. So listen, because your life may depend on it. Turn the page now. Don't look away.

And don't blink.

WEREWOLVES

A blood infection that caused lycanthropic mutation

There are species analogous to werewolves in the universe. The inhabitants of the planet Vulpana, for instance, have evolved to transform into green-eyed beasts whenever there is a full moon, as a response to their prey and, indeed, everything else on their planet undergoing an equally violent metamorphosis. And there have been cruel experiments in transmuting humanoids into wolf-like creatures.

CREATED BY
Russell T Davies

APPEARANCES
Tooth and Claw (2006)

THE WEREWOLF MUTATION

But the most common form of werewolf is, in fact, a microscopic blood-borne alien mutagenic virus that transforms its host's physiology to its own design to ensure its own survival. Interestingly, while many alien life forms are the source of Earth myths and legends, this virus works the other way round. It accesses the brain centres of its host and searches for local superstitions and tales of supernatural creatures,

and then transforms its host into the form most likely to arouse fear. The virus has also developed another survival strategy, as the transformation only occurs in response to certain frequencies of reflected solar radiation — moonlight. After a brief period in 'beast' form, the host returns to normal with no memory of their moonlit malignity. It is a kind of 'lupine wavelength haemovariform'.

The process of mutation can take a dozen generations or more, with each successive host having a more advanced form of the infection. On Earth, the process took over three hundred years, where the infection adopted the form of a humanoid wolf about three metres high. It had taken the local legends about werewolves and formed itself in their image.

The infection centred on a local monastery and became the subject of a form of cult. The monks not only worshipped the 'wolf', but also kidnapped local children to act as its hosts. They endeavoured to control it by conditioning it to be repelled by certain substances, such as mistletoe, in a kind of Pavlovian response. Their ultimate goal was to pass on the viral infection to a person in power, such as the reigning monarch, and bring about the Empire of the Wolf. Whether this idea came from the virus or the monks, it is impossible to tell; by this point the line between man and monster had become meaningless.

Fortunately the 'wolf' has some weaknesses. Silver bullets are the proverbial 'silver bullet', and magnified moonlight will kill the virus within its host and restore them to normal; in removing the contagion, moonlight is the best disinfectant.

WIRRN

Intelligent spacefaring parasites that can absorb their host's knowledge

The Wirrn are a species with an extraordinary life cycle. It is analogous to that of Earth parasitoid wasps, but if anything even more gruesome. Wirrn are endoparasites: they use other species as living hatcheries for their young. They lay their eggs inside them so their larvae can emerge and use their host's still-living body as a ready source of nourishment. The larvae are shapeless, bright green blobs covered in glistening transparent pustules of compressed air. They move by slithering upon a trail of secreted mucus and can, if necessary, liquefy and re-aggregate their multinucleate cells in order to pass through narrow gaps.

CREATED BY
Robert Holmes

APPEARANCES
The Ark in Space (1975)
The Stones of Blood (1978)

Once they have had sufficient nourishment, the larvae enter a pupal stage, selecting somewhere with lots of sunlight as solar radiation is essential for their metamorphosis. After a few hours, the fully grown imago forms emerge, over two metres high, with six legs, two antennae, ferocious mandibles and large compound eyes designed for abyssal darkness. They have adapted to live in the vacuum of space and can survive for years by recycling waste gases. When they are experiencing the effects of gravity, Wirrn use their legs to prop themselves up on their abdomens. They only need to visit planets occasionally for food and fresh oxygen, and to find hosts to breed.

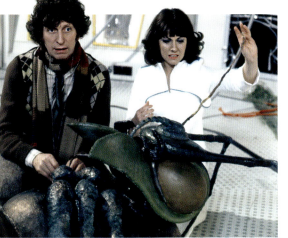

Unlike parasitoid wasps, Wirrn larvae don't just absorb their hosts physically; they absorb them mentally, too. At one time, this made little difference, as their hosts were dull-witted herbivores, but then humans came to their lands, and the Wirrn began to use them as hosts. The Wirrn that emerged had human intelligence and were determined to find more human hosts to further their knowledge. The result was a desperate war between humans and the Wirrn that lasted a thousand years and ended with the Wirrn breeding colonies in the Andromeda galaxy being destroyed.

But some Wirrn queens escaped, fleeing across the stars in search of new places to breed…

A LITTLE LEARNING

The Wirrn have another ability, which may explain how they first acquired human hosts. When they are in their larval stage their cells are sufficiently amorphous to 'infect' other creatures in the manner of a virus. Basically, if a human touches the larvae their cells will mutate into Wirrn cells and they too will acquire the larvae's absorbed knowledge in addition to their own. Once the mutation is complete they will be indistinguishable from a pupated Wirrn but, having greater intelligence, will be designated swarm leader.

ZARBI & CREATURES OF VORTIS

Zombie ants, humanoid butterflies and a giant spider intent on conquest

CREATED BY
Bill Strutton

APPEARANCES
The Web Planet (1965)

Vortis was once a world full of life. A flower forest covered its surface in a cocoon of peace. In its low gravity and rarefied atmosphere, its creatures tended to gigantism. There were the Zarbi, doleful, unintelligent giant ants that foraged the forest floor, communicating in ultrasonic chirrups. They were bred as cattle by the Menoptra, beautiful humanoid butterflies covered in white fur, with large compound eyes and antennae. The Menoptra worshipped light and carved huge monuments and temples as resting places for their dead. But they never needed to work, spending their lives in flights of thought and tending their young; flat, white-eyed larvae resembling woodlice. These larvae would retreat into chrysalises, before emerging to stretch their gossamer wings and take their first flight into the light. It was a paradise.

And then the Animus came. A creature from another world, somewhere between a spider and an octopus, but with great intelligence. It settled itself on the magnetic pole of Vortis and set about draining power from the planet. Over the centuries it shrouded itself in a vast web, the Carsenome, which grew like a fungus, stinging to the touch. It turned the streams of Vortis to acid, dissolving vegetation as raw material. Any damage to the fungus rapidly healed.

The Animus increased Vortis's gravity, bringing new moons into its skies. It could project its will through its affinity with gold and used it to enslave the Zarbi, which soon adapted to the new gravity by growing thick hind legs (though the creatures remained clumsy). It enslaved the Menoptra larvae, using their defensive stings as guns. The Menoptra themselves were barely able to fly and the possessed Zarbi attempted to enslave them. Some Menoptra fled to the planet Pictos, which had been drawn into orbit around Vortis. Others remained, evolving to live below ground, their eyesight fading in the gloom, their wings atrophying through lack of use. These creatures, the Optera, even forgot that they were descended from Menoptra, worshipping them as gods.

But the Menoptra have been making plans. Soon they will return to Vortis, armed with stalagmites and a new weapon, a living cell destructor called the Isoptope. They intend to destroy the Animus, and liberate their world…

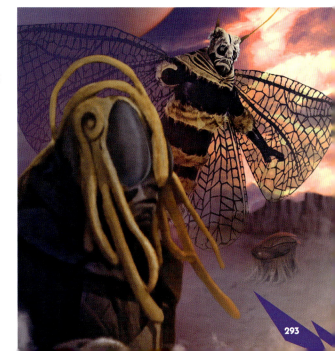

294

ZELLIN & RAKAYA

Two ancient and powerful beings that fed on human nightmares

The primeval era of the universe was a time of immortals. Omniscient beings of unlimited power that could transcend reality itself. The Guardians of Light. The Eternals. The Celestials. The Elemental Shades. These beings played games with the lives of mortals for their own entertainment. They destroyed worlds simply to pass the boredom of eternity. They considered themselves gods to be worshipped.

CREATED BY
**Charlene James
and Chris Chibnall**

APPEARANCES
Can You Hear Me? (2020)

Zellin and Rakaya were two such creatures. They placed a wager regarding two planets: which of them could bring their planet to destruction first? And so began a period of war between species and between worlds. Until, after thousands of years, the peoples of those two planets realised they had been the subject of a cruel game. They joined forces against their gods, setting their two planets on a collision course. They trapped Rakaya in a geo orb, suspended between the worlds. It would be a prison for eternity, held in place by astronomical forces and secured with a quantum fluctuation lock. Zellin fled, vowing to return and release his partner.

Billions of years later, long after the peoples of those two planets had died out, Zellin returned. He found Rakaya still trapped in the geo orb. He couldn't free her, but he could feed her what she needed to stay sane — the mental pain and anguish of mortals. He travelled the universe, taking on the form of a human being for his own amusement, manipulating the dreams of mortals to become their worst nightmares. He could then siphon their pain by detaching a finger and sticking it in their ear. When he had gathered enough pain, he could send it to Rakaya through a psychic link.

But the problem remained of how to break the quantum fluctuation lock. Only a Time Lord would be capable of that, and there was only one suitable candidate. So Zellin laid a trap for the Doctor. He travelled to fourteenth-century Aleppo to bring to life a creature from a woman's nightmares. He kidnapped Ryan's friend Tibo, appeared to Yaz in her bedroom, and gave Graham visions of Rakaya, trapped and calling for help. The Doctor would not be able to resist coming to the rescue.

THE CHAGASKA

The Chagaska was a creature drawn from the nightmares of Tahira, a Syrian woman, and is an amalgamation of creatures from that region, being part bat, part bear and part wolf, but with extremely long, finger-like claws.

ZOCCI & VINVOCCI

Spiky, suave and sensational with a GSOH

CREATED BY
Russell T Davies

APPEARANCES
Voyage of the
Damned (2007)
The End of Time (2009)

At just over a metre tall, with red skin and black lips, the Vocci stand out in the crowd. A Vocci is a humanoid alien with a head like a spiky red football. As the old saying goes, 'Red spiky face is a good spiky face.'

BANNAKAFFALATTA

One spiky alien to save us all — just don't call him Banna. The cheeky conker in white tie and tails could dance, jive and have the time of his life. And that's what he did, aboard the space tourist cruiseliner *Titanic* from the planet Sto to the more primitive culture of Earth. Bannakaffalatta had a secret accident in his past, and the surgery to repair his body resulted in a metal torso festooned with blinking lights. Bannakaffalatta was ashamed of his cyborg status, until a flirtation with waitress Astrid Peth reminded him that, despite cyborgphobia, he had equal rights in Sto law these days. This included marriage (he proposed to Astrid, half-seriously). Cyborg rights are rights.

When disaster struck on the *Titanic*, driven by the corruption of the spaceship's captain and the owner of the cruise line, the Doctor needed all the help he could get from the surviving passengers, and Bannakaffalatta was no exception. His short stature and proactive nature helped him get into a small gap in a tangle of girders and demonstrate that escape was possible for the Doctor and his gang. Later, when the group were under attack by Hosts and Haloes programmed to attack, he used his cyborg capacities to blast an electromagnetic pulse of blue energy at the robots and deactivate them. This used all of his power, beyond the point of rescue. Small but mighty, he did good and died happy. His E.M.P. transmitter was recharged and used to save the rest of the passengers.

VINVOCCI

The Vinvocci visually resemble Zocci, but are taller and their skin is green instead of red, and their hands are spiky, too. Using shimmer devices, they are able to disguise their true form and take on human appearance in order to blend in to a society and work quietly. They use a wristwatch to switch between modes.

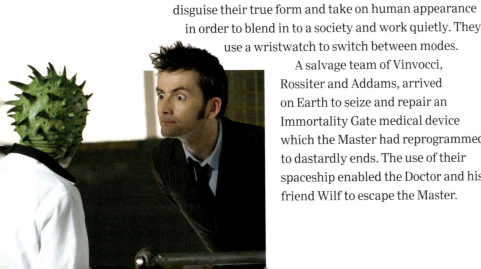

A salvage team of Vinvocci, Rossiter and Addams, arrived on Earth to seize and repair an Immortality Gate medical device which the Master had reprogrammed to dastardly ends. The use of their spaceship enabled the Doctor and his friend Wilf to escape the Master.

ZYGONS

Shape-changing genetically engineered alien cephalopods

CREATED BY
Robert Banks Stewart

APPEARANCES
**Terror of the
Zygons (1975)
The Day of the
Doctor (2013)
The Zygon Invasion/
The Zygon Inversion
(2015)**

The Zygons are one of the most striking creatures of the universe. They are broadly humanoid, with orange, rubbery skin like salamanders, covered in vestigial suckers. Their oversized brain cavities are an indicator of their vast intelligence, while their faces seem incongruously small and half-formed. This is because the Zygons are the result of centuries of genetic modification.

They were originally sea-dwelling cephalopods like squid but altered their genes to increase their brainpower, which in turn led to further scientific advancement. Their science focused on biotechnology, biocybernetics and organic crystallography, and when they developed space travel it was in living spaceships that they had cultivated from their own tissue and with which they had a symbiotic relationship; their spaceships served as hatcheries for their young. Unfortunately their spaceships' organic nature also meant they were very unreliable, with Zygons crash-landing on Earth on several occasions.

The Zygons were a peaceful species until their home world was destroyed in a stellar catastrophe in the first days of the Time War. They were forced to create a great refugee fleet, with millions of Zygons held in embryonic form, determined to find new worlds to colonise. Usually, this meant conquest, as worlds would have to be restructured to suit the Zygons by increasing their temperature and water coverage using slave labour and Zygon technology. But not all Zygons took this view; some believed they could survive by peacefully assimilating themselves into other cultures.

UNANSWERED QUESTION

Given that Zygons transform into human forms wearing clothes, that must mean their clothes are part of their metamorphosed body. So what would happen if they lost a shoe? The answer is the part of their body that was the shoe would undergo molecular dispersal, leaving no trace, and they would regrow the absent cell tissue like a starfish or an octopus.

IMITATIVE METAMORPHOSIS

The Zygons who believed the future for their race was peaceful assimilation developed a specific technology to enable this: they could pass as members of other species by transforming into them. Unluckily, this technology was only in an early stage at the time of the evacuation and relied on the 'original' being held captive in their spaceships, as their 'body-print' needed to be refreshed every few hours. As a result, it tended to be of more use to those Zygons intent on conquest.

The process was not infallible: if a disguised Zygon was injured or killed, it would revert to its natural form. Other Zygons could, though, use the body-print link to disperse a slain Zygon's molecules without trace. Over the centuries, the Zygons refined the process so that originals could be restrained by extrusions of Zygon matter and Zygons could maintain live-links with the originals' minds.

Then, in the early twenty-first century, as part of Operation Double, the Zygons found a way of keeping a duplicate viable without needing to refresh the pattern. Unfortunately, they also improved their technology in other ways: Zygons could now take body-prints from human minds telepathically.

OFFENSIVE ABILITIES

The Zygons retain two natural weapons from their squid-like ancestors; venom sacs located in their tongues and the ability to generate an electrical charge in their hands. This can stun a victim or reduce them to a tumbleweed of hair and skin.

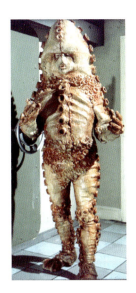

THE SKARASEN

As they altered their own genetic make-up, the Zygons made themselves dependent upon lactic fluid provided by another native of their planet, an extremely large and savage amphibious reptile known as the Skarasen. Horrifically, the Zygons who crashed on Earth near Loch Ness modified a Skarasen embryo to become a weapon — an armoured cyborg capable of withstanding a nuclear missile strike, with eyes that served as remote cameras and with claws and molars powerful enough to destroy a conference centre in a mating-signal-induced frenzy.

DEEP COVER

The Zygons of Loch Ness may have guided the Forgill family over several centuries. We know that their Skarasen was first sighted in the Middle Ages and that a monastery was built by the Loch in the eleventh century, which then became a castle with a secret passage leading to the Zygon ship. Whenever it became necessary to intervene in human affairs, the Zygons would render the head monk or clan chief unconscious with their nerve gas, transport him to their ship, take on his likeness for a brief time and then return him none the wiser. Mostly, the Zygons kept such occasions to a minimum, with Broton the Zygon only taking on the body of the Duke of Forgill in response to the arrival of an oil company. When he (as the Duke) claims that his family have served for centuries he is referring to his Zygon ancestors.

MAKING MONSTERS

Behind the scenes — and behind the sofa — with the creature creators

Many methods are used to create *Doctor Who*'s monsters, ranging from costume and make-up to digital effects. For *The Eleventh Hour*, CGI was used to upgrade Olivia Colman with some sharp dentistry.

The Weeping Angels combined prosthetic make-up, grey body paint, a heavy-duty rubber dress, fake fingernails and fibreglass wings. Good luck standing still in all that clobber!

Being a monster isn't an easy job. This Silent is shocked to learn that it takes three people to get him into costume for the cameras.

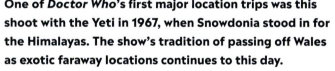

One of *Doctor Who*'s first major location trips was this shoot with the Yeti in 1967, when Snowdonia stood in for the Himalayas. The show's tradition of passing off Wales as exotic faraway locations continues to this day.

By the 1970s, *Doctor Who* was using ambitious prosthetic make-up for its monsters, including the very first Sontaran.

All monsters need a hand. Some need two. The Ood usually make do with gloves, but the Elder Ood was given the honour of specially sculpted digits.

Cybermen.
Practical)

SReid '66

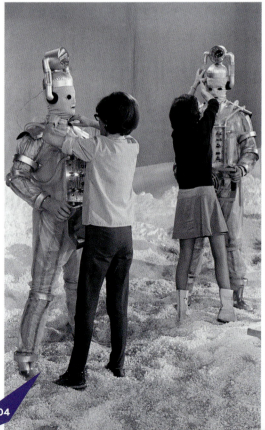

Sandra Reid designed the early Cybermen back in 1966. They were fairly low-tech, with the sticky tape holding their helmets together visible on camera. A young Peter Capaldi was captivated by the designs and got to act alongside them as the Doctor in 2017.

More than any other *Doctor Who* monster, the Cyberman have been redesigned over the course of their appearances, and continue to evolve. This chrome-plated overhaul for 1988's 25th-anniversary story *Silver Nemesis* had them dancing with joy.

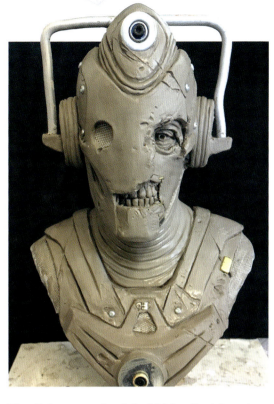

When the Cybermen were revived in 2006, many concepts were considered, exploring everything from architectural sleekness to plastic-wrapped body horror. The final design drew inspiration from Art Deco and the robot seen in the classic silent film *Metropolis* (1927).

The Cyber comeback in 2020 called for a host of new designs. These included the partially converted Ashad, an army of Cyber Warriors, and the part-Time Lord CyberMasters.

The art team drew inspiration from classic designs.

The stylish CyberMasters had detailing based on Time Lord patterns.

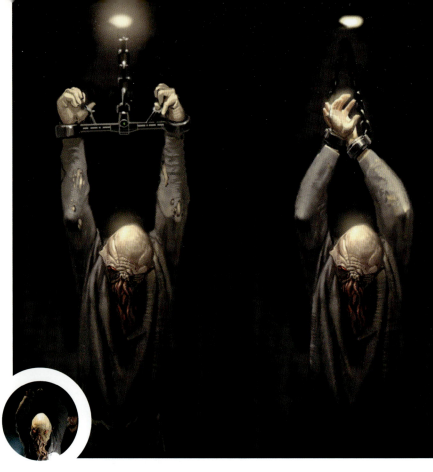

The Slitheen from *Aliens of London* were based on the idea of giant green babies.

The telepathic Ood were one of the most effective creature designs seen in *Doctor Who*'s revival, borrowing from the Sensorites of the First Doctor's era, souped up with some slimy tendrils.

Early ideas for the Empress of the Racnoss in *The Runaway Bride* included this regal design with a cobweb veil.

The Star Whale from *The Beast Below* went through many concepts, including this whimsical squid-like design. So not really a whale at all, then.

Concept artwork of the Sycorax spaceship from *The Christmas Invasion*. The artists drew inspiration from the creature design and seashells to create this environment.

Monsters are often a collaboration between costume and prosthetics designers, such as the elegant Thijarians from *Demons of the Punjab*.

When work begins on creating a new monster, the designers will often make a miniature model as a prototype. These gruesome early designs for the Monks from *The Lie of the Land* were based on mummified humans.

The intricate prosthetic design for the Morax Queen from *The Witchfinders*.

Tzim-Sha – Tim Shaw to his mates – returned from exile in 2018's finale *The Battle of Ranskoor Av Kolos* looking worse for wear.

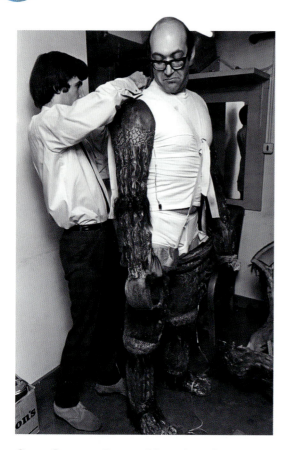

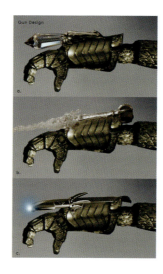

Returning monsters on *Doctor Who* are often seen in new variations as writers expand on the original ideas. Over the years, the Ice Warrior ranks have grown to include various Ice Lords and, most recently, the formidable Ice Queen Iraxxa in *Empress of Mars*.

Carry On actor Bernard Bresslaw played Ice Warrior leader Varga for the Martians' first appearance back in 1967. The heavy fibreglass armour screwed together with bolts and made sitting down impossible. Bernard looks delighted about all this.

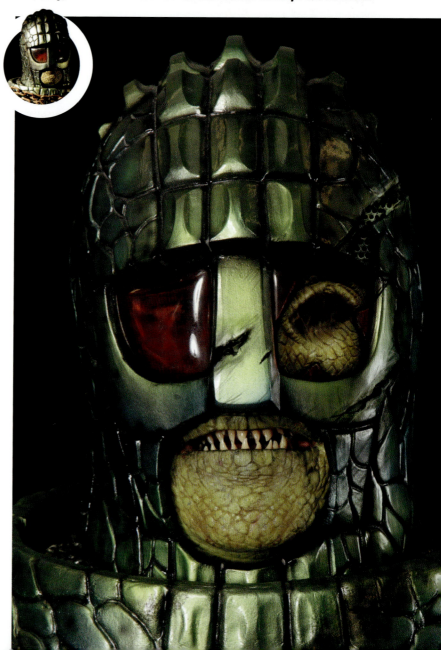

When the Silurians returned in 2010, the team considered revamping the original design from 1970 as a complex animatronic mask. But the dialogue-heavy scripts prompted a rethink to prosthetic make-up, allowing the Silurian actors to give a greater range of performance.

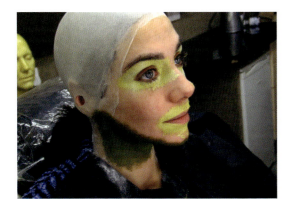

It's not easy being green. The actors playing monsters often suffer for their art, spending long hours in the make-up chair as their prosthetics are painstakingly applied and painted before filming.

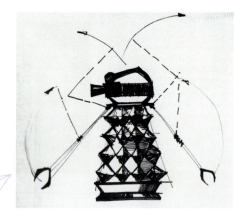

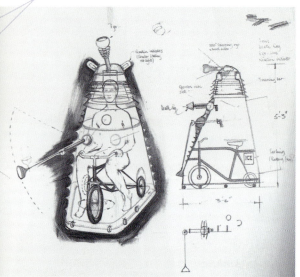

The Daleks made their first public appearance in December 1963. This took place *before* the creatures were seen on television, ruining the surprise for the patrons of Shepherds Bush Market. Spoilers!

Raymond Cusick's first ideas for the Daleks drew from geodesic architecture, but the faceted design was too complicated to build. He simplified his ideas to the familiar pepperpot silhouette, intended to house an operator on a child's tricycle. The blueprint even included a handy ice box for cooling!

The Dalek Emperor faced civil war in 1967's *The Evil of the Daleks*, which climaxed with an explosive battle filmed at Ealing Studios. The Doctor declared the Daleks' 'final end'. He should have known better.

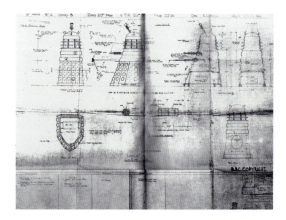

The Daleks received a dome to bumper overhaul when *Doctor Who* returned in 2005. The new casing used a cast of an original 1960s Dalek as its starting point.

The blueprints for the first Daleks feature a few details not seen on TV, such as the rear hatch for equipment, a detail later incorporated into the Paradigm Daleks.

The Daleks were supersized for their battles against the Eleventh Doctor, with bigger, bulkier casings and brash colours.

Inside each Dalek is a bubbling lump of hate, which sounds exactly like actor Nicholas Briggs speaking into a ring modulator.

In 2019's, *Resolution* the Dalek mutant slithered to the centre of the action, in gruesome detail.

V.1 V.2 V.3

V.4 V.5 V.6

Daleks spanning the show's entire history assembled for *The Magician's Apprentice* in 2015.

Published in 2020 by BBC Books, an imprint of Ebury Publishing
20 Vauxhall Bridge Road, London SW1V 2SA

BBC Books is part of the Penguin Random House group of companies
whose addresses can be found at global.penguinrandomhouse.com

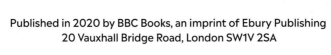

Doctor Who is a BBC Wales production for BBC One.
Executive producers: **Chris Chibnall** and **Matt Strevens**

First published by BBC Books in 2020

www.penguin.co.uk

A CIP catalogue record for this book is available from the British Library

ISBN 9781785945335

Publishing Director: **Albert DePetrillo**
Managing Editor: **Nell Warner**
Production: **Sian Pratley**
Project Editor/Interior design: **Paul Lang**
Cover design: **Ben Morris**
Interior illustrations: **Lee Johnson**
Copy editor: **Steve Tribe**
Proofreader: **Paul Simpson**
Additional material: **Stuart Manning**
Thanks to: **Neil Corry**, **Gary Gillatt**, **Tom Spilsbury**, **Gabby DeMatteis** and **Ross McGlinchey**
Behind the scenes photography and concept art courtesy of:
Ray Holman, **Millennium FX** and **Robert Allsopp and Associates**
While every effort has been made to trace and acknowledge all copyright holders,
we would like to apologise should there have been any errors or ommissions.

To all the writers, cast and crew of Doctor Who since 1963 – thank you for the monsters!

Printed and bound in Italy by **Printer Trento**

Penguin Random House is committed to a sustainable future for our business, our readers and our
planet. This book is made from Forest Stewardship Council® certified paper.